In the picturesque tourist town of Fredericksburg, Texas, Tally Holt has opened a new candy store with a vintage twist . . .but there's no sugar-coating a nasty case of murder . . .

Tally Holt has poured her heart, soul, and bank account into Tally's Olde Tyme Sweets, specializing in her grandmother's delicious recipes. Tally's homemade Mallomars, Twinkies, fudges, and taffy are a hit with visiting tourists—and with Yolanda Bella, the flamboyant owner of Bella's Baskets next door. But both shops encounter a sour surprise when local handyman Gene Faust is found dead in Tally's kitchen, stabbed with Yolanda's scissors.

The mayor's adopted son, Gene, was a handsome Casanova with a bad habit of borrowing money from the women he wooed. It's a sticky situation for Yolanda, who was one of his marks. There are plenty of other likely culprits among Fredericksburg's female population, and even among Gene's family. But unless Tally can figure out who finally had their fill of Gene's sweet-talking ways, Yolanda—and both their fledgling businesses—may be destined for a bitter end . . .

Books by Kaye George

Revenge Is Sweet

Revenge Is Sweet

Kaye George

LYRICAL UNDERGROUND
Kensington Publishing Corp.
www.kensingtonbooks.com

LYRICAL UNDERGROUND BOOKS are published by

Kensington Publishing Corp.
119 West 40th Street
New York, NY 10018

All Kensington titles, imprints, and distributed lines are available at special quantity discounts for bulk purchases for sales promotion, premiums, fundraising, educational, or institutional use.

Special book excerpts or customized printings can also be created to fit specific needs. For details, write or phone the office of the Kensington Sales Manager: Kensington Publishing Corp., 119 West 40th Street, New York, NY 10018. Attn. Sales Department. Phone: 1-800-221-2647.

Lyrical Underground and Lyrical Underground logo Reg. US Pat. & TM Off

First Electronic Edition: March 2020
ISBN-13: 978-1-5161-0540-3 (ebook)
ISBN-10: 1-5161-0540-0 (ebook)

First Print Edition: March 2020
ISBN-13: 978-1-5161-0543-4
ISBN-10: 1-5161-0543-5

Printed in the United States of America

To Friendship, an awesome cat

Acknowledgments

I must thank the following for invaluable help with this book, and many more I've left off, I'm sure: Leslie Budewitz, for helping make a scene work; Brenda Miiller at the Fredericksburg Police Department; Peg Cochran and Daryl Wood Gerber, for early critiques; and all my Facebook friends who are Maine coon lovers, including Reine Harrington, Amy Mata, and Bret and Kimberly.

Chapter 1

Tally Holt hummed tunelessly as she stirred the marshmallow crème mixture for her Whoopie Pies, her spoon clanking on the metal bowl and keeping up a rhythm of sorts. Warm summer sunlight streamed through the paned windows of the shop kitchen, laying bright distorted squares onto the taupe granite countertop. The buttery yellow of the kitchen's walls matched the sunlight this fine early July day.

The name of her shop, Tally's Olde Tyme Sweets, might have been a bit cumbersome and, according to Tally's mother, ridiculous, but Tally liked it. She thought people would take note of the odd spellings. Already, people were stopping to gaze at her sign. She hoped that, after they'd gone home from a trip to Fredericksburg, Texas, they would remember it the next time they came.

If her lovely shop was still here. It *would* be here.

She'd gotten off to a slow start a few weeks ago, mid-June, but business picked up every day. Looking ahead to the near future, she knew August would be better, and by September the charming Texas Hill Country tourist town would be overflowing with shoppers and she meant to entice her share of them inside. She had to. She had invested everything in this venture.

The soft chime on the front door broke into her thoughts, although the shop wasn't open for the day yet.

"Oh yum, I smell chocolate! Right?" Yolanda Bella burst into the kitchen after coming through the sales room. That was the way she usually entered a room, bursting into it. Today she wore an orange peasant blouse over a neon-yellow broomstick skirt. She managed to make it look good, tying everything together with a necklace of large amber chunks and a pink headband that struggled to tame her wild, curly mane of dark brown hair.

Jeans and tees were Tally's style, but she loved the way Yolanda always looked.

"Don't you touch them." Tally pointed to the chocolate cookie wafers she'd taken from the oven minutes before. "I have exactly enough for this filling." She gave the bowl of fluff some more strokes.

Yolanda pursed her lips, but said she wouldn't dream of it.

No, Tally thought, you'll just *do* it. She thought it lovingly, though. Yolanda Bella was her best friend forever, almost like a sister. She was also the reason Tally was in Fredericksburg this summer. They had been in school together whenever Tally's family had been in town, until Yolanda went away to a Dallas boarding school. They had stayed in touch even then, getting together at every school break. The big city hadn't stuck, and Yolanda had come home immediately after she graduated. She had never left again, though Tally had taken off for Austin a few years later.

Now Yolanda edged ever closer to the cooling Whoopie Pie cookie crusts and Tally shuffled to put herself in the way, still stirring the marshmallow filling mixture, which was beginning to smooth out. Yolanda hadn't noticed the batch of Mary Janes cooling farther down the counter, waiting to be rolled thin. Tally was surprised she hadn't detected the peanut buttery smell, since they were nearly ready to eat. They only needed to be rolled out and cut. The peanut butter must have been overpowered by the chocolate smell.

"You can help me fill these Whoopie Pies and I might give you one," Tally said with a sly smile.

Yolanda had no interest in baking or candy making, which Tally well knew. "You know you'll give me one anyway." She tossed her head toward the goodies.

That was true.

"Listen, I had a great idea," Yolanda said, giving up on swiping a naked cookie wafer. Instead, she pulled out a wooden stool to perch upon. "You know those dessert carts in expensive restaurants? Where the desserts are made of wax or something?"

"I think they're plastic, but okay? What about them?"

"Maybe you could get some of your candies replicated for my shop window. Using your candy in my baskets is working out great. If your candy were displayed at my place, maybe pieces of your mint fudge, or maybe those chocolate-covered caramels you made yesterday, would it help people picture our products better?" She fingered the thick amber of her necklace, still gazing sideways at the wafers.

Not a bad idea, Tally thought. "Do you want to look into the fake display candies, or should I?" she asked.

Yolanda sighed and dropped her chin to her hand, propped on the counter. "I might as well do it. My business is so slow lately, I need something to keep myself occupied."

Yolanda's hope, Tally knew, was that the two shops would help each other out. It was hers, too. Business should pick up for both of them when they got their partnership going smoothly. Tally started scooping dollops of marshmallow filling onto the chocolate cookies.

"Mm, that smells good," Yolanda said, perking up and, no doubt, looking forward to a finished Whoopie Pie.

Tally plopped a top cookie onto one and handed it to her.

"Thanks a million." Yolanda slid off the stool with a swirl of her yellow skirt. "I'd better get to my shop and check up on Allen and Gene."

"What are they doing now? They finished redoing the doors, right?" Gene Faust did handyman work for both of them and had recently hired Allen Wendt, who was new in town, to help him out.

"Yes, my doors turned out great. But now my sink is backed up."

"It takes two of them to unplug a drain?"

Yolanda grinned. "I don't mind. They're both nice to look at."

Tally sobered. Yolanda had a bad habit, in the past, of picking the wrong guy. She'd done it more than twice. More than three times, in fact. "Be careful. I don't want you to get hurt again."

"Never. Never again." Her curls bounced as she shook her head with vehemence. "I've learned not to trust guys that I don't know."

"That's the trouble. We *do* know Gene."

Yolanda headed for the front. "Don't believe everything you hear," she called over her shoulder. "He's not like that."

Tally wondered what *that* was. Gene Faust was the son of the mayor, yes, but he'd been adopted as a teenager, a wild, in-trouble teenager. General opinion in the town at the time was that his adoption was a publicity stunt, since Mayor Faust had long championed helping troubled youth. That stance probably got him elected—and kept getting him re-elected year after year. Gene was certainly troubled before the Fausts rescued him from a series of foster homes and stints in juvenile detention. And it was true that he hadn't been publicly picked up and charged with anything since then, but was that the mayor's influence on Gene? Or was it the mayor's influence on the law enforcement authorities? Gene didn't exactly behave himself, ever.

Tally vividly remembered the handsome, blond, gray-eyed Gene stealing cars and bicycles frequently when they were in junior high. He hadn't been old enough to drive, but he looked old enough, and being underage hadn't stopped him. Tally vowed to pop into Yolanda's basket shop frequently and keep track of things while Gene was working there.

* * * *

Yolanda walked the short distance to her shop with eager steps, but she halted before going through the front door of Bella's Baskets. She had defended Gene to Tally, but she had to, didn't she? No one else would.

She knew he was in despair sometimes, wondering if he'd ever live down his former reputation. She knew other things about him, too, things that not many other people did. For instance, his adoptive father, Josef Faust, the mayor of Fredericksburg, had regretted adopting him for some time now. Gene had confided that to her. His father had even gone so far as to try to have the adoption annulled. At least twice a week he threatened to disinherit Gene, and over the most minor infractions. A dented fender when Gene borrowed his beloved BMW, returning his wife's vintage red Mustang convertible on empty, or even leaving all the dirty pots on the stove when it was his turn to do dishes. No wonder Gene didn't always behave properly. His father didn't expect him to. And, even worse, his mother didn't care. She seemed to dislike Gene even more than his father did.

Maybe Yolanda was able to understand Gene's family problems so well because of her own. She was the older of two daughters, no brothers, and the child of a rich, strict father and mostly emotionally absent, but disapproving mother. Her father expected his two children to grow up to be as rich as he was. He had made all his money in real estate, buying and selling at the right times. Yolanda thought he had been extremely lucky in his transactions, but he attributed his success to his business acumen.

As for Yolanda's basket shop, Bella's Baskets? The shop she was passionate about and had poured all of her energy into for the past year? It was not a rousing success yet. It wasn't even breaking even. Mr. Bella was subsidizing it, and he did not like the fact that his own last name was on the sign. A basket shop? To him, it was a frivolous, unprofessional undertaking. His daughter should be selling real estate.

Nothing interested her less than real estate.

Her little sister, Violetta, on the other hand, was already helping with open houses. She was twenty-six and had an MBA, though not a real estate license. Yet. She was studying for it. Yolanda sometimes wondered if her sister was genuinely interested in business and real estate, or if she found it an easy way to show up her big sister. There was a seven-year age gap between them, and they'd never been close.

She had to admit that her family was a better one than Gene's, though.

She tossed her head, flipping her hair over her shoulder, and went into her shop, which was fragrant with the scent of a vanilla candle she'd left burning.

* * * *

As Tally finished wrapping the individual pieces of the Mary Janes, popping only two into her mouth to savor the molasses–peanut butter combination, she glanced at the kitchen clock, the one she'd picked up at a flea market, with a rotund aproned baker using his arms for indicating time. It was nearly ten o'clock, and Andrea would be there soon. Andrea Booker was one of the two young women Tally had hired to help out with sales. So far, she had worked hard and been an asset. She kept her long, mousy brown hair neat and, though she was quiet, almost shy, she interacted well with the customers. She was a runner and Tally saw her around town jogging sometimes when the shop wasn't open. She had also seen her riding around with Gene a couple of times with his convertible top down.

If Yolanda started getting too close to Gene, she would have to mention that. Tally even debated warning Andrea off. Gene was probably taking advantage of her youth and inexperience. But, then again, maybe she shouldn't parent her employees.

The other hire was Mart Zimmer, who came in part-time during their midday peak hours. She had been in Andrea's high school class and they knew each other slightly. She was more outgoing than the quieter Andrea, both of them thin with brown hair, one long and straight and one curly, and both of them taller than Tally's five foot three. That was handy when Tally needed things from the higher cupboard shelves.

Tally listened for Andrea to arrive through the sales room in the front of the store. Mart would come in later. She heard, instead, Andrea's name being shouted from the front. She rushed to crack open the kitchen door to see what the commotion was.

Andrea stood with the front door open, her left arm gripped by a middle-aged woman, her large bag dangling from her helpless hand. The older woman had the same build Andrea did, both of them the same height and both with the same straight brown hair, the older woman's shorter. Her features were so distorted by anger that Tally couldn't tell if their faces resembled each other or not.

A young couple was emerging from Fischer & Wieser, a cute stone building across the street, with carriage lights beside its front door. They almost dropped their bag of sauces and jellies gaping at the altercation. Others on the street turned to stare at the commotion, too.

"Don't run away when I'm talking to you, young lady." The woman's voice was harsh and grating as she shook poor Andrea. "I asked if you had done the vacuuming and you told me you had. I looked into the coat closet this morning and nothing has been moved."

Andrea had been staring at the woman, apparently her mother, at the beginning of the tirade, but her gaze dropped to her own feet by the end of it.

Tally knew Andrea lived with her parents. A sedan idled at the curb with the driver's door ajar. Had the woman driven here so she could scold her daughter on her way to work?

The harridan continued. "Tell me, Andrea, how you vacuumed the corners of the closet without moving any of the boots. You tell me that."

Andrea's reply was too soft to hear, but the woman eventually gave her one last glare, got into the car, slammed the door, and sped off.

Tally ducked back into the kitchen so she could pretend she hadn't heard the exchange. Andrea, Tally thought, meek and mousy, wasn't someone who could weather blows to her self-esteem easily. She wondered what life would be like with that woman for a mother. What a difference between Andrea's mother and her own.

At the thought of her mother, Tally's cell phone sang out as if it were psychic.

"Tally, is that you?"

"Yes, Mom. I'm answering my own phone."

The sarcasm sailed on past her mother. "Guess where we are, dear?"

That would probably be impossible. They had spoken two weeks ago, when her mother was in Memphis. The one in Egypt, not the one in Tennessee. A month before, her parents had phoned from Bern, Switzerland.

"Antarctica?" guessed Tally.

"Don't be silly. It's too far away. We're in Bali. The local musicians are fabulous."

Tally's parents were performers. They toured—acting, singing, and dancing, finding work wherever they landed. The Holt family had started out here, in Fredericksburg, but they had all been on the road for years, starting when Tally was in middle school. As she and her brother both neared the age for high school, they had both been farmed out to an aunt and uncle in Austin. Her parents wouldn't know how to put down roots. Tally wanted to learn how now, she had decided.

"That's nice, Mom."

"We're going to try to do a modern dance performance, using cowboy and cowgirl costumes, with local musicians on the beach tomorrow. We're calling it 'Straight from the Holtsters,' but the subtle nuance gets lost in translation. They don't carry many holsters here. Anyway, wish us luck."

"Okay. Good luck." Her lack of enthusiasm must have made it over the airwaves between Texas and Asia.

"Oh, come on, you can do better than that."

"I mean it, Mom. I hope you have a blast. I'm at work and we're opening in a few minutes. Gotta run."

As exasperating as her mother was, she wasn't mean. Tally always knew her mother loved her, even if she had her own indirect ways of showing it. Absentminded, scatterbrained to the point of not remembering her own children's birthdays, but never mean or nasty.

Poor Andrea. Tally would try to think of something nice to do for her to cheer her up.

Chapter 2

By the end of the morning, business at Tally's Olde Tyme Sweets had slowed down somewhat. They had completely sold out of all their taffy, even the tart green apple flavor. Tally had worked in the kitchen for a bit, then entered the sales room to help out Andrea and Mart. Since, after fifteen minutes or so, she could tell she was redundant there, she slipped into the kitchen, then to her office to go over her sales figures. It had been a few days since she had done that. She sat down with a cup of raspberry herb tea and got to work. Her first try showed that some money was missing. She drummed her fingers on the wooden desk in annoyance and started over. However, when she came up with the same figures three times in a row, she gave up. She would ask Yolanda to go over the numbers. She was much better with math.

At about noon, she emerged to tell Andrea she could take a break and let Mart take over.

Tally paused to admire her shop for a moment. The walls—decorated in muted, swirling pinks and lilacs with dark chocolate brown accents, the glass candy case—gleaming and full of her handmade confections, the sturdy wooden floor (actually easy-care laminate)—rustic wide planks to match the wainscoting and the cabinets. She loved it all, even the light fixtures made to resemble Mason jars, which had been here when she moved in. She'd had most of the décor changed, but had left those charming lights exactly as they were.

"Do you want to go out to get lunch?" Tally asked Andrea.

"No, I'm not hungry. I'll stay here and work."

"You could rest a few minutes in the kitchen. Mart and I can handle this."

"Yeah, we really can," Mart said. "It's kinda not that busy."

Andrea studied Mart. "Are you feeling better? You didn't look good when you got here."

"I'm fine. I guess I have a little stomach upset this morning."

Alarm bells went off for Tally. "You can't work if you're sick, Mart. You'll pass it on to the customers."

"It's nothing. It was something I ate last night. Really, I'm fine."

Mart appeared perfectly healthy, she had to admit. Better than she had earlier. Tally turned her attention back to Andrea.

Tally had put a comfy chair in the corner of the kitchen and placed a reading lamp and a table full of books next to it. She loved to take her own breaks there, but Andrea had never taken advantage of the mini-library of mysteries.

"You should go sit in the reading chair in the kitchen," Tally urged. "You can put your feet up on the ottoman and have a glass of iced tea or something."

"Why? Do I look tired?" Andrea pouted and sounded defensive.

"I've noticed how hard you work, and I want to make sure you like it here. I'd like you to keep working for me. We don't need three people selling all the time."

"We totally don't," Mart agreed, shaking her bouncy, curly hair. She left them to help out a customer at the front of the store, a lone woman with indecision distorting her face.

"I'm not considering quitting," Andrea said.

"I didn't think you were," Tally said. "It's not that." It was hard to do a favor for Andrea! "Do you want to go out and shop a bit?"

"No, I'm saving my money. You go shop. I'll stay here."

Tally thought she might just do that. "Maybe I'll leave, then. I do have a couple of errands. I won't be gone long, but text me if you need me to come back here."

"Sure."

How did doing a favor for Andrea end up with Tally taking time off? How exasperating.

In the kitchen, the sun was still streaming in, glinting off the granite countertops and making the yellow walls look like sunshine itself. She took off her service smock and snatched up her purse. As she returned through the front of the shop to leave, she noticed Andrea was engaged with a young family and they were loading up on goodies. Mart was ringing up the sale she had finished making for the woman.

Tally pushed the door open, setting off the soft chime. As soon as she was in the glare of daylight, she reached into her purse for her sunglasses.

Low, gray clouds were gathering, but none of them blocked the hot summer sun yet.

Tally wanted to talk to Yolanda, to ask her what to make of Andrea, but first she took advantage of her break to stroll in the other direction. She passed the quaint tourist shops that bordered Main Street: the wine-tasting parlors featuring local Texas wines, a haberdashery called Keep Your Head, a kitchen shop called Cook Up Trouble, art galleries and jewelry stores galore, to name only a few. Yolanda used wares from several of these for her baskets. The warmth that caressed the top of Tally's bare head felt soothing. As deliciously soft as the cream cheese mints she had made yesterday.

A chattering group of shoppers swept past her on the sidewalk, elbowing her aside. She sidestepped, eavesdropping. Their conversation told her they were intent on buying homemade candles in the store on the next block. The tourists would soon become thick on the sidewalks, intent on buying gifts and souvenirs, even this early in the season. Some of them might even be starting holiday shopping soon. She trusted they would also be crowding into her vintage candy shop and Yolanda's gift basket boutique.

Tally made her way to the candle shop to replenish her own supply. Coming out and turning around, she retraced her steps and went into Bear Mountain Vineyards, which was next to Bella's Baskets. This shop felt cool, like hers did. Not dark, exactly, but not as glaring as the sidewalks baking in the July sun. She hoped that was the feel her own place had. She strolled the aisles, floored with older tile and lined with wooden wine racks. The small, neatly hand-lettered signs on each row of bottles told a little something about the grapes.

"Looking for something special?" asked the shopkeeper. Tally had met him as she was moving in last month. His name was Kevin Miller, an unimposing man of medium height with short dark hair and a stylish scruffy beard. He gave an overall dark impression since he dressed all in black, slacks and a short-sleeved polo shirt.

"I'd like to browse around for a few minutes. It's nice to be out of the heat, and I want to bring something to my friend at the basket shop."

"Yolanda, right? Sure. Take your time." He stepped aside to let her stroll the aisles unimpeded.

A bottle of a deep red blend caught her eye. The label had a picture of Enchanted Rock, a favorite tourist place outside Fredericksburg, and the description was alluring, "Medium oak, full-bodied, excellent accompaniment to aged cheeses, black cherry bouquet." Tally loved Enchanted Rock. When she had been younger, she had hiked there every chance she got and knew the trails well. If she went there today, she was sure she would still be able to pick out the hard-to-follow paths. She bought two bottles of the wine.

"I like this one. I think you will, too," Kevin said as he checked her out. "Enjoy them. Tell Yolanda hi from me."

After another brief foray into the hot sun, she ducked into Yolanda's place next door, intending to offer her a bottle of her find. She also wanted to bend Yolanda's ear about Andrea and see if she had any ideas about something nice to do for her, providing Yolanda wasn't too busy with customers. True, she knew even less about Mart, but Mart wasn't there as much and had an easy, comfortable way about her. Not downtrodden and pitiful-looking, like Andrea.

Yolanda had no customers, but was standing close enough to her handyman, Gene Faust, that Tally thought she might be able to see his tonsils when he spoke. They pulled apart as Tally entered.

Yolanda eyed the distinctively shaped paper bags that Tally gripped by the bottle necks. "You have something for me?"

"Maybe."

Tally spoke to Gene. "Are you going to be long?" Maybe he would get the hint and leave them alone. She didn't want to be rude, but she did want to look out for her friend. In her opinion, Yolanda needed protection from bad boy Gene.

His smile vanished, and he gave Tally a sullen sneer. "I have to finish up. Don't know how long it'll take."

"You're unplugging the drain, right?" That's what Yolanda had said. How long could that take? "Where's Allen?"

"He had to leave to get some supplies. I got the drain flowing, but a pipe has to be replaced. It's old and corroded. Going to spring a leak any time."

Yolanda smiled at Tally and tossed her head. "It's always something with these old buildings."

* * * *

Gene moved to the sink and crawled under it. Yolanda's store was one big open area with a short counter for ringing up sales. She had knocked out a wall to make it that way, wanting the customers to see her making up their baskets. She thought they should appreciate the artistry that went into creating a beautiful arrangement. It was painfully obvious that Tally wanted Gene to leave them alone, but Yolanda couldn't tell him to do that. It would be rude and he'd been hurt so much.

She felt herself drawing closer to Gene, since he had started doing work for her in the shop. She did sometimes wonder if their relationship was based on her pity for him. That wasn't the healthiest basis. Would he have asked her for money if she hadn't expressed her concern over his well-being? His business wasn't going as well as it should have been, and his parents refused to loan him even a dollar. Exactly the opposite of her parent/money problems. She bit her lower lip, contemplating the comparison. Life was strange.

* * * *

Tally could tell that Gene wasn't going to leave anytime soon. She handed one of the bagged bottles to Yolanda.

"Maybe we can share some of this later," Tally said.

Yolanda leaned close and darted a look at the front, indicating she wanted to tell Tally something that Gene wouldn't overhear, so they both moved to the front door.

"Gene told me something that Andrea told him," Yolanda whispered. "I think you ought to know."

"Okay, what is it?" Tally hated gossiping behind her employees' backs, but she also didn't like them keeping secrets from her.

"Andrea says that Mart has a venereal disease and shouldn't be working in a food job."

"She what?" Tally bellowed. She lowered her voice to continue. "I'll check on that."

"And that she's piling up a bunch of money and is going to run away."

Was Mart stealing money from her? Was that why she couldn't get her figures to balance? Her shoulders slumped. "Thanks, Yo. I'll check on that."

"I've been thinking of closing early today," Yolanda said in a normal tone of voice. "My orders are caught up. I'll come over to your place as soon as Gene is done here."

"See you then."

Tally walked back to her shop, turning a couple of things over in her mind. One was how close Yolanda and Gene had been when she came in. She needed to find out what was happening. Gene was bad news, and she didn't want Yolanda tangled up with him too tightly. She remembered some of the guys she'd started going around with after she came home from boarding school. Tally always thought they were attracted to her friend's money as much as to her. Yolanda's parents were free with their allowances to her and their younger daughter, Violetta. The bad guys flocked to Yolanda, though, never to her quieter, shyer, bookish little sister. The other thought, of course, was Andrea tattling on Mart to Gene. Could she be spreading lies so Gene wouldn't take up with Mart? That was possible. It was also possible that she was telling the truth, but Tally didn't want to believe that. It seemed she didn't need to tell Yolanda that Gene was seeing Andrea, anyway. Yolanda should be able to deduce that.

The sidewalks still teemed with shoppers and tourists. None of them were going into her shop or Yolanda's. Maybe they needed better exteriors to entice them in. She knew Keep Your Head used heads with cute hand-painted expressions on their faces to display the hats. And Cook Up Trouble had a miniature kitchen in the window to show off pots and utensils. They appeared outsized on the tiny stove and countertop, but that was the charm that made people stop and look.

"Tally," Andrea said as soon as she came in the door. "The fridge has quit. I'm afraid the chocolates are going to melt. Where have you been?"

Tally raced to the large stainless refrigerator in the kitchen and cracked the door open. No light came on and no cold air tumbled out. "Do you know how long it's been off?" Why hadn't Andrea texted her?

Andrea had tailed her into the kitchen. "I'm not sure. I went to get some more Clark Bars and they felt too soft." Those were made from Tally's treasure trove of recipes from her granny, as most of her wares were.

With both of them tugging they managed to roll the fridge out far enough to check that it was still plugged in.

Tally whipped out her cell phone and called Yolanda. "Is Gene still there?"

"Sure, he has to replace a pipe and Allen hasn't gotten back yet with it."

"Can you tell Gene to come over here right away? My refrigerator conked out."

"Oh no! I'll get him."

Gene walked in two minutes later. The look he gave Tally was haughty, not friendly. It said something like: *Oh, so now you need me, right, Miss Hoity-Toity?*

His expression for Andrea said something altogether different. Tally didn't like that.

Hoping it would help, Tally groveled. "Gene, could you possibly get this running? I'm afraid my goodies will melt, especially the chocolate."

He stared through half-closed eyelids and smirked. He knew she needed him and that she didn't like him, she could tell.

"Please? Could you get it fixed soon?"

"That depends on what's wrong with it, doesn't it?" He sauntered to the appliance, cracked the door, as Tally had done, then closed it and pulled the refrigerator farther out from the wall. "Do you ever clean behind here?"

"I haven't yet. We only moved in a few weeks ago." The appliance had come with the shop, and she had no idea how old it was.

"The last people didn't either, it looks like." He drew a small flashlight out of his back pocket and shone it around. "Get me a vacuum."

Tally didn't like his clipped tone, ordering her around like that, but before she could hustle to get her mini vacuum from the other side of the room, Andrea was handing it to him. She would ignore his manner as long as he got her appliance working before she lost her precious candies.

A flock of tourists chose that moment to swarm the store, setting off the front-door chimes several times. Tally returned to the salesroom to help Mart wait on them while Andrea lingered in the kitchen another moment. Tally was dying to sneak a peek into the kitchen and see what was going on between them, but she was too busy. Andrea emerged after a minute or two, a dreamy softness in her large brown eyes. Was she up to hanky-panky with Gene in the kitchen?

Tally ignored the small warning signal her brain had sent her and happily sold box after box of her handmade Mary Janes, Twinkies, Mallomars, even some individual pieces of taffy and fudge. Her Baileys Truffle Fudge was, as usual, a big seller. She was especially proud of that one, as it was her own recipe. She seemed to have a knack for fudge. It was a tourist favorite, too, luckily.

Andrea was now hard at work. She seemed less reticent when she was interacting with the customers, Tally was happy to see. Not truculent at all, either, like she had seemed with Tally earlier.

Gene picked an awful moment to wander in from the kitchen. The shop was packed and his clothes were covered in dust and lint, probably from behind the refrigerator. Tally gaped at him in horror and rushed to shoo him out of the public room into the kitchen.

"You're gonna have to replace the thermistor at least. Maybe the motor, if you don't want everything to spoil."

Was his voice loud enough for the customers to hear? She didn't like the thought of them contemplating melted chocolate and too-soft fudge. She drew him farther toward the rear of the kitchen, almost to the door to the alley.

"How long will it take to get the parts?"

"Depends."

"On what?" The man was maddening. She gritted her teeth and managed a small smile.

"I'll run out to the hardware store and see what's in stock."

As he left, out the back—Tally made sure of that—she crossed her fingers that the hardware store was well stocked. The clouds she had noticed earlier had gotten serious and were shedding a brief summer shower. Gene dashed to his truck, parked near Yolanda's back door. She thought he got only moderately wet.

She checked the candies in the dark, warming fridge and decided that they would have to be cooled very soon. So she texted Yolanda, who returned a text saying that she had room in her floral cooler.

Tally stuck her head into the sales room. It was only half full, and Andrea and Mart didn't seem overwhelmed. "I have to go out for a minute. Be right back."

When Andrea gave her an exasperated look, Tally motioned her over and whispered, "I'm taking the candies to Yolanda's cooler. They're getting too soft."

Andrea nodded. "Good idea. Don't take too long. We might get busy. Is Gene here?"

"No, he's gone to get some parts."

Tally hauled her treasures, stuffed into a plastic garbage bag, out her back door, through the rain—now a light mist—and into Yolanda's shop. There was a fair amount of business at Bella's Baskets, Tally was glad to see.

"What temperature is your cooler, by the way?" Tally had forgotten to ask that. Maybe it would be too warm or too cool.

"It's supposed to always be thirty-five degrees. I don't check it, but the flowers seem to thrive." She kept a few hardy varieties for her arrangements.

"Mine is a tad above that, so this will be fine." She unpacked the Whoopie Pies, chocolate-covered caramels, and other goodies into the empty space beside the carnations and daisies while Yolanda held the door to the cooler for her.

As they finished, Allen, the other handyman and Gene's employee, pushed in through the back door carrying a bag from the hardware store.

Tally silently fumed, realizing that Gene could have called or texted Allen to pick up her items instead of making another unnecessary trip. She couldn't afford for Gene to pad his bill by taking extra hours to do the job, or billing for extra trips.

Chapter 3

"Where's Gene?" Allen asked as he set his packages on the floor by Yolanda's sink in the rear of Bella's Baskets. "I brought the pipe and the tools he needs."

Tally tilted her head up at him. The man wasn't extremely tall, but it didn't take much to be taller than Tally. Tally thought his weathered face and obvious strength were awfully attractive. Much more so to her than Gene's classic movie-star good looks that Yolanda, Andrea, and every other young woman in town were so taken with.

"He went to the hardware store," Tally said. "You didn't see him there?"

"Huh? Why did he go there? I've got everything we need. He could have paid for this stuff."

"Tally's refrigerator needed something," Yolanda said.

Allen shook his head and exchanged raised eyebrows with Tally. He seemed as bemused as she was by his boss.

"I have to turn off the water for a bit," he told Yolanda.

"Do what you have to. I can always run next door if I need anything." Yolanda turned to a basket she was beginning and pawed through her jingle bell collection to select the ideal one.

Allen crawled beneath the sink to start working on the pipe that needed replacing, clanking with his wrench and other tools, and muttering about getting his money from Gene. He seemed doubtful it would happen.

"Andrea and Mart were fairly busy, so I'd better get back," Tally said. "Come over if you need anything."

"Do you know when Gene is showing up at your place?" Yolanda asked.

"It shouldn't take him long, why?"

"He borrowed a few dollars and said he'd get to the bank today to pay me back. Ask him if he's been to the bank when he shows up."

"Will do."

Tally left by the front door and lingered on her short stroll to her place. It was a pleasant day. Puddles steamed on the pavement in the aftermath of the sudden storm. She closed her eyes and turned her face to the July sun, a stray hair wisping across her face in the slight, sultry breeze, carrying the damp of the rain. She tucked it behind her ear. When she opened her eyes, she was overcome by a feeling of contentment, despite whatever else was going on. She had returned to the town where she grew up, on the way to her very own shop, and working next door to her best friend. Even better, she had to wait for a clump of tourists to enter her place before she could go in.

She quickly grabbed her smock from the kitchen, noting that Gene hadn't returned yet, and got to work helping sell her handmade delectables. Life was so good right now, she felt like pinching herself.

"My time's kinda up," Mart said at five. "You want me to stay extra?"

"I'm sure we'll be okay," Tally answered. "We're stocked up, so Andrea and I can stay out front and sell." They were alone in the kitchen, so she took Mart aside. "Mart, are you okay? You're not sick?"

"Why do people think I'm sick? I'm perfectly healthy. See?" She stuck out her tongue as if that would prove she didn't have any diseases.

"It's…something I heard."

"From who? Who's spreading rumors about me? Is it Andrea? You know she's jealous of me and Gene. He doesn't pay any attention to her. I wouldn't listen to her either, if I were you."

Tally resisted the urge to roll her eyes. "I shouldn't have given it a moment's thought. No, I didn't hear anything from Andrea." Technically, that was true. Yolanda had relayed the information from Andrea to Tally. "Forget I said anything. See you tomorrow."

Tally would have to look up the symptoms of VDs, but Mart did seem healthy.

Mart ran out the front door and climbed in the passenger door of a waiting car. Tally ducked down to squint at the driver. The car looked like Gene's little gray convertible, a Fiat Spider, but the top was up and she couldn't be sure. Whoever the driver was, he leaned over and gave Mart a long kiss before they took off. It had to be Gene. No one else in this town owned a gray convertible Fiat Spider. She fumed, thinking about the fact that he was supposed to be working.

When she turned from the door, Andrea was standing behind her, a stormy frown of rage on her small, delicate face. Yes, Andrea was definitely jealous of Mart and Gene. But Gene wasn't innocent. He seemed to be leading everyone on.

He also should have been fixing Tally's fridge.

So, did Mart have a disease that meant Tally shouldn't be using her, or was Andrea lying out of jealousy to get Mart fired? Tally decided to come down in favor of the latter. Mart didn't look sick, but Andrea was definitely jealous.

She didn't have time to dwell on her employees, though. A merry call rang out from the kitchen. She ran there from the front room to receive a shipment from the nut farm man. How she loved handling the bulging bags of whole and half pecans, shelled peanuts, slivered almonds, and other nuts that lent crunchy goodness to her treats.

When it was almost seven, time to close up, she finally heard Gene in the other room. She ran to the kitchen to make sure it was him. He had his head inside the appliance, fiddling with something.

As she was about to return to the front, Yolanda rushed in the back door, carrying a half-done basket. The jingle bell she had already inserted tinkled as she swung the basket onto the counter.

"I need to know what you think," she said. She noticed Gene and said "Oh!" with a smile. "Did you get the cash?"

"Completely forgot. I'll get it next time I'm by the bank."

"I thought you were closing up early," Tally said, noticing the frown Gene's response had drawn on Yolanda's brow.

* * * *

Yolanda held her anger inside, not wanting Tally to see how upset she was. She grabbed Gene's arm and pulled him out the back door of Tally's shop so she could talk to him in private in the alley.

"I need that money," she said. "You promised to give it to me today. You said you positively would pay me today. I've been waiting a long time." Yolanda knew her parents would dole out any money she asked for, but she wanted to prove herself with her shop. She hadn't gotten any handouts from them yet this month and didn't plan to. She wanted so much to make a go of Bella's Baskets on her own.

"Not that long." He gave her that devastating smile. It didn't devastate her now, though. In fact, it bounced off her anger. "I'll have it. Hold your horses. Be patient."

"How much longer? I've been patient. And you did promise me. You swore you'd have it. I need to buy some things for the shop. Tally might be right about you. If I don't get that money by the end of the day, I'll go to your father."

She saw alarm creep into his deep gray eyes. Maybe she'd gone too far. But she *did* need the money very soon. It wasn't a small amount, and she couldn't afford to be without it much longer.

He reached out to stroke her hair and she swatted his hand away.

His eyes turned hard. "If you couldn't afford it, maybe you shouldn't have given it to me in the first place."

"I didn't give it to you. It was a loan." Yolanda felt her jaw clench, along with her fists. "I mean what I say. I'll go to Mayor Faust."

Gene turned and went through the door into Tally's shop. Yolanda composed herself and followed him. Where was she? Oh yes, she was bringing the basket to Tally for her opinion. She turned her attention to Tally. "I was locking the door, and I got a call for a rush job. They want this tomorrow. It's for a birthday party the next evening."

* * * *

Yolanda indicated the basket she had set on Tally's counter. "Tell me which is better."

Tally wanted to ask Yolanda what was going on between her and Gene, but she would save it for later when Gene wasn't around. She turned her attention to the basket. It was white wicker with a thick, twisted wicker handle.

Yolanda had filled it with Shasta daisies, a yellow teapot with matching cup and saucer, and some yellow cloth napkins. "This is for a sixty-fifth birthday. And she's a big tea drinker. I'll get some tea bags, and I want to use something from you, maybe your handmade Twinkies?" Yolanda tilted her head and twisted a curly lock around her little finger.

Tally's Twinkies were a different shape than the classics, but were the same golden color. She considered the taste of hers superior, but maybe that was a bias on her part.

"They'd go with the color scheme. Do you want them now?" Tally started to pull a wrapped package, ready to sell, from the freestanding freezer.

"I'll get them later so they'll be fresher, but here's my question." She set two spools of ribbon on the counter with her scissors. "Which color is best?" One spool was bright yellow with white polka dots, the other pale yellow striped with another yellow a shade deeper.

Yolanda used her huge ribbon scissors to cut a snippet of each and looped them over the handle.

Tally reached toward the handle. "Let me see what—ouch!" She had run into the point of the scissors that Yolanda brandished and it had nicked her knuckle. "Those are wicked." She squeezed a teensy drop of blood out of the joint of her index finger.

Yolanda gasped as the scissors clattered from her hand to the countertop. "I have to keep them sharp." The blades were fiendishly long. "Are you all right? Can I get you a bandage?"

"No, no, it's almost stopped. I'm fine. I wanted to see one color at a time. Are *you* all right? You're very pale."

"I...I don't like blood. Seeing it, touching it, thinking about it." She stared at Tally's cut, looking stricken and pale.

Tally pulled out a stool and ordered Yolanda to sit. Her color soon returned, and Tally held her hand behind her so Yolanda wouldn't see that her cut hadn't quite quit bleeding yet.

Andrea came into the room clutching her large bag to her chest. "Should I lock the door and turn on the closed sign? No one is here."

"Sure," said Tally. "But tell us first which ribbon you like better."

"I like the dots," Andrea said. "I have to leave right now, if that's okay with you." She walked over to Gene and gave him a poke on his shoulder. "I have a hot date tonight. Right, Gene?"

Tally managed not to let her mouth drop open, but Yolanda wasn't as successful. Tally felt the temperature drop to near freezing as a stunned silence stretched among the four.

Gene straightened up and grinned at Andrea. "I'll be there."

"I'll go switch the sign to closed," Tally said, wanting to leave the room. It was early to close, but she wanted everyone gone.

"Gene Faust, I meant what I said. I want my money today." Yolanda's voice was frigid. Before Tally could move, Yolanda ran out the back in a blur of hot colors.

A short time later, after everyone was gone and peaceful quiet reigned inside Tally's shop, she took another stab at counting her money and matching the numbers on her spreadsheet. When the numbers showed a shortage one more time, she stood and shoved her chair back so hard it rolled away and smashed against a cupboard.

She sent Yolanda a text and waited. No answer. She called Yolanda and got her voice mail. Two more calls went unanswered. Now she had another worry, and she began to fret about her friend. Tally started pacing her kitchen, then noticed the abandoned basket sitting on her countertop. The flowers hadn't wilted yet, she was glad to see. Tally and Yolanda each had keys to the other's shop, so Tally fished her key to Bella's Baskets out of her desk drawer. After sticking some Twinkies in amongst the flowers, she grabbed the basket and headed out the front door, the jingle bell rattling softly, slightly out of tune with the door chimes.

The lights in the basket shop were turned off, but it wasn't yet eight o'clock so the sun was still up, and would be for about another hour. There was enough daylight that Tally didn't need to switch on the lights, so she went straight for the cooler and stuck the basket in.

She snapped her fingers and grimaced when she realized she had left the spools of ribbon at her place. Her snap sounded loud in the dim, empty shop. Then she heard another sound. It was barely audible, but the shop was otherwise completely silent. She followed the sound of the soft snuffles and found Yolanda on the floor, slumped against her worktable, quietly weeping.

Wordlessly, Tally knelt beside her and wrapped her arms around her bereft friend.

"You can say you told me so," Yolanda said, thickly, hanging her head.

"No, I won't say it."

"You don't have to. Gene is no good. You were right. He doesn't like me. He's only after my money." Yolanda rested her cheek on Tally's shoulder.

Tally petted her dark, wild, springy curls. "I'll bet he enjoys your company, though."

"Ha." The syllable was mirthless. "He'll enjoy Andrea's a lot more. She's much younger than I am. And she works out."

"Oh, come on, young isn't always so good. Andrea jogs. I'm not sure that's the same as working out. Any man should be proud to be seen with you."

"Well, whether they should or not, they're not flocking to my side." She raised her head and looked around. "I don't see any here. Do you?" She displayed the ghost of a grin.

Good, Yolanda was cheering up. "I brought your basket over to put into your cooler."

"Tally, what's that?" Yolanda sat up straight, sounding panicked.

A drop of blood from her nicked knuckle had fallen onto the floor. "Oh, I guess it's still bleeding. Do you have a bandage?"

"My first aid kit is on the shelf behind you."

Tally got up and doctored herself, putting some antibiotic cream and a bandage on her finger, and wiping the drips from the floor.

"Did Gene get your refrigerator fixed?"

"No, and I'm upset about that. I believe he could have. But he left before he finished the job."

"Tally, I've always thought you were the naïve one and I was the better judge of people, but I might have to change my mind about that."

They sat on the floor in companionable silence, drawing comfort from each other, until daylight started to fade outside. Tally rose and dusted off her hands on her jeans. "I know what we need. A night on the town."

"Yes. I don't have to drop this basket off until tomorrow." Yolanda's smile was almost up to her normal high wattage. "That sounds good. Let me fix my face. What do you have in mind?"

The nightlife in Fredericksburg wasn't exactly glamorous, nothing like Austin or Dallas, but there were some fun places.

They dropped in to a couple of them, Crossroads and Hondo's, both on the main street where their own shops were located. Each had a live band and plenty of mirth and noise. It served to drown out some of their sorrows.

After a couple of drinks each, soaked up with nachos, stuffed roasted jalapeños, and shrimp and grits, they walked home, sated and much more content than they had been a few hours ago.

"I have to ask you something," Tally said. "Well, two things."

"Shoot." Yolanda cocked her thumb and stuck her pointer finger at Tally.

"Andrea—"

"I don't want to hear about her."

"This is in relation to her working for me. I'd like to know if you have any tips. I'm having a hard time relating to her. I know she's shy and insecure—"

"You could have fooled me." Yolanda twirled a curl around her little finger.

"You're right, she was rather forward with Gene today. She's always seemed shy to me before today. With me, she usually seems…distant, or maybe a little prickly. I'm having trouble getting her to loosen up with me."

"Do you need to be best buddies with your hired help? It might be better this way."

Tally gave that a moment's thought. They walked on, and light from the shops that were still open spilled onto the sidewalk in huge, misshapen rhomboid patches.

"What's the other thing?" Yolanda asked. "You said you had two questions."

"I need you to see what you think about my bookkeeping. Not tonight, but maybe tomorrow? It looks like I'm off somewhere."

Yolanda gave her a sideways look. "Off? Which way?" Headlight beams from a car that was turning at the next corner caught the gleam of her dangling earrings.

"The wrong way."

"So maybe Andrea is stealing your money."

Yolanda might be saying that, thought Tally, *because she doesn't like Andrea. But still...* "I started thinking that as I was telling you all this. Look, Gene borrowed money from you, money that he hasn't paid back, right?"

"I doubt he ever will, or ever intended to," Yolanda said. "I was such an easy mark." She turned her face to the stars. "I thought we had a thing going. Ha. Am I ever dumb."

"You are not dumb." Tally caught her hand and squeezed it. "He's a sleazebag. But what if he's doing the same thing to Andrea? He's persuasive, wouldn't you say?"

"Oh yes. He is. So, you think he's having her dip into your till?"

"She could be. Maybe. Or maybe not that. Not directly. But maybe he's borrowing from her and she's running out of cash and...there's all that money that she handles every day."

"Or Gene might be swiping it all by himself. Is he ever alone in your place?"

"Not exactly alone, but I'll bet he could probably manage to do it."

＊ ＊ ＊ ＊＊

After Tally and she parted ways, Yolanda couldn't stay still. She'd gone inside and dropped off her purse. She locked up and went outside again. She starting walking in the dark, pondering, trying to decide whether or not she really would go to Mayor Faust about his adoptive son. If she told him, would he reimburse her the money she was out? She could ill afford to lose it permanently, and it was beginning to seem that she might never get it back from Gene.

She tried to picture talking to Mayor Faust. He was an imposing figure. He looked a bit like the Monopoly mayor, heavyset, potbellied, and bald. But he was also tall and eagle-eyed, and without the white mustache and top hat. What would he do if she went to him and said his son had bilked her out of money and possibly was hitting on other women? He had no deep love for Gene anyway. Would he disinherit him completely? Tell her to bring charges against him?

He was running for reelection, so that might have a bearing. Maybe he'd want to hush up his son's misdeeds, fearing scandal and taint—things that would hurt his chances of retaining his office. If he wanted it swept underneath the rug, he might pay her.

Another thing to consider, though, was the possibility that Gene might be getting money from others. Andrea, for instance. It might be too much to overlook.

Yolanda walked for about an hour, thinking hard, as night grew deeper and deeper.

* * * *

The next morning, Tally was determined to get to the bottom of her shortage. She decided to ask Andrea, point-blank, if she had taken money from the shop. If she phrased it right, it wouldn't be harsh and accusatory. She hoped. She rehearsed some phrases on her short walk to work. Maybe something like, "Are you having any financial problems, Andrea?" Or maybe, "I wonder if you need any help, Andrea. Am I paying you enough?"

However, so many customers streamed in that Tally was kept busy helping wait on them and bringing out fresh candies to replenish the emptying shelves. Having to hold her bandaged finger straight was a hindrance boxing up candies as well as making change, but she was getting used to it. She had to run over to Yolanda's twice and retrieve her chilled goods from the floral cooler. Both times, she returned to her own kitchen and noticed Yolanda's ribbon and scissors still on her counter, forgotten by both of them. She kept telling herself she would return them on her next trip.

Gene showed up mid-morning, right after Mart arrived, with some more mysterious-looking parts, and got to work tinkering with the refrigerator. Allen came in soon after he did. They had a short conversation that ended with Allen fuming and Gene giving him a shrug. Tally remembered Allen complaining about getting reimbursed from Gene for purchasing parts with his own money. Was he even getting paid for his work? she wondered.

With both of them working, Tally hoped she would have a functional appliance soon. She worried about how much this was going to cost, though.

A few minutes after Allen arrived, a young woman walked in the front door and came up to Tally with a purposeful stride. "Is Gene Schwartz here?" she spat out with a frown. She looked about Andrea's age, maybe two or three years out of high school. Her soft blond curls fell prettily around her heart-shaped face.

Tally hesitated for a moment. She had almost forgotten that he used to be Gene Schwartz, before he was adopted by Mayor Faust. "He's fixing something for me." She didn't want this strange, angry woman wandering freely in her store, so she didn't direct her to the kitchen, where he was. "Can I give him a message?"

"I need to talk to him. It's important." She bobbed her head to emphasize her words. "Tell him Dorella Diggs needs to see him. I'll wait outside."

How odd, thought Tally. Maybe this was another female Gene had borrowed money from. She didn't have time to leave the floor now, though. The message would have to wait. She wasn't Gene's errand girl.

A little while later, Allen ducked into the room. "I need to leave, but Gene is finishing up. You should be good to go now."

Tally called her thanks and heard him go out the noisy back door. It had a bad squeak. Maybe she should have Gene fix that before he left.

Andrea pulled Tally aside as soon as Allen left. "I don't feel well. I'm afraid I'll have to leave." She certainly was pale and shaky.

"Do you want to sit for a while?" She wanted to feel her forehead, but she knew Andrea would not like that.

"No, I have to go." She grabbed her bag from under the counter and headed for the kitchen, her tennis shoes squeaking on the floor as she pivoted. "I'll leave out the back."

Luckily, the steady stream of customers eventually slacked off somewhat so Tally and Mart survived the next hour. A short downpour helped keep the shop from overflowing with customers.

A little before six o'clock, Yolanda came in the front door. Today she wore a red and yellow dashiki over lilac leggings. Her earrings were huge brass discs that flashed in the light shed by the Mason jar lights. Several brass hoops adorned her right wrist. "Did you know your back door is locked?"

Tally shook her head. "Maybe Andrea or Allen pushed the lock accidentally when they left."

"I have my helper working, and we're not very busy," Yolanda told Tally. "I wonder if I could go over your books while I have a few spare moments."

Tally hadn't mentioned a thing about the shortage to Andrea yet. She hadn't had a chance before Andrea started looking so ill, and she couldn't say anything before she left in such a rush. She hadn't even given Gene the message from Dorella. "Sure, go ahead." She waved Yolanda toward the kitchen office.

Yolanda stared at Tally's bandaged finger for a couple of seconds. "Is it…is your finger okay?"

"Sure, it's—" Tally glanced down. The bandage, decidedly pink, needed changing. "I have another one in my pocket. I'll freshen it. Go on back and I'll be there in a few minutes."

Poor Yolanda. The sight of blood incapacitated her. Tally quickly changed the bandage and kept working while Yolanda went into the kitchen. By some miracle, Tally hoped she could make the numbers jibe and not indicate a shortage.

* * * *

Yolanda started across the kitchen to Tally's office, but didn't get far.

Something she had never seen before stopped her. Took her strength from her. Paralyzed her.

So much blood.

She had trouble comprehending what she was seeing. Her legs started to give way.

The next thing she remembered, she was sitting on the floor next to it. There was one familiar item. She still couldn't quite grasp what she was seeing.

Too much blood.

She shook her head to clear it and took a deep breath. But evil smells entered her nose and her lungs so she blew it back out. She clamped her hands to her head.

What was she doing here? Oh yes, she was supposed to go over Tally's financial records and find out what was happening.

Her head spun, felt like it would float off her neck and bump against the ceiling. She kept a tight grip on it with both hands to keep it in place. Bring it down. Keep it sitting on her neck.

But there it was, still lying there. She grabbed the familiar object and got off the floor.

She started for Tally's office again, then shook her head again.

She needed to leave. She needed to think. She needed to hide this thing.

* * * *

It seemed like only minutes passed before Tally heard the back door squeaking open again. Was Yolanda done already? How could that be? She called to Yolanda, but didn't get an answer. She called Gene's name, too, and he didn't answer either.

"Excuse me a moment," she said to the woman, who had her arms full of Whoopie Pies. "I'll be right back. Mart, could you help this customer?" She had to see who had come in, or gone out. Mart was staying late today, luckily. It sounded like the door was unlocked now. Maybe Yolanda had left, or Gene. Had they left together? She didn't want Yolanda to forgive him and take him back.

She took two steps into the kitchen and froze. Gene hadn't left. He was sprawled on the floor in a large pool of blood. He looked very dead.

Chapter 4

Tally tried hard to swallow the bile that rose in her throat, but had to run to the bathroom, where she got sick. She reentered the kitchen and blinked, but the dead body of the handyman was still there. Gene Faust lay dead on her floor. It couldn't be a natural death, not with all that blood. There wasn't anything sharp in the vicinity that he could have accidently fallen on.

When Tally gripped the edge of the countertop and willed herself to look directly at him, she almost needed to run to the bathroom again. There was a gaping hole in his back. Had he been stabbed? She glanced at the counter for Yolanda's scissors. They weren't there.

She needed to call the police.

Her vision grayed around the edges, and her ears rang. Before she collapsed, she plunked onto the floor and lowered her head to get the circulation flowing up to her brain.

She needed to call the police.

But Yolanda's scissors! Had she killed him? He couldn't have fallen on them. Could he? Had something else killed him? Surely something had stabbed him. Was he dead when Yolanda had come through here?

She needed to call the police.

Tally texted Yolanda: *Where are you?* She waited, still sitting on the floor, for an answer. None came. She called Yolanda's number. It rang and rang. Voice mail came on. She punched the call off, getting more and more upset.

"Where are you, Yolanda?" she whispered. Should she run next door? Squeezing her eyes shut, she pondered what to do.

"I'm leaving," Mart called from the front. "The shop is almost empty. 'Bye."

Tally managed to call out a good-bye and heard Mart leave through the front.

She jumped an inch when the phone in her hand trilled. She started to silence it, then noticed her brother's number. She swiped her finger across the face of the phone and answered his call.

"Hey, Sis!" Her heart rose a bit at his cheerful, booming voice. "How's it going?"

She thought about telling him, but only hesitated a second. "Fine. It's all…fine here. Where are you?"

"On my way!"

"On your…way? Here? How close are you?" No! He couldn't come here now!

"Mom didn't tell you I was coming? I should get there tonight. Maybe about nine or ten."

No. Mom did not tell her that. Okay. Nine or ten o'clock. Better than right now.

"Sis? You there? I'm driving, so I'll come straight to your place."

Her place. Any place but the shop. "Yes, that would be perfect. Come to my place. No, Mom didn't say anything. I guess she forgot. She's excited about their new show."

Cole let loose with his infectious laugh. "Yeah, she is. Well, I'm coming, and I'm bringing a surprise. Someone for you to meet."

It was now about seven thirty. Nine o'clock would come very soon.

"If I'm not there," she said, "wait a bit and hold tight. I'll be home soon. There are some…things to clean up at the shop."

"I can help."

"No! I mean, it's nothing. I'll do it. See you soon."

She broke the connection before she had to explain anything else, then she called the police.

They arrived within minutes. She called Yolanda three more times before they got there and still couldn't reach her.

Official people swarmed over her kitchen, setting up lights and taking pictures, cordoning off the whole room so that she was moved to the front of the store to be questioned. Tally felt she could breathe much better when the body was out of sight.

The police had ushered out the remaining customers and locked the place up tight.

Gene! Dead! In her shop!

Those thoughts kept circling above her calm, rational answers to their questions. She couldn't tell them much. Several people had gone through the kitchen, but they must have been there while he was still alive. She gave them the names of Allen, Andrea, Mart, and Yolanda. Had there been any deliveries that afternoon? She was sure there hadn't been. She herself hadn't been in the kitchen for hours.

She told them that the back door was usually left unlocked, but had been inadvertently locked for a short time. What time was that? She couldn't tell them, she'd been so busy with customers.

After about an hour she was released and slowly walked home, her mind repeating the fact that someone had died—no, had been murdered—in her own shop. She'd gone half a block when she halted, remembering she hadn't mentioned Yolanda's scissors. A question entered her head—had Yolanda finished that tea basket for the woman's sixty-fifth birthday today? If so, it wasn't decorated with either of the two ribbons, the bright yellow with polka dots, or the pale two-tone yellow. Maybe she had used white ribbon. Maybe she had forgotten where she left her supplies. Maybe someone from Gene's checkered past had come into the kitchen, stabbed him with Yolanda's scissors, and run out, taking them with him.

But where was Yolanda?

Tally turned around and headed over to Bella's Baskets. It would be closed now, but maybe she was there. Tally peered through the dark front windows, but did not see any sign of Yolanda. When she went around back, the door was locked. One more text to her friend, then she headed home to be there when her brother, Cole, arrived. With a surprise. A friend for her to meet. She sure didn't feel up to that.

When Tally had come home for her grandmother's funeral in the spring of this year, Yolanda had made her realize how much she missed living in the place where she'd grown up. Her small bakery in Austin had been doing well. She wondered *How could she justify leaving a booming business to start another one?* It would be making a leap into the unknown. Yolanda had dragged her to see the shop next to her own gift basket business. It was an empty sandwich shop with a *For Sale* sign in the window.

"See?" Yolanda had said, pointing through the windows of the darkened space. "You'd be right next door to Bella's Baskets. We could work well together, your baked goods and my baskets." She gestured to her own shop window, crammed full of baskets, shiny balloons, and delicate silk flowers. Her sign swung gently on a wooden arm that stuck out across part of the sidewalk, proclaiming that this was, indeed, Bella's Baskets. To go with the name, Yolanda made it a practice to tuck a small jingle bell into each gift basket she sold.

Yolanda had half persuaded her, but Tally was still on the fence when two boxes were delivered to her Austin apartment after she returned from the funeral. The first was marked fragile and contained mostly packing material. Nestled in the middle was the ornate mantel clock that Tally remembered being over her grandmother's fireplace. As a child, she had sat on the floor in her granny's house playing with her dolls and listening to the comfortable ticking of the clock for many hours. She carefully lifted it out and ran her hands over the smooth wood, then traced the carvings around the face. She opened the door on its back and wound it. After she set it on a shelf and heard the ticking in her own apartment, tears sprang to her eyes.

Tally wiped her eyes and opened the second box to find several more things from her grandmother's estate. She was charmed by the faded one-foot-square hooked rug of a yellow rose that she had made for her granny when she was small, and by some of the dangly earrings she'd been permitted to use for playing dress up. But she was enthralled by the old-fashioned metal box of recipes. Her granny had been the best candy maker ever. And these were her old-time candy recipes.

She remembered reading through the first one, for something called Mallomars. Her grandmother had grown up in New Jersey, and after she moved to Texas, she experimented with re-creating treats from her childhood. This one was made with honey, brown sugar, some gelatin, egg whites, and semisweet chocolate, plus a few other ingredients. Even reading the recipe, she could almost taste and smell the chocolate-covered gooey treat.

She had tried that one out first, using lots of pans and her candy thermometer, and had gotten hooked on vintage candies that very night.

After careful consideration, and realizing she could get top dollar for her successful bakery business, she decided she wanted to sell vintage candy made from those precious recipes. She bought the place next to Yolanda's, and moved in about a month ago. She opened her shop in mid-June. June was not peak season here, but not low season either, until the Fourth of July weekend, which was High Season. That was a big boost. She considered that she was giving her shop a chance to get onto its feet and establish itself as a fixture, a vintage candy shop, for the high volume fall-into-the-holidays season.

She dragged herself through her front door and glanced at her grandmother's clock. It read nine thirty, a lot later than her usual time to get home from work. She was relieved that Cole's Volvo wasn't there yet. Only her own powder-blue Chevy Sonic sat under the shelter of her carport at the end of her front driveway. She kicked off her shoes and sank into her navy-blue couch. When she flicked the TV on, she caught the middle of a drama that she didn't usually watch. She clicked it off and heaved herself up to rummage in the kitchen for something resembling at least a light supper, since it was late for a big dinner.

Tally had finished assembling a ham and Swiss sandwich with lettuce and tomato when she heard a car drive up. In seconds, Cole was knocking at the door. She kind of dreaded meeting someone new tonight. She was so exhausted from the events of the day, and the questioning had finished wearing her out. The detective had warned her that she might face more of that in the coming days, too.

Taking a deep breath, she unlocked the door. Her handsome blond brother, Cole, stood there alone, carrying a case at his side. She peeked around him and squinted toward the car, up and down the street, but no one else was there. Unless he—or she—was hiding behind the big tree in her yard.

"Where's the person I'm supposed to meet? Coming later?"

"No, he's here now." Cole grinned, showing both dimples as he hoisted high the vented carrier he held. "Meet Nigel."

Inside the carrier crouched the biggest cat Tally had ever seen. "Is it a mountain lion?"

Cole chuckled. "No, he's a Maine coon. They run large."

That was an understatement. The cat was in a dog carrier. A cat carrier wouldn't have been able to contain him.

"Can I let him out inside?" asked Cole. "He's been cooped up for a long time."

"I guess." Tally stopped gaping and stood aside for Cole and Nigel to enter. "Will he pee on the floor?"

"You don't know much about cats, do you?"

"How would I? I've never had one. We didn't have any pets growing up, so how do you know what to do with it?"

"Him. He's not an *it*."

"Well, excuuuse me. Him. So, will he pee on my floor?"

"Wait here a sec." Cole set the carrier down in the middle of the living room and ran back to his car. He returned with his battered suitcase and a few other items—a bag of kitty litter, a plastic litter box, and a grocery bag. After giving his sister a hug, he set up the litter box first, then drew out bowls and filled them with cat food and water.

"Is this stuff going to stay in the middle of the floor?" Tally asked, entranced that the big tuxedo-colored cat went right to the litter box and used it, neatly scratching at the bottom of the box to bury the evidence before taking a few dainty steps to his food and digging in.

"You're right. I shouldn't start him out where he's not going .
Where should we put his box?"

"The back porch?"

Cole frowned. "Of course not! He's an indoor cat. You can't let him out."

"What made you decide to get a cat anyway? And such a big one?"

Cole plopped onto the couch, and Nigel, finished with scarfing up his food, jumped into his lap to clean his paws. Cole gave a soft "Oof!" when Nigel landed.

"I didn't exactly decide," he said. "It just happened."

Tally sat beside him and tentatively touched the top of the cat's head. It was soft and silky. "Don't tell me. A woman left him behind when you broke up with her."

"That's basically it."

Cole went through women like, well, like this cat would probably go through cat food and kitty litter.

"What did you say he is? Is he wild? Part cougar? Part mountain lion?"

"All cats are part cougar and mountain lion, but no, he's tame. Maine coon is a real breed."

"How often does that litter box have to be changed?" she asked. It didn't look big enough for this monster cat, tame or not.

"You should change it about twice a week, but you need to scoop every day."

Tally sat straight up. "Wait a minute. What's this 'you' business?"

"Right. I mean, generally, people need to do that."

The way Cole said it, though, Tally had an inkling that wasn't what he meant at all—until she objected. Was he thinking of leaving this cat with her? A cat hardly fit Cole's lifestyle, which kept him on the road for weeks at a time. Tally never knew if his love-'em-and-leave-'em habits were a result of his job as an itinerant sculptor or a result of his personality and his reluctance to stick to one woman. Maybe his inability to commit was a result of their nomadic upbringing. Tally sometimes worried she was a bit like her brother.

"I have to tell you what's going on here, Cole."

"What? Is something the matter? Why so serious?"

"It is serious. I don't know how to say this. It's…" Tears started flowing, even though she was trying to hold them inside.

"Sis. Tell me." He put his arm around her shoulders.

"A man was murdered in my shop today." She felt the muscles in his forearm tense.

"How did that happen?"

She told him everything she could. About finding Gene's body and about the police and the crime scene people coming, and about her trying to figure out how it could have happened. Her tears stopped as she related everything to him. She was glad he was here. He was comforting. When she finished telling him the entire story, they sat in silence for a few moments. Tally realized she was very tired.

"I'm beat. I need to go to bed. Do you want to stay here, Cole? You can have the couch." She didn't have a guest bedroom, but could always make room for her brother.

"That would be great, at least for a couple of nights. I have to be on the road in a few days. Heading to Albuquerque for work."

"I guess Nigel travels well? Albuquerque is a bit of a drive."

"Yeah, nine or ten hours. I'll get my other suitcase."

He hadn't answered her about the cat traveling to New Mexico. *If* the cat was going to travel to New Mexico. Would having a pet suit her own lifestyle? She didn't think so.

* * * *

The next morning, the cat was crouched outside her bedroom door like a huge inanimate stuffed toy when Tally emerged after showering and dressing. Cole was fast asleep on the couch, snoring with his mouth open. Tally bent to pet Nigel, and the cat bumped his head into her hand, forcing her to scratch his ears. He started to purr like a buzzsaw. Tally had to admit she was impressed with him.

"Nice kitty. Nice Nigel," she crooned, trying to match his rumbling. "I have to leave for work, so you take care of Cole for me."

She ducked out the back door rather than the front, so as not to disturb Cole, whose snoring was louder than the cat's purring.

Kevin, the shopkeeper at Bear Mountain Vineyards, ran out as she walked past his store.

"What's going on over at your place?" he asked. "No one seems to know."

The authorities hadn't told her not to say anything, so she could probably tell him. "A man was killed yesterday."

"Killed? Really?"

"In my shop."

Kevin was stunned into silence for a moment.

"Yeah, killed in my shop," Tally repeated.

"Who is it? Who killed him?"

"It's Gene, the mayor's son. He was doing some work for me. But I don't know who killed him. I don't think anyone does."

"Let me know if I can do anything."

She thanked Kevin and went on toward her place. A policeman was coming out the front door of her shop when she arrived.

"Is it all right to go in?" she asked.

"Sure. I'm taking the caution tape down now." He held a strip of bright yellow that had been stretched across the front door to seal it. "Crime Scene got busy and processed everything yesterday and last night. You might want to have someone get in there and clean up, but the scene is released."

"What... what do you think happened? To Gene, I mean?" She closed her eyes so she wouldn't see the memory of his body, but it didn't work.

"He was murdered."

"But how, and who did it?" Could they tell he'd been stabbed with scissors, she wondered, with a slight shiver of guilt for not mentioning Yolanda's scissors.

"Can't say. Sorry. Not while it's an ongoing investigation. Someone will be in contact later to take your statement."

"I talked to the police last night."

"They'll need you to sign an official statement sometime today."

She watched him get into a squad car and drive away.

Her shop felt foreign, changed, when she went inside. She stopped two steps inside the door, unable to take another step. But she had to. She had a business to run. The walls hadn't changed color; they still swirled with pink and lilac. The glass candy case gleamed, standing on the sturdy wide-planked floor. The cute Mason jar light fixtures hung overhead, as usual. But everything was dimmed, diminished, and duller than she remembered, seen through a dark aura hanging in the air.

She shook herself and marched into the kitchen to face the spot where Gene's body had been. Giving a shudder, she left. She went to Yolanda's and let herself in with her key to fetch her merchandise from Yolanda's cooler.

"Is...everything okay?" Yolanda asked as Tally sped by.

"We need to talk, but I have to open right now." Tally fled, but not before she saw Yolanda's condition. Red nose and eyes, unkempt hair, and even an outfit that was, for her, awful—a tan skirt and a plain black top with no jewelry in sight.

Tally was on her hands and knees scrubbing when Andrea came in.

"Here, let me help you," she said. "Did you see the television coverage last night?"

Tally shook her head. "Was it awful?"

"They didn't say much, but it was mentioned." Andrea got beside Tally on the floor with a brush and scrubbed at the bloodstain beside her. Andrea sniffled as she rubbed at the brown spots.

Tally got up and handed her a few tissues, for which Andrea thanked her. Poor kid was taking Gene's death hard. "You don't have to do this. I can handle it."

"No," Andrea said. "I'll help. I want to. What a shock, Gene murdered right here."

Tally let out a breath and nodded. The soap and water had loosened the bandage on her finger, so she put more cream on it and a new bandage. It seemed to be healing awfully slowly, but it was a deep puncture. She had rammed her finger into the point of the scissors, after all.

When the floor was clean, Tally stood and stretched. "We'd better get to work. I guess we can open for business. We might even get some gawkers. Might as well try to sell them something."

Andrea grinned at that. Over her tearfulness now, she didn't seem too broken up over Gene's death. But was her cheerfulness forced? Covering up some deep feelings for Gene?

Mart came in ready to work and the three tried to act like it was a normal business day.

That turned out to be difficult, but not in a bad way for Tally's business. The place was swamped. Dozens of people surged in, milling around. At first, when she saw how much traffic they were getting, she was afraid that most of them would gawk and leave. And maybe most of them did. But a lot of them noticed her products and decided to try them out. Enough that it was a record sales day within a couple of hours.

At about mid-morning, as Tally was getting ready to head to the kitchen for an overdue break in the cozy chair in her reading corner, Cole came through the front door. Mart brightened up when she saw him, and Tally thought Cole reciprocated.

"I came to sample your wares, Sis."

"You and everyone else in town." She introduced her brother to her employees and left them together with only slight misgivings. Since Cole would only be here for a few more days, she didn't think that would give him enough time to break Mart's heart. Would it?

This was a situation Tally would have to keep close track of. She couldn't have her brother's adorable dimples plowing through her employees' hearts.

Chapter 5

Tally was proven wrong almost immediately. When it was time for Mart's lunch break, Cole came and picked her up, idling his Volvo at the curb as he ran in to fetch her.

"Be back in a few," Mart called as she dashed out the door.

Tally drummed her fingers against her jeans, making *skritch*ing noises and wondering if this was something she should nip in the bud, for Mart's sake. After all, Cole had been through six—or was it seven?—women in the last six months. As far as Tally could tell from long distance, each one had fallen hard for Cole. While the relationship was on, he professed to be head over heels with each one, but when it was over, he moved on and acquired a new girlfriend within a few days. Some he met through clients, some from online dating services, and some, Tally suspected, were his clients. Cole, she had to admit, even though he was her brother, was a lothario, a regular love-'em-and-leave-'em kind of guy. Whether or not this was another result of their itinerant upbringing, Tally had no idea. But she'd seen him in action often enough, from middle school on, to know it was his thing.

He flirted with everyone, and when a cute female fell for him, which was often, he dove right in. Wined her and dined her. Dazzled some of them. That made them fall even harder. She remembered one girl in high school, and another in college, who both went into deep depressions when he'd had enough.

Cole's standard breakup method wasn't nice. Tally had talked to him about that many times. He wouldn't tell the woman directly that he was done with her. He would simply start dating someone else. Or move away, be off on his next road trip and not tell her good-bye.

Yes, Tally would have to warn Mart about her brother. She'd done it before, for other women. Now she felt responsible, like she had to defend her employee, arm her for what was inevitably going to happen between them. Oh, how she sometimes wished a femme fatale would toy with him and show him how it felt.

She was drawn out of her thoughts by the clamor of the door chimes and a fresh barrage of customers. Soon, she needed to retreat to the kitchen to make more goodies. After about an hour, Yolanda came in the back door. She looked only slightly better than she had earlier.

Tally pasted on a bright smile and greeted her. "Beautiful day out! How are you?"

Yolanda dragged herself to a stool at the prep island, plopped her elbows on the counter, and dropped her head onto her two fists.

"Come on, smile," Tally said. "It'll make you feel better." Tally finished combining the peanut butter and powdered sugar for Mary Janes, then pulled the hardened sugar and corn syrup mixture from the refrigerator and started spreading the mixture on the cooled candy base.

"You think so? Do you know that the police came into my shop this morning? Two of them. They questioned *me*! Like they suspect me or something."

Tally gave her friend a sideways glance, wanting to come at the subject obliquely. "So you know about...Gene?"

"That he's dead? Yes. The police told me that. But they seemed to be suspicious of me. Like I killed him or something. I'm not saying I didn't want to, but how could I kill someone? I couldn't do that."

Tally hugged her friend. "I know you couldn't." She stepped back to look at her, brushing off a stray blob of peanut butter and sugar that had landed on Yolanda's shoulder. At least she wasn't wearing a favorite outfit, or even an attractive one. Tally stuck the other half of the candy mixture into the microwave to soften, then carefully poured her peanut butter filling over the rest.

"So, how did he die?" Yolanda said. "Do you know? *Did* someone kill him? They wouldn't tell me."

"Yes, I do know. He died right there." She pointed to the spot on the floor with the candy thermometer she was cleaning. "I walked in and found him."

Yolanda gazed at the floor, and a visible spasm ran through her. She crossed her arms and hunched her shoulders. "And?" she said.

"And, yes, someone murdered him. Unless he fell onto a sharp object. But there wasn't anything there for him to fall onto."

"Sharp object? Was he stabbed?"

Tally nodded, unable to speak. She wanted to ask Yolanda about her scissors, but she also didn't want to. So she stuck the dough into the fridge to chill and changed the subject completely.

"You know the plastic models you were talking about the other day?" Yolanda gave her a blank stare. "He was stabbed with a plastic model? Of what?"

"No, no. Nothing to do with…Gene. I was wondering if you'd found out anything. You were going to research having my candies replicated to put in your window? Remember?"

Yolanda lifted her head, uncrossed her arms, and came alive, a bit. "Oh yes. I found out a little information. I did some printouts of prices to compare. Come over later and I'll show you."

"Are you all right? I tried and tried to get hold of you last night, to tell you about Gene."

"My…phone was dead. Sorry." Yolanda gazed past Tally's shoulder when she told that obvious lie. She'd been kicking the legs of the stool, and Tally finally noticed.

"You have new shoes?"

Yolanda lifted one shoulder with no enthusiasm. "I've had them awhile. I don't believe I've ever worn them before." They weren't her usual flamboyant style—plain black ballet flats.

How was Tally going to bring up the scissors? She had to know where they were. She *wanted* to know that they hadn't been used to kill Gene. She scrubbed her mixing bowl with more than her usual force. "So, did you get that basket done?"

"Basket? Oh yes, that basket. Not yet. I'll deliver it today. The customer called, and I said I'd be there in an hour. She said that would be okay."

"Will you be able to finish it?" *Without your scissors?*

"Sure. It's almost done. It only needs the ribbon. Did I leave that here?"

At last, an opening. "Yes, you did. Here they are." Tally wiped off her hands on her apron and picked up the two ribbon spools she had stuck into a drawer to keep them clean during the flurry of candy making. "I don't see your scissors, though." Tally swiveled her head to gaze around the kitchen. "I thought you left those here, too."

Yolanda drew back the hand she had stretched out to take the ribbon. "Gosh. I wonder…where…they could be."

Yolanda sounded like a robot when she said that. Her hand shook slightly, too. Tally was horrified at her first thought, but tamped it down. Her friend did not *kill* Gene. Was she shocked because she realized the scissors might be the murder weapon?

"No idea. If I see them, I'll let you know. Do you have another pair?"

"Oh sure. I have others." Yolanda reached out again and this time took the ribbon. "Thanks. I'll go finish that basket right now. I need to get it delivered."

She hopped off the stool and fled out the back door. Tally was left with the scent of a batch of homemade Twinkies wafting from the oven. That smell usually made her feel comfy and cozy, but, for some reason, it left her thinly forlorn and cold inside today.

* * * *

Yolanda blinked back tears on her way to Bella's Baskets. It might be reasonable for the police to suspect her, but Tally? It seemed like Tally wasn't believing what she said. Yolanda hadn't been completely truthful, she knew, but if her best friend suspected her of murder...

Her life was such a mess right now. She'd been dating a user. Her business was teetering on the brink of going under. Her family clearly thought her little sister was so much better than she was.

She pushed open the door to her shop. It took a moment for her eyes to adjust from the bright July sun to being indoors.

When they did, she saw a strange woman standing in the middle of the floor. Rats! She had forgotten to lock the front door again.

"Can I help you?" Yolanda put on a smile, hoping her eyes weren't red.

"Yes, I need a party basket. My granddaughter is turning sixteen, and I want to wow her. I'm giving her a car and would like to tuck the keys in the bottom."

Yolanda perked up as ideas started flooding in. "Oh yes, that would be great. We could use carnations, get it? *Car*-nations? Maybe some driving gloves, a car charger for her phone."

"What good ideas! I'm glad I came to you for this."

"What kind of car? I can maybe get some coasters with the make and model on it."

Partially energized after the woman left, Yolanda decided to deliver the basket with the yellow ribbon, show Tally the fake candy prices, then close the shop and go home. Maybe a long, hot bath would wash away some of her anxiety.

* * * *

Andrea came into the kitchen a short time later. "Did your friend leave?"

"Yes," Tally said, wondering how she knew Yolanda had been there. "Were we talking too loud?"

Andrea blinked. "No, I don't think so. But I heard you. I wanted to ask her something if she was still here."

"Ask me. I'm going over to look at some printouts in a few minutes, as soon as she gets back from a basket delivery."

Andrea waved her off. "No, that's okay. I'll ask her later." Andrea stared at her toes.

"Oh, you have new shoes, too?" Tally said. "Didn't you just get new ones?"

"This is an extra pair. I haven't ever worn them here before."

"Do you need a lunch break? You've been working nonstop."

"Yes, I would like one. I need it." Andrea whipped off her apron and hung it on a hook on the wall. "I won't be gone long. Thanks." She went out the squeaky back door.

That was rather abrupt, Tally thought. After trying so hard to get Andrea to take a break the other day, she'd scooted off now like she was late to something important. Andrea didn't usually use the back door. Tally glanced out the door and down the alley. Andrea was already nowhere to be seen. Had she gone into Yolanda's shop? Yolanda was probably out delivering the basket by now. Andrea had said she wanted to ask Yolanda something. What could that be?

Tally mentally shrugged, shoved another batch of Twinkies into the oven, took the timer with her, and went to fill in at the front of the store.

* * * *

That evening Tally and Cole had dinner together at her house. She was glad to cook for him and spend some time with him. He'd been with Mart for lunch and then again after the shop closed at seven o'clock. She had so many questions. She wanted to know if he had more news about their parents, and, most of all, what his plans were for that cat.

"That cat" was, at the moment, rubbing his broad, black furry side against Tally's legs as she carried two plates of tuna casserole to her kitchen table.

"Nigel," she said, trying to be stern with him, "you're going to make me trip."

Cole laughed. "You have to be an agile walker with him around. He doesn't let people get very far without his help."

"Help? I call it a hindrance."

"But he's so cute. Right?"

Tally looked down at the cat's wide-eyed, innocent face, above a blob of wild, white, soft fur. "Is he part lion?"

"I suppose every cat is part lion. They're all felines."

"I mean, is he *recently* part lion?"

Cole laughed again. "He's cute. That's all I know."

Tally somehow made it to the table without spilling anything. She set the plates down and sat. "You get our drinks. I don't want to chance another trip."

"Ha. Another trip—I get it."

Tally didn't, since she hadn't tripped yet. Her slight frown at his bad pun evaporated in an instant. She had never been able to be mad at her younger brother. A little upset sometimes, but never angry. He was five years younger, only thirty, and she could always find excuses for his behavior. Sure, he was spoiled, but that's because he was the baby. Sure, he didn't have a solid plan for his future, but he was still young and had plenty of time to make one—and to settle down. Sure, he treated women badly, but...that one was harder for her to rationalize. She often brushed it off as a product of their traveling all over the world with their parents' performing career. If she dug deeper, though, she would see that she hadn't been affected in the same way. However, maybe she'd been affected in other, equally crippling ways. After all, her personal love life was, well, nowhere. Missing.

But for now she had to find out about Mart. After Cole had gotten some food in his stomach, Tally started in. "So. Mart. You're seeing her?"

"Nothing serious."

"That's good, because I'm not quite sure you're the only one she's seeing."

"Really?" Cole raised his head from his plate and widened his eyes in mock surprise. He knew? And he didn't expect her to be a one-man woman? "She's...having some trouble."

"She is?" Her employees never told her anything, obviously. "What kind? Health kind? Money trouble kind?" Was Mart stealing from her?

"Kind of. I mean she needs money for the trouble she's in."

"Did you give it to her?" That wasn't good.

He nodded.

"I'll tell you the truth, Cole. I'm asking because someone is filching money from my till and it might be her. Are you sure she's not using you?" There was a lot of that going around. Gene taking money from Yolanda, Mart taking money from Cole, someone taking money from her, Tally. "Gene was taking money from Yolanda that he never intended to repay, and I think Mart was seeing Gene as well."

"He's the guy who died in your shop, right? So I guess Mart isn't exactly seeing him."

"I mean before he died, silly." She took a few bites of the tuna casserole, crunching the potato chip topping. "Think about this. What if Gene and Mart were partners in crime? What if they were both swindling money from people?"

"I wouldn't call it swindling. It's borrowing. But why would they do that? To run off together?"

Tally considered that. "It's not an impossible theory." Gene's bad boy behavior had been making it harder and harder for him in this town. It made it hard for Josef Faust, too. Surely Gene would be a hindrance for his career if it got around that he blithely took people's money. For instance, Yolanda had told Tally that she'd lent him money Yolanda could ill afford to lose. Had Gene been planning on running off with Mart as soon as she took enough money from the shop—and now from Cole, whom she'd just met? "How much did you give her?"

"Look, Sis, she really does need the money. It's for something specific."

"And you're not going to tell me what?"

"I can't. It's very personal."

"I need to know if she's contagious. Whether or not she should be working with food."

"No, nothing like that."

And that was the end of that discussion.

"Is your finger bothering you?" Cole asked. "You can't even bend it, can you?"

"The cut is right on my knuckle, so that's where the bandage has to go."

"You could put it on so you could bend your finger, though." Cole pushed his chair back and stood. "Where are your bandages?"

Tally told him they were in the medicine cabinet of the bathroom. Cole got some supplies and rebound her finger so that it was curved.

"That's much more comfortable," Tally said, holding her hand up and inspecting the job he'd done. "Very nice. Thanks."

"No problem. I cut myself a lot working on sculptures. I know all the tricks."

Her doorbell rang.

"Who is that this late?" Tally said, annoyed, getting up to answer it.

She opened the door to see her landlady, Mrs. Gerg. The woman was short, a lot shorter than Tally, who wasn't tall. She was sturdy, though, and her clothes were sturdy, too. The crop pants and short-sleeved top she wore tonight looked like they were made of brown burlap. The only thing that wasn't substantial about her was the poor woman's hair. You could see her pink scalp through the thin gray curls clustered about her round head.

"Oh, hi, Mrs. Gerg." She knew why the woman was there.

"See what I found for you, dear." Mrs. Gerg thrust a small box toward Tally. Tally took it and inspected the heavy wooden box, carved with dragons. The lid, which didn't fit well, started to slip off, but Tally caught it before it hit the porch floor.

"I know you like boxes and thought you would love this." Mrs. Gerg beamed as Tally tried to show appreciation for the gift.

"Where did you find it?"

"You would never believe it. It was at that house three blocks over, with all the kids' toys in the yard all the time. Who would suspect they had Asian treasures in their house?"

Mrs. Gerg was a yard sale addict. She must walk miles a day on the weekends, going from one sale to the next and picking up trinkets at many of them. She'd started bringing Tally some of her finds as soon as Tally had moved in. It was true, Tally had a small collection of various sized and shaped boxes on a chest near the front door, but she would soon run out of room for them if Mrs. Gerg kept bringing more and more boxes to her.

As for this being an "Asian treasure," Tally thought she would find that it was a cheap reproduction of something that was not very grand to begin with, if she dug around for information on it. Which she wouldn't do. That would be ungrateful.

"Thank you so much, Mrs. Gerg." She set it next to the square porcelain box with a delicate butterfly on top that Mrs. Gerg had brought her a few days ago. "It's Wednesday. Were they having a sale today?"

"Oh, heavens no. I got this last weekend and didn't have a chance to go through everything yet. I might have one more box from that day when I get through sorting it all out."

Tally very much wanted to tell her she didn't need any more boxes, but didn't have the heart.

"I saw that young woman out running again," Mrs. Gerg said, leaning in for confidentiality. "I see her all the time. She's going to wear out those young knees. You can't run all the time like that without damaging something."

Tally knew she was talking about Andrea.

"Should you say something to her?" Mrs. Gerg asked. "She works for you, doesn't she?"

"Yes, she does, but I can't tell her what to do when she's not in my shop. I think she'll be okay."

"Well, all right, if you say so. I might stop her and talk to her about it someday, though," she said with a wink. "Is your finger okay?"

"Oh yes, it's fine. I only have a little cut."

The woman was a busybody. She walked all over the town and probably knew a lot about everyone.

Tally thanked her again and told her good night. As she walked away, Tally noticed her shoes. They were flimsy black flats considerably run down at the heels. In spite of their condition, they didn't impede her progress at all. The woman probably wore out several pair a year, walking so much. Tally hoped she could pick up more shoes at yard sales.

After she and Cole finished eating and Cole left to do whatever it was he was doing, she thought long and hard about their earlier conversation. What on earth was Mart's personal problem that Cole couldn't tell her? Could she be pregnant? She'd been sick one morning. That could be morning sickness. At least she knew that if Mart was carrying a baby, it couldn't be Cole's. He hadn't been here long enough for that. All of her speculation, she knew, was based on the shaky assumption that Mart was being truthful with Cole.

She stroked the huge cat that was sprawled in her lap, purring.

"What do you think, Nigel? Who's going to get hurt here, Cole or Mart?"

He stared into her face with his gorgeous amber eyes and wrinkled the black fur on his forehead. Was he considering her question? If only he had the answer.

Chapter 6

When Mart came in to work around eleven o'clock the next morning, Tally tried to detect any signs she might be pregnant, but didn't see them. She wondered if she'd been with Cole last night when he left after dinner. What a mess! Messes! Messes even beyond the awfulness of Gene's murder. Gene had been seeing Yolanda and Andrea, at least, and maybe Mart, too. Was Mart leading Cole on? Her thoughts halted right there. If Mart was toying with Cole, it might teach him a lesson—serve him right. She wouldn't warn Mart against getting serious about Cole; she would let the relationship take its course. She wondered about the fact that Mart didn't seem to be grieving for Gene as Andrea seemed to be. Maybe it wasn't even Gene she had seen in the car with Andrea the other night… but maybe it was.

Andrea, meanwhile, was working, taking frequent breaks in the kitchen to give in to her quiet weeping. Tally had tried to tell her, both that morning and the day before, to take a day or two off, but she wanted to work. "It keeps my mind occupied," she'd said.

At noon Tally got a call from Detective Jackson Rogers to come in to the police station and sign her statement. "I'll be there in an hour, if that's okay," she said. He assured her that one o'clock would be fine. She'd had to pick up brown sugar on her way in this morning, so her car was out back. She'd gone through more brown sugar than she'd thought she would, and her next delivery wasn't for a couple of weeks yet. She told Mart, who was working beside her, that she had to go to the police station.

"Have you signed a statement?" she asked Mart, who blinked at her blankly. "You know, about where you were and what you were doing when Gene…died?"

"No, nobody asked me to. I was working in the front of the store the whole time. I didn't go to the kitchen at all."

"I know that, but they asked for the names of my employees, so I thought they might get statements from both of you."

"Maybe they're skipping me because of my parents."

Tally raised her eyebrows. "Your parents?" She didn't know anything about Mart's family.

"Yeah, they're good friends with the Fausts. I've known Gene since he came to live with them. My parents are really upset about him being dead like that."

So Mart thought her parents had pull with the mayor so she wouldn't be questioned. Interesting.

Tally left a few minutes before one o'clock to go to the police department on East Main Street at the edge of town, driving through another brilliant sunshiny day, the sky filled with high, wispy cloud fragments. She asked for Detective Rogers at the front desk and was directed to a small office down a short hall, where he motioned her to the chair in front of his desk. As she took the form from him, she noticed his eyes were exactly the same intriguing shade of gray that Gene's had been. What a world of difference, though. Gene's expression had never been as earnest as that of Detective Rogers, nor had he ever looked nearly as intelligent. This man looked like no one could put anything past him.

Since she had been contemplating her single state lately, she took a couple of seconds to wonder if the detective was married. He was attractive in a hard, lean, cop type way. A glance told her he didn't wear a ring, which might not mean anything. She deliberately turned her attention from those deep gray eyes to the piece of paper before her.

"If you'll please write out your version of what happened the day Gene Faust was murdered. In your own words," he said. "Exactly like you told me at the time."

What had she said? She had told him that Yolanda went to the kitchen. Had anyone else gone after her? Of course. The killer had. But who was that? Tally squeezed her eyes closed, in despair. Yolanda had been the last one in the kitchen that she knew of before Tally walked in and found his body. She wrote that down, but it made Yolanda seem securely guilty.

In an attempt to muddy the waters, she wrote that Dorella Diggs had come into Tally's Olde Tyme Sweets looking for Gene and had seemed angry. She wrote that she didn't see where she went after she left out the front door. Dorella could have gone around to the back. Andrea had left through the back when she said she wasn't feeling well, though that had been earlier. Would she have seen Dorella? Tally wrote that Andrea left through the kitchen, right under the part about Dorella.

She hesitated. Should she mention Mart, even though she hadn't been in the kitchen at all while Gene was there? She drummed her fingers on the paper for a minute, then wrote that Mart had been in the salesroom. She laid the pen on the pad of paper and told the detective she was finished.

"Sign your name at the bottom."

After she signed and he read over her statement, he asked if she was sure she couldn't recall anything else.

"Like what?"

"Maybe some customers who interacted with the deceased. What about his assistant, Allen Wendt? Where was he?"

"I'm not sure. He was there earlier, but left."

"How much earlier?"

"A couple of hours? Maybe more. Let me think. He came in soon after Gene got there, about eleven or a little past."

Rogers looked at her statement and ran his finger down the page. "And what time was Ms. Diggs there?"

"Right after Allen. She wasn't in the kitchen that I know of, but she wanted to talk to Gene."

"And she was angry, you say?"

"I think so. It seemed like it. I forgot to give her message to him, so he never knew she was there." Unless she had gone around to the back.

"And you say your two employees weren't in the kitchen at the time either."

"That's right. Andrea had gone and Mart stayed out front."

After she left the police station, she parked behind Tally's Olde Tyme Sweets and walked around the block to gather her thoughts, recalling the argument between Gene and Allen. So both Allen and Dorella were mad at Gene, but it didn't seem like either of them had killed him. If neither Allen, Dorella, Andrea, nor Mart had killed Gene, who had?

"Not Yolanda!"

The two women laden with shopping bags who were walking toward her gave her odd looks as Tally realized she'd spoken out loud. She repeated it silently, in her mind. *Not Yolanda.*

That became her mantra as she got busy working in the shop. She'd been in the salesroom only a few minutes when Allen came in the front door. She wanted to ask him what he'd been spatting with Gene about.

"I came by to see if there's anything that needs finishing up," he said. "I don't know what Gene was doing when he…died."

"It looks like everything was completed. He hadn't quite packed up his tools yet, though. The police left them, and I shoved them into the corner."

"I'll take them, if you want, and give them to his parents. I'll see if anything else needs doing, too."

She heard Allen banging the tools around, putting them into Gene's metal toolbox. But when he ducked his head into the salesroom, she stopped him.

"Wait, Allen. Andrea, I need to talk to Allen. Hold the fort a minute."

Andrea looked a little better. Maybe she was getting over the shock.

Tally went into the kitchen with Allen.

"I'd like to deliver his tools to his parents," she said. "I need to offer my condolences." And maybe see if they were anywhere near when he died. She knew his parents didn't deeply love him, maybe even disliked him.

"Sure." Allen set the toolbox on her countertop.

She eyed the none-too-clean thing, telling herself she would thoroughly clean the countertop later. She waited for him to take his leave, but he was hesitating.

"Are you going to need a handyman?"

"I guess I will. Are you taking over Gene's business?"

"Not exactly. But I'm volunteering to do your odd jobs if you don't have anyone else in mind."

Of course she didn't. She hadn't had time to think about that.

"I've had some cards printed." He handed her a shiny card with his name and phone number in white over a gray-tone picture of tools spread out on a black surface.

Her hand touched his as he gave it to her. Such a warm, strong hand, she thought. Why had *that* thought sprung into her mind?

"Th-thanks," she said, stammering slightly. "I'll call you."

"That would be great." His smile hit her harder than his touch had. Then he walked through the front room and out the door, setting off the chimes, before she could find her voice and say, "That's not what I meant."

She turned the card over a few times, thinking that Allen had gotten them printed awfully soon after Gene's death. Or had he printed them before that? Knowing that Gene would be unable to keep working?

* * * *

Yolanda punched the screen to end the call with her father and gazed out her window to calm herself. Her shop had been empty for the last hour, but passersby had been stopping to look at her display. They would soon start coming in.

She hated the humiliation of having to ask him for money. Again. But she needed supplies. All those things she had mentioned to the grandmother, the things for her granddaughter's new-car basket. She had gotten the job and now had to come up with the goods. Those custom-made coasters were going to cost more than she'd thought. She would be able to recoup her expense when the basket was paid for, but she had to make the basket before she got paid.

Of course, her father had used his most condescending tone, sneering at her "little hobby."

"No, Dad, it's not my 'little hobby.' It's my job. It's what I'm doing for a living."

"What kind of living loses money every month?"

"I'm gaining traction. I'm getting more and more business. I'll make of go of this, but I started out with zero capital."

"Whose fault is that?"

Yolanda could almost feel the steam boiling from her ears. She had asked him for a start-up loan, but he had refused, telling her it would be easier to wait and fund her as she got off the ground. She should have known that, with him, getting off the ground involved groveling.

Sometimes she wished she had parents like Tally and Cole had. Absent parents who wandered the globe. For the twentieth time, she kicked herself for not going to a bank for a loan. Tally had done that, and she should have, too. She should have tried, even though her mother had told her she wouldn't be able to get one. She would have to come up with a business plan and get money from someone other than her tight-fisted, sarcastic father soon.

At least he hadn't found out that she had given money to Gene and hadn't ever gotten it back.

* * * *

At five p.m., both Andrea and Mart were on the sales floor, and Tally didn't need to be at work in the kitchen right then. There was a lot of inventory ready to go. Besides, she was itching to take the tools to the Fausts and see how they were dealing with their son's death. If they weren't a bit distraught, she'd tell Detective Rogers to take a look at them. Anything to remove his focus from Yolanda.

She told her two employees she would be gone half an hour or so, hefted the toolbox from the floor, where she had set it as soon as Allen left, and toted it to her car. Everyone knew where the mayor's family lived: in a Colonial two-story house on Travis Street complete with columns supporting the grand balcony above the porch that swept across the entire front of the broad mansion. She parked on the street in front and toed the picket gate open, grasping the toolbox with both hands as she made her way to the front door. She managed to press the doorbell with a knuckle on her right hand and was treated to a grand chime concert. It sounded like the doorbell had set off the beginning of a symphony.

Mrs. Faust opened the door and frowned at Tally doubtfully, as if to say, *"Do I know you?"*

"Hi, Mrs. Faust," Tally said, and then introduced herself and told the woman how sorry she was for her loss. She shifted the heavy metal box to her left hand and extended her right.

Mrs. Faust acted reluctant, but limply took Tally's hand. Tally didn't know her first name since everyone simply called her Mrs. Faust. It occurred to Tally that maybe it wasn't easy being married to the mayor and having no identity of your own.

Tally held the cumbersome box in front of her with both hands. "This is your son's. It was left at my shop."

"Your shop?" Recognition opened her eyes and raised her plucked eyebrows. "You mean the place where he died?"

"Yes, he was working for me that day. At Tally's Olde Tyme Sweets."

"I've seen it and driven by. Never been in. I've heard some good reports. Did you bring me any samples?"

"Mrs. Faust, I'm not selling my sweets to you right now, I'm returning your dead son's belongings." Tally was ruder than she liked to be, but this woman was aggravating her. Why on earth would she have brought candy samples to her? She had never met Mrs. Faust before one on one, but she completely disliked her at the moment.

"Oh yes, you can set it..." Mrs. Faust glanced around the hallway behind her. "I don't know. Maybe here?" She pointed to the hardwood floor beside the door.

Tally walked through the entrance and started to set it on the floor. "On the carpet so it doesn't scratch the wood," Mrs. Faust added.

Tally set it down and eyed her. "If you'd ever like to see the place where your son died, I'd be happy to let you do that."

Mrs. Faust stared at her.

"Are you curious about what happened to him?" Tally asked.

"Not really. I think it was unpleasant."

"Well, yes, he died. Of stab wounds. He was murdered. You don't know anything about it? Have the police asked you where you were when he was killed?"

"Oh my, no. They wouldn't do such a thing."

"They wouldn't? Why? Where were you? Do they already know?"

Mrs. Faust put an even haughtier expression on her wrinkled face. "I was getting my hair done at Fancy's Curls. I always get it done there on Tuesday afternoon. Are you finished here?"

"Yes, I am."

The woman's indifference to her own son wasn't even thinly veiled. She just didn't care.

Tally stomped her way back toward her car, trying to stop her head from exploding with the anger she felt toward the coldhearted woman.

Chapter 7

As Tally got to the Fausts' front yard gate, which she had left swinging open, she was met by the mayor himself. He was striding up the walk with a golf bag slung over his shoulder. Their garage was around the corner. Apparently he preferred to access the house from the front rather than go through the backyard.

"Good afternoon, Mr. Mayor," she said.

He squinted at her. She wondered if he was nearsighted. But he opened his eyes wide when he recognized her. "It's Tally Holt, isn't it? You work in the place where Gene was killed."

"Yes, that's me. I came by to return your son's tools. They were left in my shop." At least he called his son by his name. "I'm so sorry for your loss."

"Thank you, young lady. It's been a hard blow." His eyes were now eagle-sharp, even if they did sit in a comically round, bald head. It felt uncomfortably like his eyes were penetrating into her brain. "Were you there when it happened?"

"I was in the shop. In the front. He was killed in the kitchen."

"And you didn't hear anything?"

Was he interrogating her? "We were busy, full of customers. They chatter and make a lot of noise." Why was she justifying herself to this man? She wanted to ask where he had been while his son was being stabbed. Maybe she would give him the same treatment he was giving her. She glanced at his clubs. "Do you golf a lot? Were you golfing when he died?"

"As a matter of fact, I was. I spend a lot of time on the golf course. It's necessary to network in my job. If you'll excuse me?"

He brushed past her, bumping her sore finger. She clicked the gate latch shut and started to get into her car. Before she closed the door, as she was reaching for her seat belt, she stopped at the sound of screeching.

"What do you think you're doing here?" Mrs. Faust was tensed in the doorway, ready to spring on her husband like a puma, it looked like to Tally.

"I need to get some things." Mr. Faust's voice was raised, too.

"Get them all. And don't come back."

She saw him push past her to get into the house. "You just *think* you'll get this house," he said. "The judge is my friend, not yours. You'll get pennies."

That sounded like they were divorcing!

"At least that thug you adopted is gone. If he'd had his way, we'd probably both lose everything. What an idiotic thing to do, adopting a juvenile delinquent."

The mayor turned to face his wife, and Tally could clearly see his face. "He might have done better if he'd had a mother, instead of…you. You never gave him a chance."

"I'm not the one who petitioned to have the adoption annulled." She shoved him aside and slammed the door closed with both of them inside.

Tally let out a breath. The show was over. But it had been quite enlightening. If she hadn't disliked Gene so much, she might have felt sorry for him, being brought into that household.

* * * *

That evening, she was surprised when Cole showed up at Tally's house at about eight thirty.

"Have you eaten?" she asked him.

"No, not yet. I was going to, but something happened." Nigel ran over to Cole and started twining around his legs, purring loudly. The cat was heavy enough to knock a person over if they weren't careful. Cole showed his dimples when he saw the cat.

"I assumed you'd be with Mart tonight."

He reached down to give Nigel a rub. "I assumed the same thing. She said she'd meet me for dinner an hour ago, but she never showed."

"Did she call? Text? Anything?"

"Only after I texted her when she was an hour late. Said something came up. Never said what it was."

Tally managed not to smile at Cole's exaggerated doleful expression. "So, how many times have you been stood up in your life?"

"Stood up? Never."

"Now you know what it feels like. Maybe she thought you'd ask her to repay the money she *borrowed* from you."

"I never mentioned that. Do you have anything to eat? I'm starving."

Tally bit back any further I-told-you-sos and made him a peanut butter–honey sandwich, having picked up takeout on her way home and eaten as soon as she'd gotten in from work an hour ago. Her kitchen still smelled like the wonderful pulled-pork BBQ she'd had, but Cole didn't seem to notice.

"I was thinking, Sis," Cole said between bites as he sat in front of the TV, "do you think we should tell Mom and Dad what's going on here?"

Tally sat beside him and drummed her fingers on the end table. She had been wondering the same thing.

"Do you still do that? Stop, okay? It's annoying."

"Sorry." Tally put her hands in her lap.

"Hey, I'm kidding. But what do you think?"

Tally drummed her fingers silently on her leg. It helped her think. "If we told them, what would they do?"

"Good point. They would either cut their trip short and come here, or they wouldn't. If they didn't come, would you be upset?"

"Probably. But if they came here, what could they do?"

"Right. And they're so excited about this latest cowboy thing. Although I'm pretty sure they're in the wrong country for cowboys."

"They are excited," Tally agreed. "You're right. Let's leave them alone. We'll tell them all about it when it's over."

"Good idea."

As he was crunching the last of the carrots she had laid on his plate, Cole's phone beeped. He frowned when he saw the display.

"A text?" Tally said.

"Yes. From Mart," he said around his final bite of peanut butter.

"Well, what does she say?"

"She wants to meet tomorrow." He set his phone down on the couch beside him.

"Are you going to?"

"I don't know."

"Maybe you should. And you should try to get some of your money back."

He swallowed the bite and shot a thoughtful look at her. "I might just do that. Before, she mentioned something about…"

Tally waited. "About what?"

"She was talking about a former boyfriend. It sounded like he had asked her to marry him, but then was coming on to one of her coworkers. She says she can't trust men anymore."

"She said that? A coworker?" Tally jumped up and took Cole's empty plate into the kitchen.

"What are you doing, Sis?"

"I need to think about this." She tried to picture Mart's job application. She remembered that her name was actually Martha and that she lived out of town on a ranch, probably with her parents. It was the job history section she was trying to recall. She didn't think she had any. She'd hired Andrea full-time because she had worked for a couple of years in shops around town. But this was Mart's first job out of high school, so Tally had taken her on to work part-time. Tally was pretty sure Mart had never had another job, not even during high school. So, if she was speaking the truth to Cole, her coworker was Andrea. Tally had seen the sparks between Andrea and Gene herself. That might mean that the man she was angry at, the one who had made her distrust men, had been Gene. *If* she was telling Cole the truth. Tally didn't know why she was reluctant to trust Mart, but she was…

* * * **

As soon as Tally got to work the next morning, she looked up the job applications. It was exactly as she'd remembered it: If Mart had ever had a job before this one, it wasn't mentioned on her application. The section for experience was blank.

Around lunchtime, Andrea was in the kitchen eating and Tally and Mart were working in front with a full room of customers when Cole came in.

The sparks that flew between him and Mart were not the same type that had flown between Andrea and Gene. Tally saw thunder on both of their brows.

"Come on, I'll take you to lunch," Cole said. "You wanted to meet, right?"

Mart turned her head away from him. "Not right now. Maybe tonight. I can't leave."

"Sure, go ahead," Tally said, stirring up trouble, she knew. "I'm sure Andrea's almost done eating. We'll be fine." Tally felt devil's horns sprouting on her forehead as she acted all innocent, countering Mart's excuses to Cole. She wanted her brother to get his money back.

Mart drew in and let out a huge breath. "I can't. I don't want to. You can't make me." She even stuck out her lower lip, like a pouting toddler. It was almost comical. Tally was surprised at her childish behavior.

Cole stepped closer to Mart. Now the customers were starting to stare at them. "You don't have to do anything except return the money you got from me under false pretenses. Or I'll go to the police."

"It's not false pretenses! I really *am* pregnant!"

A collective gasp came from Tally and the fascinated customers. Tally grabbed Cole and Mart's upper arms and pulled them into the kitchen.

"Andrea," she called, bursting into the room with Cole and Mart in tow. "Please cover the sales floor for a few minutes. I'll explain later."

Andrea glanced at them, full of curiosity, and trotted out of the room.

"Okay," Tally said, wanting to shake both of them, but dropping her grasp on their arms instead. "What exactly is going on?"

"This doesn't concern you," Mart said, rubbing her arm and still pouting.

Tally started to flare up, but settled herself down. "You're right. It doesn't. It concerns my brother and the money he gave to you. If you repay him the money you owe him, it's no concern of mine. If you don't, you'll have to look for work somewhere else. I suspect you've been stealing money from the cash drawer, too."

Mart gaped at Tally. "How did you..."

That had been a shot in the dark, but it had hit the target. Mart *was* dipping into the till. "Were you and Gene pulling the same pranks? Were you both getting money from unsuspecting dupes *and* stealing from me? Why do you have such a need for money? You have a place to live and an income." Tally stopped for breath, realizing she had been shouting. She hoped the customers hadn't been paying attention.

"Tally," Cole said. "Leave us and let us talk this out."

Tally could see that her attacks were making Mart more stubborn. She had to admit she had gone overboard. Was Mart really pregnant? With Gene's baby? And was she trying to get money for...the baby? An abortion? She decided that she didn't want to know. As softly as she could, she said, "Fine, you two talk about it. I need to get back to work."

She felt Mart's angry eyes boring into her back as she left.

The sound of their raised voices soon drifted out to the salesroom. An amused expression crossed Andrea's face when she heard Mart's words coming from the kitchen: "It wasn't Gene. Okay, I'm not sure. It might have been Gene. He said he'd marry me, but then, at the last minute, he dumped me!"

Mart's voice sounded frantic to Tally. Maybe Gene had preyed upon her. After all, she was barely out of high school and Gene was older, and a veteran of the juvenile justice system with several stays in the detention center. It was an uneven match from the get-go. But now she had to decide whether or not she should fire Mart.

Cole's voice reached her. "I don't care what *you* need. *I* need my money back or you'll be sorry you ever met me. When people lie to me, it makes me—"

"I didn't lie!"

"So you *did* repay me yesterday? When was that? Where was that? I don't remember it. Watch it, little woman, or you'll end up like your buddy Gene."

Tally heard the back door squeak, then slam shut, and she went to check on Mart.

Mart stood in the middle of the room, her arms rigid at her sides and her fists clenched. The murderous expression on her usually sweet, young face made the hair on the back of Tally's neck stand up. *What would this young woman be capable of?* she wondered. *And what did Cole's parting words imply?* She pushed them aside, unable to think about that right now.

The back door swung open, and Yolanda walked in, a questioning look on her face. "What was that?"

"What was what?" Mart asked. "I have to get back to work." She hurried through the doorway into the salesroom.

"Tally?"

Shaking her head to clear the nasty flare-up from her mind, Tally looked at her friend and tried to get Mart's hostile expression out of her memory. She was pleased to see Yolanda in a caftan of bright greens, blues, and aquas, set off with large pieces of turquoise jewelry. She hoped her friend was feeling better. Somebody should be in a good mood. There were too many negative vibes floating around.

Chapter 8

"Is Cole all right?" Yolanda asked when she got inside Tally's kitchen. She had passed him in the alley on her way to the back door and he hadn't even noticed her. Not that it was unusual for Cole to ignore her. His reappearance in Fredericksburg was dredging up all the bad memories of their younger years from the depths of her mind. She had had a crush on the handsome, blond, dimpled god. He, however, had never seemed to know she existed, even though she was his sister's best friend. Walking past him, saying hi, and having him stare straight ahead was nothing new. The humiliation that bubbled up within her was the same old feeling, too.

Tally was standing in the kitchen, staring at the back door when Yolanda came through it. The room was redolent with the lingering scents of some candy Tally had probably made in the morning. Something sweet, maybe with chocolate and brown sugar. "I heard shouting from outside," Yolanda said.

"They really got into it, didn't they?"

"Who was arguing? Was it Mart and Cole?"

"Yes, they were beginning to be an item, but it seems like that's over."

"Ooo, nasty breakup. Sorry." Maybe that would serve Cole right. She shook off her bad feelings, pulled a stool out from beneath the island counter, and climbed on, hitching up her caftan. She spread some papers on the countertop. "Here's what I found."

Tally sat next to her friend, and Yolanda shoved one of the papers in front of her. "Something like this should be doable."

Yolanda didn't think Tally was actually seeing any of the illustrations. She put a finger on one. "How about this? Doesn't it look like your own Truffle Fudge?"

Tally finally looked down and focused on the paper, a printout from Yolanda's computer. "I guess. But how hard can it be to make a square piece of plastic and color it brown?"

"That's beside the point. We're not going to make plastic fudge. This company does."

"How much do they charge for that?"

"Not much." Yolanda moved her finger so Tally could see the price. She glanced at the offensive wound on Tally's knuckle, but it was covered nicely with a bandage and she was relieved to see that it was clean and dry.

"Oh, not bad," Tally said. "And you get two dozen pieces?"

"Right. We could put a few in each basket to give the idea. Scatter them around."

"Wouldn't it look like you don't get much fudge in each basket?"

"The other pieces could be hidden under lots and lots of ribbons and flowers and stuff, for all they know."

"What else do they have that we could use?"

Yolanda fanned out the other printouts and they went over them, agreeing on some and rejecting others. Yolanda had been amazed to see that the company had Whoopie Pie replicas, even a Clark Bar in its distinctive red wrapper. She got a smile out of Tally when she showed it to her.

"I'd sure like to see these in real life," Tally said.

"Me too. Maybe we could order one or two to see how nice they are—how realistic they look and feel." Yolanda paused a moment, not wanting to spoil Tally's mood any further. "But seriously, tell me what's going on with Cole. Something between him and Mart?"

Tally explained to her that they had been out together a few times. And that Mart had borrowed a lot of money from her brother.

"Really? Just like Gene did with me? That's strange. Do you think they were coordinating it?"

"I've thought of that, but I really don't know," Tally said. "Mart was seeing Gene, I'm pretty sure, before he died. Maybe she learned from the master."

"The master criminal. You sure were right about him. At the risk of speaking ill of the dead, Gene wasn't a good person." She shook her head slowly.

Tally leaned over and hugged her friend around the shoulders as they sat side by side. "I shouldn't have said that. I didn't know him very well."

"You knew him well enough. You're good at reading people, Tally. Did you know about his father?"

"The mayor? That he adopted him as a teenage kid who was going off the rails?"

"No, not that. Everyone who lives here knows that. Did you know that the mayor, his own father, threatened to annul the adoption a year ago when Gene got caught shoplifting some things in Dallas? At least that's what Gene told me."

That must have been what Mrs. Faust had been yelling about at her front door when the mayor was there. "Annul the adoption? That's pretty cold."

"I thought so too. Now, though, I wonder if it was true or if he was trying to make me feel sorry for him."

"I believe it," Tally said. "I saw both his parents yesterday. Neither one of them are a bit broken up about his death. His mother almost seems to be glad he's gone. She shouted something about him and an annulment when I was there. His father isn't much better. He's putting on an act of being sorry Gene is dead, but I'll bet he's not. His campaign for reelection will be a lot easier without Gene around stirring up trouble."

"It's a mess, isn't it? The way the police talk to me, it feels like they suspect I killed him. I'm sure they don't, though—I mean, how could they? But they badger and hound me, like they think I'm going to confess or something."

"Of course they don't think that," Tally said, but her words rang hollow, even to Yolanda.

* * * *

They decided to buy the package of plastic fudge and a couple of Clark Bars, which were individually priced, and Yolanda left to put the order into her own computer at Bella's Baskets. She paused outside the door, seeing Cole at the end of the alley, behind the hat shop on the corner. She couldn't help but notice him, the way the sun gleamed off his blond hair. He was with a woman, but it couldn't possibly be Mart, since she was inside Tally's store. Yolanda walked toward her own back door, in their direction, trying to get a good look at the woman who was behind Cole. They were talking earnestly, gesturing, but not in anger.

Neither of them noticed her, concentrating only on each other. Yolanda could hear their words now as she drew closer.

The woman said, "You were with her day before yesterday, weren't you?"

"We broke up today, Dorella. I'm not attached to anyone."

Now that Yolanda was closer, the woman sounded distraught. Yolanda saw Cole reach for her and decided to make her presence known so she wouldn't embarrass them. "Hi, Cole! Who's this?"

Cole turned, not embarrassed at all. "Yolanda! This is Dorella Diggs. She's offered to show me around Fredericksburg. There are some new wineries she knows about." He cocked his head toward Dorella.

"I thought it would be fun to pop into some of them," Dorella said. "The ones in town and the ones close by. Nice to meet you." She smiled slightly. "You have that basket store, don't you?"

Yolanda nodded.

"I've seen you around town, I'm sure." Dorella had a pretty face and softly curling blond hair. She had to be much younger than Cole.

"Good to meet you, too. Gotta get to work." Yolanda walked to her back door and left them, marveling that Cole was a fast rebounder. It had been minutes since he'd had the dustup with Mart.

* * * *

Tally kicked off her shoes and wiggled her toes in the carpeting as she came in the front door of her house at the end of her workday. Nigel greeted her at the door by crashing into her legs with the side of his body.

"Hey, that's not a gentle rub, big guy," Tally said, reaching down to pick him up. "Oof! Are you heavier than you were this morning?"

By the time she'd carried him into the kitchen, she decided he probably was. Especially when she saw what had happened there. An empty box of crackers that had been on top of the refrigerator lay overturned on the floor with a few lonely crumbs spilling from it.

"You ate all of these?" Tally was amazed. The box had been nearly full. "What's wrong with these last crumbs? Why didn't you clean those up?" She decided they shouldn't feed Nigel that night. Maybe not tomorrow morning either. Letting Nigel jump down with a thud, she picked up the empty box, threw it into the recycle bin, and swept up the crumbs.

She heard the front door open and it startled her until she remembered that Cole was staying with her. Still, she was relieved when he sang out, "You home, Sis?"

"In the kitchen." She put the broom and dustpan in the closet. "You hungry?"

"No, just had dinner."

Tally shot him an incredulous look, her eyes opened wide. "You're with Mart again already?"

"Oh no, we're quits. And I'll probably never get my money back."

"I hope you learned something."

"Yes, Mother. I will be more careful after this. She told me she was never pregnant after all."

"She lied to you about that?"

"To everyone, I assume. She can't be trusted in the slightest."

Tally took a container of cottage cheese from the fridge and scooped some into a dish, topping it with applesauce for her own meal. "Where did you eat?"

Cole flashed his dimples at her. "Don't you mean, 'who did you eat with?'"

Tally cocked her head. "Not Mart? You've moved on already?" So Mart had dumped him, but it hadn't had the effect Tally thought it would. He wasn't broken up at all.

"I met her a couple of days ago stopping for lunch. She works at Burger Burger."

"So I probably don't know her. I've seen it, but I haven't been there. What's her name?" She sat and started in on her bowl of cottagey applesauce while Cole fetched a beer from her fridge.

"Dorella. She's local, lived here all her life."

Tally wondered what that would be like, to live in the same place your whole life. Wait, that name rang a bell. "Dorella? Dorella…Diggs?"

"You know her?"

"Not really. But she came into the store a few days ago. It was the day…"

"What? The day what?"

"Never mind. It was a few days ago." She wanted to process this before she blurted out that Dorella had been involved with Gene, and that she had been in the shop near the time he had died. "So, Mart isn't returning the money she borrowed?"

"No, and I don't believe she ever intended to. It's gone." He shrugged and tipped the beer bottle up to his lips.

"I'm so sorry about that. She admitted that she has taken money from me, too."

Cole slammed the bottle onto the table. "No! Are you going to press charges?"

"I don't know. I have to decide. Cole, she scared me today. She gave me a look that made me cringe. It made me wonder if she could kill someone. Do you think she killed Gene?"

"I thought she wasn't there." He tore off a paper towel and wiped up the froth that had spilled over when he banged the bottle down.

"I don't know if she was or not, when I think about it. She can be cold-blooded. I saw her kiss Gene in front of Andrea, which made Andrea furious. That was mean. And I heard her say that she might be pregnant with Gene's baby and Gene had said he'd marry her. He can't when he's dead, but maybe he told her he wouldn't and that set her off. If she got angry enough, she might be capable of murder."

"I have to agree with you there. He probably did tell her he wouldn't marry her, because she told me she wanted to abort the baby before she admitted she wasn't pregnant. That's what the money was for. I'm sure she was trying to trap Gene into marrying her. She does have a hard side to her."

Tally thought he might be saying that because she'd had the audacity to break up with him, but maybe he was right. "What should we do?"

"I guess I should tell the cops what she told me about Gene and her."

"And I should tell them that she's been stealing money from me."

Tally lay awake for a long time that night. In the deep silence, she could hear the steady ticking of her grandmother's clock from the living room. It helped her to bring her thoughts down to solid ground. She didn't want to talk to the detective about Mart, but felt she had to. She knew she should fire her, and didn't want to do that either. What would Mart do when she did that? Would she go after Tally next?

Chapter 9

Saturday dawned late, delayed by black storm clouds sweeping in with chilly showers from the west. Tally drove to work to keep herself dry, her windshield wipers *chunk-chunk-chunk*ing on high the whole way. She ran in the back door from her parking space behind the shop, the wind whipping her hair, her clothes, and her umbrella, which almost turned inside out.

Andrea was already there. She had to have come in the front door of the shop, since the back was locked, and Tally had to use her keys when she arrived. Andrea's mother's car was in the back, too, so she must have had to walk around. Andrea had a key to the front door, but not to the back one. "It's a gully washer today, isn't it?" Andrea said.

"It is. Texas rains come down hard."

"But they don't last long."

"I don't remember having this much rain in July," Tally said.

"We don't usually. You're right." Andrea grabbed a tray of candies from the kitchen fridge and went to the front to put them into the display case.

Tally fiddled around in the kitchen, agonizing over facing Mart when she came in. Andrea had left a backpack on the floor, and Tally moved it next to the bathroom so she wouldn't trip over it.

She was afraid she was going to have to fire Mart. The shop wasn't due to open for fifteen or twenty minutes yet. She called out to Andrea that she was going to dash to Yolanda's place, then she picked up her dripping umbrella and ran out the back and through the storm again.

The wind wasn't as fierce as it had been moments before, and the rain was already letting up. Tally hoped it would stop completely and the sun would dry up the puddles. The shop would do better business without rain, she was sure.

Kevin from Bear Mountain was in the alley dumping plastic bags in his trash bin. "Hey, are you doing okay? You and Yolanda?" He dashed over to meet her behind Bella's Baskets.

"We're holding up, I guess. It's hard, though. The police need to find out who killed Gene, then we'll all rest easier."

"It looks like they've questioned everyone who has shops on both sides of the street. If I hear anything, I'll let you know."

"Thanks, Kevin."

"Tell Yolanda hi."

"I will."

She rapped on Yolanda's back door and pushed it open. Yolanda looked up from the basket she was finishing with a bright red, shiny bow. It only clashed slightly with her pink and purple sleeveless dress. The garnets she wore were on the small side for Yolanda-jewelry.

"Flashy," Tally said. "What's that one for?"

"A four-year-old's birthday party."

"A basket for a four-year-old? I wouldn't think they'd be interested in that sort of thing." Tally looked closer and saw that it was full of doll clothes. "Is there a doll in there somewhere?"

Yolanda laughed. "Yes, buried underneath the clothing. Her parents wanted to present it this way. This little girl's favorite color is red."

"That's a refreshing change from pink." Tally shook the drips off her umbrella and propped it beside the back door.

"Aren't you about to open?" Yolanda asked. "Do you need something?"

"Boy, do I." Tally slumped, her elbows on the counter where Yolanda worked, and dropped her chin into her hands. "Advice again. On an employee again."

"Is it still not working out with Andrea?"

"Not Andrea this time. Mart."

Yolanda snipped off the last of the excess shiny red plastic and started wrapping the basket in cellophane. "Yeah, I thought she was dating Cole, but I saw Cole with someone else."

"Dorella?"

"I think that was her name. So if Cole is two-timing Mart—"

"No, nothing like that. They've broken up. But she did take Cole for a ride, got a bunch of money out of him. And the worst part is that she admitted she's been stealing from my till in the shop." Tally drummed her nails on the counter in annoyance. "Taking the money that I have to use to pay her. That's not smart, when you think about it."

"Oh no! What are you going to do?"

"I kind of hoped you'd tell me what to do." Tally told her that Mart had gotten the money from Cole for an abortion for a baby that might or might not have been Gene's. She said Gene was going to marry her, but had decided not to at the last minute. Then it turned out she wasn't pregnant at all. She'd lied. "Or so she says. There's no way to verify anything with Gene dead." Yolanda's mouth fell open. "So...*she* killed Gene?"

"I have no idea. Well, it might be possible. I don't even know if she's telling Cole the truth. She probably is, because I'm sure she's the thief in my place. Why else would she say that? But what should I do? Tell the police that she's a crook? Cole is going to tell the detective about her taking money from him and what she says about Gene. He told me that I should report what I know to the detective, too."

"He's right. You should. Why wouldn't you?" Yolanda went to her front door to unlock it and flipped her sign to *Open*.

"I know. I should. I'm honestly a bit afraid of antagonizing her. If she's a killer, why wouldn't she kill me?"

"Because you didn't get her pregnant—*or not pregnant*—and leave her at the altar?" Yolanda grinned, but Tally didn't see the humor.

Tally met Allen coming in as she went out the back door. He gave her a huge smile, and she cheered up a bit.

"You look great today," he said.

She didn't think she did, but it was nice of him to say it. "Thanks." He, on the other hand, *did* look pretty great.

"I finally got the part," he called out to Yolanda. To Tally he explained, "She wanted another shelf for her cooler."

Tally basked in the glow of Allen's handsome smile for a moment, then left.

She trudged slowly toward her place, feeling that gravity had suddenly increased, barely noticing that the rain had stopped. It would be eleven o'clock soon, which meant that Mart would be at work. Too soon.

* * * *

"Oh good, I need that," Yolanda said, holding out her hands for the large box Allen held. It was damp from him taking it through the rain from the hardware store to his truck, and to Bella's Baskets. He'd gotten wet, too. He shook droplets from his hair and ran a hand through it, tousling his thin, straight strands.

"I'll put it into the cooler," he said. He busied himself opening the box and extracting the metal shelf from the packing while Yolanda shifted plants around to accommodate the extra shelf.

"I have a lot of small things that will fit on this new shelf." She set some larger plant containers on the countertop.

"Let me get this heavy thing." Allen reached for one that was still in the way. He picked up the container, then froze, bent over with his head inside the flower cooler. She heard him suck his breath in sharply.

"Are you all right?" Yolanda asked. Maybe he had hurt his back bending over and lifting like that.

"I…I'm okay. But…" He shoved the vase back into the corner and straightened.

"What? What is it?" Yolanda tried to see what was behind it.

"Don't touch anything." He whipped out his cell phone but, before he could dial, Detective Rogers came in the front door. "You! I was just calling you," Allen said.

Yolanda swiveled her head back and forth between the two men. "What's going on? Allen, what's in my cooler?"

"Yes, what's in the cooler?" the detective asked.

Allen addressed him. "I guess you should come see this, Detective Rogers." Yolanda felt cold fingers running up her spine.

* * * *

Tally cheered up and hummed to herself while she walked back to Olde Tyme Sweets. She had, of course, noticed before how good-looking Allen Wendt was, but in an objective, non-personal way. With that high-beam smile he'd given her, it had become a bit more personal. His hands were strong, but they looked gentle, too. He never seemed angry or upset, always cheerful and…friendly? More than friendly? She floated through her back door, an inch and a half off the floor, and called out for Andrea.

"I'm back," she sang, and started for the front.

Rounding the island counter in the center of the room, she paused. An odd odor, almost putrid, was coming from the bathroom at the side of the room. She would check it out, but first she needed to see how Andrea was doing.

Her employee had opened the store a half hour ago, and with the sun now beaming down on Fredericksburg, people were flocking in. Tally smiled at the thought of the profits they would make today—if Mart didn't steal them. She vowed to keep an eye on her after she came in. Tonight, she would decide about telling the detective about Mart.

"How's Yolanda?" Andrea asked as Tally entered the salesroom.

She realized Andrea thought Tally had been soothing Yolanda, other than the other way round.

"She's doing great."

"Oh, sorry. With the way you dashed out of here in the rain, I thought she might need something."

"I had a quick question for her." Tally tied on a smock and walked up to a pair of middle-aged women who were agonizing between Whoopie Pies and Mallomars.

"Can you tell us a bit about these?" the taller one said. "They both look delicious, but we've never had either of them."

From the way the woman pronounced "about," like "aboot," Tally wondered if they were Canadian. She had had a high school teacher from Alberta who'd said that, and she had adored the teacher.

"Sure." Tally took a package of each off the shelf. "Mallomars are like a cross between a cake and a cookie on the inside. Covered with chocolate on the outside, of course, as you can see. They're made with honey, brown sugar, some gelatin, and other things." She held up the Whoopie Pies. "These are really sandwiches made with two chocolate cookies and a marshmallow sort of filling. Think of them as puffy, glorified Oreos."

They turned to each other, wide grins on their faces. The shorter one said, "It looks like we'll have to take a package of each." They took the boxes from Tally and trotted over to the counter to pay.

Tally started toward another small knot of people hovering over the Twinkies, feeling her cell phone vibrate in her pocket on the way.

She hiked up her smock and pulled it slightly out to glance at the caller—Yolanda. She waited on her customers, then got another text from Yolanda. Thinking she had better see what was going on, she pulled her phone all the way out of her pocket.

When Tally and Yolanda had been in middle school together, before Yolanda went off to boarding school, they'd established some secret codes. They hadn't known what ASAP stood for, but Yolanda's father had often used it when he was referring to things that were urgent. So the two young girls had decided that would be their SOS code. The distress code letters jumped out at her: *ASAP*

"Be right back," she called to Andrea and ran into the kitchen to call Yolanda. No answer She texted her: *What's wrong?*

Yolanda texted within seconds: *At police station. found weapon my place. being questioned. can u come.*

Tally's hand went numb, and she almost dropped her phone.

Chapter 10

Once more, Tally left Andrea tending the store as she rushed out to her car in the alley. What must Andrea think? She couldn't dwell on that, though. She had to see what was going on with Yolanda. Even with the unemotional nature of a text message, Yolanda's distress had come through. Tally's tires slipped, then caught hold and screeched on the wet pavement as she sped away.

When Tally pushed through the door to the police station, she stopped to catch her breath. She had driven as fast as she could—the police station was located on the edge of town, and a tractor had lost a load of hay on Main Street and delayed her twenty minutes while the farmer and several motorists cleared the road.

A severe-looking woman with thick glasses sat at a desk behind a window. She was the only person in sight, so Tally asked her where Yolanda Bella was.

"Wait a moment. Let me look." The woman tightened her lips, accentuating the wrinkles around them, and paged through some papers on her desk, then consulted her computer screen. "It says that she's over at the jail right now."

"She's in jail?" Tally screeched. "In jail? She can't be. What for?" She knew her voice was too loud, too high-pitched. She had to calm down.

The woman's level, no-nonsense stare through the thick lenses quieted Tally. "She's just in that building. Not in a cell, necessarily. Would you like me to find out if you can see her?"

Tally hadn't thought of the possibility that she wouldn't even be able to see Yolanda. How could she find out what was going on?

"I'll call the detective," the woman said.

Within a few minutes Detective Rogers came into the lobby. He motioned Tally to a hard plastic chair and sat beside her.

Tally immediately started babbling, her voice rising again. "I have to see Yolanda. Is she all right? What's happening?"

"Whoa, wait a minute, Ms. Holt." He held up both palms. "Ms. Bella is fine. We need to ask her some questions. You won't be able to see her until she's released."

"When will that be? I can wait here."

"I wouldn't suggest that. It might be some time." His voice was quiet, but firm.

"Well, what's she being questioned about? You know she had nothing to do with Gene's murder. Nothing."

"I can't tell you any more, but I think you should go home and wait to hear from her."

"How long will it be? Are you going to grill her for hours and hours? All night? That's what they do on TV shows when they're trying to break someone."

"I don't have any time estimates right now. Go home, Ms. Holt. This has nothing to do with you."

Tally sat straight up. "It certainly does. She's my best friend. If she's in trouble, I need to know."

"Give us some time. Go home."

"I have to go back to work," she said, and got up and marched out before she could say something she might regret.

When she got to the shop, she deflected Andrea's questions about where she'd been and what she'd been doing with vague statements about Yolanda having some ordering problems at the store.

"I need some help here since Mart didn't come in," Andrea said.

"She didn't come in? She should be here by now. I'll call her."

"I did, but she didn't answer."

Tally called her, too, but she didn't get an answer either. She felt relieved that she wouldn't have to confront Mart today.

Shortly after two o'clock. Yolanda sent a cryptic text: *Released going home.*

When, another hour later, Tally went to the shop kitchen to replenish the Whoopie Pies, the odor she had noticed earlier had gotten chokingly worse. Now she could tell it was coming from the employees' restroom. She cracked open the door, started gagging, and slammed it shut. Trembling with fear, she opened it again and switched the light on.

Now she knew why Mart wasn't working.

* * * *

It was ten o'clock that night by the time the crime scene people finished up with Tally's Olde Tyme Sweets shop. Mart's body had been removed a few hours before that. Tally had called Cole and told him she was delayed, but didn't tell him why. There would be time for that later, when she was more composed. After all, he'd been fairly close to her for a short time.

The first thing Tally had done was dial 911. Then she went out front and told Andrea that they needed to close the shop.

"What's wrong?" Andrea's eyes grew wide with alarm. "Is something wrong?"

Tally nodded. "Mart is…she's in the bathroom."

"Is she sick?"

"No, Andrea, she's dead. It looks kind of like someone stabbed her with my candy thermometer." It looked very much like that, since the temperature-gauge end of the instrument had been sticking out of her chest, the sharp end buried deep in it. It wouldn't have been possible to trip and end up like that.

"Oh no." Andrea grabbed her backpack from the floor. "I feel sick. I'll be right back." She ran out to the alley and returned a few minutes later.

* * * *

The police arrived and took over the scene. It was a very long day, and nobody could leave the shop.

Detective Rogers, who had stayed the whole time, came over to Tally and Andrea, who were huddled in the corner of the kitchen where they'd been for several hours after being told to stay put.

"We have your preliminary statements, and we're wrapping up here, so you're free to go. We'll want formal statements at the station tomorrow."

"I don't suppose I can open the shop tomorrow," Tally said.

"Given that this is the second fatality on the premises, we'll have to hold it closed for at least a day. You should be able to open Monday, though."

She had planned on being open on Sunday to take advantage of the increasingly busy tourist season, and to carry on business seven days a week for the rest of July and the first part of August. One Sunday missed wouldn't be too bad. She hoped.

She had picked off her bandage, and her cut was oozing again. Maybe she had picked off a scab, too. She didn't remember.

Dispirited and exhausted, Tally slogged toward the back door, following Andrea, who had bustled out in two seconds. The parking spaces behind the store were dark. Tally looked up at the streetlamp that was supposed to light the area, but it was apparently burned out. Someone loomed next to her car, a silhouette in the darkness. She stopped to figure out who it was as Andrea roared off, spinning her tires as she left.

When the noise had died away, she took a step closer to the shadowy figure.

"Tally? What's going on?"

Her shoulders sagged with relief as she recognized the voice. It was Allen Wendt.

"Allen, you scared me. What are you doing lurking here in the dark?"

"It's not usually this dark." They both looked up at the burnt-out streetlamp. "I saw the lights on in your shop, and the police cars and crime scene van, and had to stop. Have they discovered something new?"

"Someone, not something." Tally opened her car door, splashing a stripe of light across the inky blacktop.

Allen frowned and took a step toward her. "Someone? They found Gene's killer?"

"You know, I halfway thought she might have killed him. But she was killed in a very similar manner. She was also stabbed with something lying around, something sharp."

"She? Who? *Another* killing?"

"Yes." Tally sank to her car seat, her legs giving way from weariness. "Mart Zimmer, my employee. Someone killed her in the bathroom. Stabbed, just like Gene."

"Oh no! Oh, Tally." He put a strong, warm hand on her shoulder.

Tally reached up and clasped his hand, then turned her eyes on him. Her tears, stemmed successfully for hours now, started to flow. He pulled her to her feet, and they stood gazing at each other for a moment. He held out his arms, then Tally fell into them and they embraced as she sobbed.

Chapter 11

Tally and Allen ended up on the relatively quiet far end of the noisy bar in one of the restaurants that stayed open late, having a couple of cocktails. She found him to be a good listener. She told him about trying to find Mart when she didn't show up at work, and tried to recall when it was that she'd first smelled the awful odor in the shop's bathroom.

"I probably need to tell the detective when that was," she said, "as soon as I figure it out. Have you given statements to the police about Gene's murder?"

"Not yet. I mean, not one that I signed. I've been told I will have to."

"We're supposed to do that tomorrow for poor Mart. You probably will, too. When I came back from Yolanda's..." She drummed her fingers on the bar, trying to recall exactly how everything had happened. She had stuck a new bandage on her finger, and it was feeling much better. Maybe it would be healed soon.

Then it came to her. "It was right after I came into the shop from Yolanda's. I put off figuring out what that smell was. Something that had spoiled, I thought."

"Are there spoiled candies that would smell like a dead body?" Allen said with a smile.

"Maybe some ingredients. Spoiled milk?" She sipped her gin and tonic, refraining from guzzling it. "But no, not really."

Allen stared at the pretzel bowl while he played with a couple of pieces, shedding salt on the bar top.

"Allen, I'm very worried about Yolanda. The detective wouldn't tell me anything. All I know is that she was being questioned. This was before we found Mart, so it had to be about Gene. I can't imagine why they would hold her that long. It was hours. She's home now, so I ought to look in on her."

"Can I go with you?"

Tally didn't really want him to, since neither of them knew him that well. "I think that wouldn't be—"

"Wait a minute. There's something I have to tell you." He finished pulverizing the pretzel with his strong fingers. "I was there."

"Where?"

"I was at her store when the detective came in."

"So you know what this is about?" She swiveled her stool to face him. He nodded. "I know exactly what it's about."

Tally waited for him to tell her, then waited some more. "You have to tell me."

"I'm not supposed to."

"Says who?"

"Detective Rogers, of course. They don't want anything made public yet."

"So they have evidence against Yolanda? They can't!"

Allen dropped his head and stared at the pretzel crumbs. "They do. I want to help her. I don't believe she put it there. It wouldn't make sense. She wouldn't have let me move things around in the cooler if she'd known it was there."

"What? If she'd known *what* was where? In her cooler?"

"It looked like the murder weapon. It was her ribbon scissors."

Tally swayed, felt like she might fall off the bar stool. Allen reached over and steadied her. She now realized that this was what she'd been afraid of. Yolanda's scissors had been missing right after the murder, and they'd never turned up. Yolanda had been evasive when Tally had asked about them.

"Just because her scissors were hidden, doesn't mean…" she said.

"There was dried blood on them."

"If she had killed someone with them—okay, *Gene*, not *someone*—she wouldn't have left the blood on them, would she?"

"She also wouldn't have stuck them in her own cooler. I was helping her move things out of it to install a new shelf, and surely she would have stopped me before I found them."

"*You* found them? And called the detective?"

"No, no. He walked in the door right as I found them, the very moment. I had started to call him. Then he was behind me. Yolanda almost fainted. Terrible timing. But I feel responsible. I want to help Yolanda if I can, to make up for the trouble I've caused her."

Tally made up her mind to let Allen come along, and they wended their way to Yolanda's Sunday House. It wasn't nearly as close to work as Tally's little rental house, so Allen drove his white pickup. Tally thought it was surprisingly neat for a single guy's car. Nothing crinkled under her feet when she climbed in. Her own two-door Chevy Sonic was much messier. Things on the floor definitely crinkled when a passenger stepped into her car.

* * * *

Yolanda was roused from her crushing lethargy by a knock on her door. She glanced at the clock. Midnight. Her instinctive alarm sharpened at the sound, overshadowing the horrible ennui that had weighed her down and glued her to the couch, unable to move, since she'd been home.

She approached her old-fashioned wooden front door cautiously and peered out the peephole. Seeing Tally, her spirits lifted. But...on reflection, did she want to see her friend right now? Did she want to see anyone? She cracked the door open, and Tally opened the screen door and pulled her into a hug. Yolanda was horrified to see Allen Wendt standing behind Tally.

"What on earth are you doing here?" Yolanda stiffened in Tally's arms. "And what are *you* doing here?" She directed the last question to Allen.

"Can we come in?" Tally asked.

She couldn't leave them on the tiny porch this time of night. Talking out there would disturb her neighbors. She motioned both of them in, with misgivings. Stewing in her anxiety was taking up all her energy right now and she didn't have much left for her friend.

After Tally and Allen sat on her brocade couch and she slumped into the wingback chair, Yolanda asked, "Is something wrong? It's midnight."

"Of course something is wrong," Tally said. "What happened at the police station? Do they think you killed Gene?"

"What's he doing here?" Yolanda didn't look at Allen.

"We've been talking about everything that's happened," Tally said. "Allen feels bad and wants to help."

Yolanda turned to Allen, sitting up straight. "You give the police evidence against me and now you want to help?"

"I had no idea that pair of scissors was there."

"You sure happened to find it at the exact wrong time."

"I know. I didn't know Detective Rogers was going to come by with more questions right then. It was all bad luck. When I saw him, I wanted to act like I never saw them and keep them hidden from him, but it was too late. I feel bad and want to help you out if I can."

"So you don't think I killed Gene?" She glared at both of them, back and forth, daring them to say it, dreading what they thought. Wouldn't anyone think she had killed him when the murder weapon had been found hidden in her shop? If she didn't know differently, she would think so, too.

"Of course not," Tally said. "Why would you leave it there, let Allen find it, if you had put it there? That doesn't make sense. So, *do* the police think you killed him?"

"It's my pair of scissors. My fingerprints are on them. I heard them say that enough times."

"Of course they would be—they're yours."

"But...they're in the blood. The detective says that's damning evidence."

"In the blood? What does that mean?" Tally asked.

"It means," Allen broke in, "that her fingerprints got put there after the blood was there." He gazed at Yolanda, his gaze level and calm. "You handled the scissors after Gene was stabbed."

The small room grew silent. A couple of cars passed by in the street outside. In the distance, a siren wailed, then faded. Yolanda felt faint.

Tally came to sit on the arm of Yolanda's chair. "Yo," she said, "what's going on? What happened?"

Yolanda couldn't stem the tears that finally started flowing. All during her interrogation and for the past few hours at home, she'd been too numb to cry. She started shaking with exhaustion and cold. Tally slipped a comforting arm around her shoulder, and Yolanda leaned into her friend. "Yes. Yes, yes, yes, they think I killed him. How could they not think that? There's a ton of evidence against me."

"A ton?" Tally rubbed Yolanda's bare, quaking shoulder.

"A ton. We broke up, I was angry with him. Everyone knew that. People heard us argue. He took my money, he two-timed me, he treated me horribly. And my prints are on the murder weapon. I'm so cold. I've been cold all day."

Yolanda rubbed the goose bumps on her arms, exposed by the sleeveless dress she still wore. The air-conditioning had been set on high at the police station. "So, your scissors are definitely what killed him?"

Yolanda nodded, taking the tissue Tally handed her to wipe her nose. "Go ahead. Ask me."

"Ask you what?"

"Ask me how my prints got on the weapon, in the blood."

"I can't imagine. I know you're afraid to touch blood. You hate it. You almost faint when you get a tiny cut."

"That's true. But not this time."

"What do you mean?" Tally's hand stopped rubbing her shoulder.

"This time I didn't even notice the blood. I grabbed the scissors. I saw them there, sticking out of him, and it was mine, my pair of scissors. I couldn't leave it there. I grabbed it, stuck it into your cupboard, and ran out."

She heard Tally let out a breath. Allen whistled.

"You saw him dead? And didn't tell anyone?" Tally said.

Yolanda couldn't speak anymore. "Please go. I have to be alone." Her shivering hadn't quit. If anything, she shook more. She had to get out of this light dress and put on her warm, fleecy robe.

"But…did you put it in your cooler?" Allen asked.

She shook her head and croaked out, "No, I didn't bring them there. I put them where I didn't think anyone would notice. On a bottom shelf at Tally's. Not in my cooler."

* * * *

Tally and Allen talked for a bit in his truck after leaving Yolanda.

"Do you believe her?" Allen asked.

"How can you ask that? Of course I believe her." Her head was pounding, and she felt dizzy. This couldn't be happening. The world felt unreal right now.

"So, how did the weapon get into her cooler?" Allen asked. "Scissors don't walk."

"Can you take me home? I have to get to bed." She rubbed her temples, trying to ease her sudden headache.

"Sure." Allen's rugged face was grim as he started the truck up and drove her home in silence.

Tally was never so glad to see Nigel. She gathered up the giant blob of fur and carried him to her couch, where he purred in her lap for a good half hour. He didn't seem to want food right now, for a change. What a good kitty, Tally thought.

There was no sign of Cole. She wondered, dully, if he had taken off yet. She fully expected him to leave soon. He'd gone through a few of the local girls and would then move on, if he stayed true to form. How could they be brother and sister? Him, the love-'em-and-leave-'em guy. Her, the hardly-ever-have-a-date gal. And when she did go out with a guy, he dropped her off, mad, at her door.

She blinked, hard. She would *not* cry. Not about that. She should be crying about Yolanda. What to think? If what Yolanda said was true, it made sense that her fingerprints were on the scissors. But if she put them on Tally's shelf, why weren't they still there *on* the shelf? It didn't make sense. Who would have moved them? Hidden them where they would eventually be found?

Nigel yelped as she jumped up and knocked him off her lap. Of course. The person who murdered Gene had moved them. Okay then, if that was what happened, how did that person know where they were? Surely no one saw Yolanda hide them. No one else had been there.

When Tally had found the body, she had assumed the killer took the weapon when he—or she—departed. The police would naturally think that, too. But, before the murder, the scissors had been right there on top of the counter. Anyone could have grabbed them and stabbed him. That had to have happened before Yolanda went through the kitchen. So, who was there? That was what she had to track down. She had to reconstruct where everyone had been before Yolanda found the body.

Tally sank deep into the couch, and Nigel, instantly forgiving her—what a sweet boy—jumped into her lap for another petting session. Tally absentmindedly stroked him, trying to cast her mind back and figure out who was where, and when. She had given the police the names of the people who had been around: Allen, Andrea, Mart, and Yolanda. And maybe Dorella. She mentally crossed off Yolanda, then Mart. Since she was dead.

Chapter 12

Before Tally got out of bed Sunday morning, her cell phone rang from the nightstand where it was charging.

"How soon can you get to the station?" Detective Rogers asked.

"I'm not up yet. You closed my shop, so I'm sleeping in. Or I *was* sleeping in."

"How soon can you get here? I need you to identify some evidence."

More evidence? Against Yolanda? "What is it?"

"I'll show you when you get here. When will that be?"

How annoying. "An hour." She wasn't going to jump into clothes and rush down there for that rude man. She would eat breakfast, shower, dress, walk over and fetch her car from behind the shop, then drive out.

"I'll be waiting," he said.

When she got there, the detective made a production out of revealing what he wanted her to see. He ushered her into his stale-smelling office, invited her to sit, and offered her something to drink. When she impatiently declined, he summoned a young man to bring something from somewhere. Detective Rogers then took the bag from the man and held it open without touching what was inside.

She leaned over to peer inside and saw a single tennis shoe. She directed a questioning look at Detective Rogers.

"Do you recognize it?" he asked. "Does anyone you know wear Chuck Taylors?"

"I don't recognize it. But all tennies look pretty much the same to me. It's not mine, if that's what you're asking. Yolanda doesn't wear tennies." She did, but hadn't worn any lately, so it couldn't be relevant.

"Who else does?"

"Most of the people I know, at one time or another." She bent down and inspected the shoe more closely. "What are those spots? Is that blood?" Did it belong to the killer? She felt something crawl up the back of her neck.

"Yes, it's blood."

"Whose is it?"

"We're having it analyzed. Don't know yet."

She searched wildly for an innocent explanation for those rusty spots. "So...someone could have cut themselves shaving, or opening a can of soup."

"And then discard one of the shoes in the alley behind your shop."

"Why would someone throw away *one* shoe?"

"Good question," he said with a grimace. "The killer must have been pretty rattled. Or extremely crafty. We're looking for the other one, but haven't found it so far."

That made her pause. When he put it that way, the tennis shoe became more important. "So you think this shoe belongs to the killer. And it was discarded after the crime. So the killer had to have fled out the back. And left one shoe behind?"

"Not necessarily, although that's the simplest explanation. It could have been put there later. We didn't find it right away."

Leaving one shoe behind didn't sound simple to Tally. "When did you find it?" She hadn't known they'd searched the alley, but she hadn't been out there watching them when they were going over the place. "The killer's DNA is on it, right?"

The detective smiled grimly. "I'm sure the owner's DNA is on it."

"Well, whose DNA is it?"

Now he chuckled. "Do you think we put a drop of DNA on a slide, hook it up to a computer, and a picture and full dossier appear on the screen?"

Actually, she was picturing something like that.

"It takes days and days to get a DNA analysis back. Sometimes weeks. Or more. I'll try to put a rush on this. Then, after that, we have to match it to someone. Not everyone's DNA is on record since this isn't a futuristic police state."

"Oh." That would make everything harder. Not that she wanted to live in a futuristic police state. That sounded awful.

"A shortcut would be to find someone who knows who this shoe belongs to," he said.

* * * **

Tally drove home wondering why on earth someone would discard one shoe after killing someone else. But why leave it in the alley? And why only one shoe? Detective Rogers was most likely right, though. It was the killer's shoe. Nothing about Gene's death was simple.

If the shoe was connected, she had something concrete to work on. She was determined to figure out who could have done it—and then, gradually, by process of elimination, who actually did do it.

Who to start with? She cast her mind back to the many mysteries she had read. Aha—a light bulb lit above her head, figuratively. The police always suspected those closest to the dead person, right? Family. She would see what more she could find out about Gene's parents. They should be easy to eliminate. Parents didn't kill their own children, did they? Not that Gene was actually their child, but she couldn't see killing an adoptive child either, unless something was very wrong with that parent.

After she'd been home for half an hour, her doorbell rang. It was Mrs. Gerg, her landlady. Tally hoped she hadn't brought her another box from a yard sale.

"Hello, Mrs. Gerg. How are you today?"

"I'm fine and dandy. There are so many yard sales today. Even more than yesterday. I hope you don't mind that I didn't bring you anything." She held a large, round plastic container. It looked like she *had* brought Tally something.

"No, that's fine," Tally said, uncertainly.

"I brought this instead." She shoved the container toward Tally, who took it.

It was hot. She noticed that her finger was bending some and wasn't sore anymore. The bandage had fallen off sometime during the day. She was glad to be rid of that sore finger.

"I had to come see if you were all right. I noticed your shop is closed and wondered if you're sick."

"No, I'm not sick. I had to close the shop because…"

"Oh, because that young man, the mayor's son, was killed there?"

"No, that was a few days ago." She might as well tell her. Everyone would know eventually, even without Mrs. Gerg spreading the word. "Someone else died there yesterday." Or maybe the day before that. She hadn't been told exactly when Mart had been murdered.

It was a good thing Tally had a good hold on the container, because Mrs. Gerg let go and took a step back, almost falling off the porch. "Someone else?"

Mrs. Gerg was horrified, rightly, that another person had been killed there. "And I didn't hear about it?" Mrs. Gerg added.

Oh, thought Tally. *She's more surprised that she didn't know.* Actually, Tally was surprised about that, too. Now, for sure, everyone in town would know.

"Is it that girl who works for you? The one who jogs down my street in the evenings?"

"No, it's the other one. Mart Zimmer."

"Oh my." She glanced upward to process the information. "I was afraid you were sick, so I brought you some chicken soup." Mrs. Gerg pointed to the plastic tub Tally held.

"That's awfully nice of you. I'm not sick, but I'd love to eat the soup, if you don't mind."

"It's yours. I made it for you. Take care now." Mrs. Gerg stumped down the two steps from Tally's porch with her short legs and walked away briskly, on her way, Tally thought, to seek out more yard sales. And more boxes for her. And spreading the news as she went.

* * * *

Tally was still working on a way to approach Gene's parents again on Monday morning when his mother walked into her shop, soon after she unlocked the front door and opened up. She seemed overdressed to be shopping, in a mauve silk pant suit, but maybe, Tally thought, a mayor's wife always dressed to the hilt.

"Good morning, Mrs. Faust," Tally said. She had planned to stay in the room, working the sales counter. Andrea hadn't come in yet, but should show up any minute. She was certain the mayor's wife had never been to her shop before. She wondered what she was doing here now. Tally had offered to show her where Gene died, but she hadn't acted interested. She decided not to bring that up.

She wanted to blurt out, *Did you kill your son?* But instead she asked, "Are you looking for something special?"

"I believe so. The garden club is meeting at our house tomorrow and I'd like to serve something different."

The garden club? With her son just murdered? Tally showed her some of the newest items, the Twinkies and the Baileys Truffle Fudge.

"Could I have a taste of that?" She pointed to the fudge.

What was wrong with this woman? She wasn't a bit upset being in the building where Gene died.

"Sure thing. Hang on a sec." Tally scurried to the kitchen to get a small piece of the fudge so she wouldn't ruin the batch on display in the case.

"My goodness. That's terrific," Mrs. Faust said after she tasted it. "I'd like a pound of that. I'm baking white chocolate cookies, and I'll have these on the plate for contrast. The colors should be complementary. I'll still have to decide on the wine to serve. I wonder, though. That might be a problem with this variety of tastes."

"When is Gene's funeral going to be?" Tally felt bold asking that question, but it distressed her that Mrs. Faust hadn't even mentioned him. If Tally had lost a son, she doubted she would be hosting a garden club and worrying about wine choices a few days later. She shivered at the coldness of the woman.

"Oh, the funeral? I'm not sure. You'll see it in the paper. Josef is handling that."

"I see." So, she wasn't even helping plan her son's funeral. Colder than cold. Frigid. No wonder Gene had gotten into so much trouble. She couldn't imagine her own mother showing so little concern for her if she died.

"Josef says we can't plan anything until the body is released anyway," Mrs. Faust said, gazing out the front window.

"The body?" Had the woman called Gene *the body?*"

"That's what Josef says. The authorities are talking to him, you know." She said it like Josef was privileged to be talking to them. Tally hoped they were talking to him as a suspect. And to Mrs. Faust, too.

Tally busied herself measuring and wrapping Mrs. Faust's purchase. She was angry about the woman's cavalier attitude and decided to delve into it further. "Where were you again when he died?"

"Let's see, that was Tuesday, wasn't it?"

"Yes. Tuesday afternoon. Did you hear about it right away?"

"Oh, heavens, yes. The whole town was buzzing instantly. As if he hadn't given us enough grief when he was alive."

His death gave *her* grief?

"I was at the hairdresser's that day. I have a standing appointment at three o'clock every Tuesday afternoon."

The police hadn't said they knew exactly what time he died, but it was some time in the afternoon. She had found his body at around seven o'clock, but Yolanda had to have found him earlier, before six, maybe around five forty-five, if she remembered correctly. Would Mrs. Faust, were she so inclined, have had time to murder her son after a three o'clock hair appointment and before five forty-five? That would depend.

"Where do you get your hair done?" she asked. "I'm looking for a place," she added quickly. "I haven't had a cut for weeks." That much was true. "I use Fancy's Curls on South Adams Street."

"I'll have to try them. Thanks for telling me." Tally handed Mrs. Faust her batch of fudge, avoiding touching her. The woman was creeping her out. She wondered if her skin would feel cold, like lizard skin. She certainly wasn't going to touch it. She was going to check her alibi, though, just in case the police hadn't followed through.

While the shop was still empty, Tally called Fancy's Curls and made an appointment for Tuesday at nine, an hour before her shop opened. She didn't want to be there when Mrs. Faust was, in the afternoon, but she wished she had thought to ask Mrs. Faust who she used.

Andrea came in through the front door, dropped off by her mother this time, and asked if Mrs. Faust had been in. "I saw her driving off."

"She was getting goodies for a garden club meeting at her house. Isn't that cold? She cares more about her garden club than about her dead son." Tally immediately wished she could take back her words. That was an insensitive thing to say to the woman who had dated Gene.

"She's no prize," was Andrea's terse reply as she tied on her smock and got to work.

* * * *

Allen Wendt called a few minutes before closing to ask if Tally would like to join him for a drink at Java Joe Corral around the corner.

"What time will you be there?" she asked, wondering if she wanted to do this or not.

"You close at seven. How about eight?"

An impulse seized her to find out more about the Fausts through him. That might be a good avenue. "How about quarter after seven? I'll walk over right after I close up." She could get Andrea to handle the end-of-the-day tasks. She had done it before. What drove her impulsive decision was that Allen had worked closely with Gene. He might know something about his strange family.

As soon as she settled on a bar stool next to him, she started off asking Allen about his family, planning to segue into Gene's situation. "Where are you from?"

"Here and there. I've never really settled down."

"That's interesting." Well, it sort of was. She spun slightly on her bar stool and sipped the wine the bartender had set in front of her. "Where does your family live?"

"They never settled down either. How about you? Are you from here?"

Okay, she would approach it from a different angle. "I grew up here. I left, but came back when Yolanda talked me into opening my store next to hers. I knew Gene when he was younger. I'd almost forgotten his name was Schwartz before he was adopted. He used to make the news quite a bit, being in trouble a lot."

"I guess he ended up in the news, too, didn't he?"

Tally shivered. Yes, he did. "How well did you know him?"

"Not well at all. I got the job through a want ad in the Austin paper online."

"Yolanda didn't kill him. I know that," Tally said, leaning toward him and lowering her voice. "I need to know more about him to find out who *did* kill him."

"Whoa, girl. You're going to play detective? Is that a good idea? That Rogers guy seems like a serious sort. He might not like that."

She was sure he wouldn't. "I'm not telling him, and I'd appreciate it if you didn't either. But what about Gene? Was anyone angry with him lately?"

"Besides me?"

Tally leaned away, surprised he'd said that. "Why were you angry?"

"He owed me money. It was beginning to look like he was never going to be able to pay me for the work I've done. His credit was no good at the hardware store. I doubt he had any funds."

"What did he do with his money? Yolanda and I paid him for his work and I know other people did, too."

"Beats me. It's obvious that he underbid some of the jobs. I've heard him on the phone with his father asking for money. His Honor, the Mayor, as far as I can tell, never loaned him any."

"His mother doesn't seem to have liked him. Did anyone like him?"

"I felt bad for the guy, with those parents. They weren't supporting him in anything he did. He was kind of out on a limb by himself, and the limb was breaking. But still, I do need to get paid when I work."

Tally gazed into her dark red wine, feeling an acute pang of pity for Gene, in spite of the fact that she hadn't liked him. An alarm went off in her head. Allen was angry at Gene, and he was not very far away when he died. On the other hand, Allen had bought her a drink, so he wasn't broke. Was he telling her the truth about Gene?

A booth became available, and they moved to it to have a bite to eat. They talked about the town and some of the German oddities, like the

Sunday Houses and the museum devoted to Admiral Nimitz, a famous World War II naval commander who had been born in Fredericksburg. They also talked about all the German names of places. Tally felt herself relaxing with Allen, in spite of the mystery he insisted on surrounding himself with. He was attentive and pleasant, and not at all bad to look at. When their food was finished, he offered to walk her home and she accepted. She had walked to work that morning, so her car was still in her driveway.

The streetlamps cast flowing bars of light across the sidewalk as they strolled, the songs of tree frogs and cicadas flowing down over them. The evening air was soft on Tally's skin.

Allen talked about a project he'd done in another town, his voice silky and low. The customer had designed a storage shed that couldn't be built, but the guy wouldn't take no for an answer. Allen had to figure out how to engineer the thing so it would resemble something like the amateur drawing, but would still have four walls, a roof, and a door. The customer didn't want a boring old rectangle, but more of a diamond shape, to fit in an odd corner of his lot. She couldn't help stealing glances at Allen's face as he talked. It wasn't quite handsome, but was attractive in a rugged way. When he talked about his work, she saw a spark of animation that made it interesting.

At her front door, he thanked her and said maybe they could do it again.

"What's that?" he asked when a yowling racket started up inside her house.

She laughed. "That's Nigel. He knows I'm out here and his din-din is late."

"Puma? Tiger?"

"No, he's merely a cat." She opened the door and scooped Nigel up to meet Allen. Nigel sniffed his outstretched fingers and licked one.

"I must have some barbeque sauce on my finger," he said, smiling at the cat. "You're sure that's not a puma?"

"He's a Maine coon. They're large, but they *are* domesticated pet cats."

"He's big, all right." Allen stroked Nigel a couple of times, said good-bye, and left.

Tally didn't know if she wished he'd kissed her good night or not. The only thing she felt at the moment was an emptiness inside.

Chapter 13

Yolanda half listened to her stylist at Fancy's Curls talking about the fish her son had caught last weekend while she strained to hear the woman two chairs over. Her voice was loud, but the place was full of chatter, so she couldn't make out every word.

Tally had called Yolanda last night and said she wanted to find out everything she could about Gene's parents. Neither of them seemed to even like him, let alone love him. Yolanda doubted that would prompt them to murder him in Tally's shop. But Yolanda agreed to scout out the hairdresser on the off chance she hear something that would lend a clue to the murder.

Just now, by an amazing coincidence, Yolanda deduced that the woman two seats over was talking about Gene's mother.

"She's always been mad at Josef for adopting him. He was a hard-case juvenile delinquent, you know."

"I know," the stylist answered. "She comes here to have her hair done. She was here the day he was killed."

"I couldn't believe it when he threw it right in the water. I mean, we hadn't even weighed it yet."

Yolanda nodded to Khristie, her own hairdresser, and strained to hear the other conversation.

"Was she?"

Now Yolanda held her breath, listening. Did Mrs. Faust have an alibi in the hairdressers' shop? Or did she get her hair done and then go kill her son?

"It was nine pounds if it was an ounce," her own stylist said, continuing the fish saga.

The customer in the other chair continued, "So at least she didn't kill her own son."

"I'm not so sure. She hated him."

"What time was she here, though? You said she was here when he was killed."

"I don't know if it was exactly when he was killed. She showed up late because her car wouldn't start. Or so she said. She also left early for some reason. She ended up getting a trim when she was scheduled for a perm."

Yolanda wondered if the stylist was trying to make more out of the situation than it warranted, to make herself the center of attention. Several patrons were staring at her, wide-eyed. The one between them and Yolanda said, "So you think she killed her own son?"

"I didn't say that. Only that she wasn't here as long as she was supposed to be. She mentioned to me in the grocery store that the police had asked her about that day and she said she was here all afternoon."

Yolanda's own hairdresser asked, "Have you told the cops that?"

The gossiper stuck her chin out. "They didn't ask."

A chorus piped up, telling her she needed to talk to the police.

It occurred again to Yolanda that she didn't have the world's worst parents. Even if Gene's mother didn't kill him, she was an awful mother. His father could just as well have killed him, too, since neither of the older Fausts wanted him. And they had, after all, adopted him. Why, if they didn't want him? Was it truly a publicity stunt by the mayor, as so many people said? How awful to play with a person's life like that.

The shop had grown quiet as each of the five hairdressers returned to concentrating on their clients, one by one. Yolanda's stylist finished her up. Yolanda paid and headed for the door, almost bumping into Tally, who was coming in. She grabbed her friend's arm and whispered, "I'll talk to you later. I have some dirt on Gene's mom."

* * * *

Tally nodded and went to the desk to see who could do her hair.

It would obviously be the colorful young woman who had just finished Yolanda, since hers was the only chair empty. Tally kept her ears open wide to try to catch stray remains of whatever had been being gossiped about before Yolanda left—the "dirt" on Gene's mom. Should she ask outright if this woman, whose name tag said she was Khristie, also did Mrs. Faust's hair? No one seemed to be talking about Mrs. Faust at the moment.

Khristie's own hair was striped with bright stoplight red, so Tally was relieved when she didn't suggest the same for her. Tally asked for a shampoo and a trim, though, so she would be there as long as possible, barring red stripes or a perm, neither of which she had ever gotten in her life.

At the shampoo bowl in the rear of the shop, she couldn't hear any dirt at all. But when she returned to the chair at Khristie's station, a woman beside her was talking to her hairdresser about Mrs. Faust. She wasn't the same one who had been there when Tally arrived. This woman had a very short, almost mannish cut. She probably had to come often to keep it that length.

"So it's possible she killed her own son? And she's the mayor's wife?" the short-haired woman asked.

"No, I don't think so," the hairdresser said. "They were just talking about it, that she wasn't here when she was supposed to be. My schedule has her here for her original time. I never changed it."

The client continued, "If anyone killed him, anyone in the family, I would think it would be the mayor. I've heard his re-election campaign is asking for a lot of donations, and the talk around town about his son isn't helping anything. The word is that people didn't like his son and weren't donating."

What word was that? Tally wondered. *Did everyone know Gene had been two-timing several women? Did they know about his finances?*

The short-haired customer continued without need for prompting, luckily for Tally. "He's been seen out at all hours and drinking more and more lately. And a different woman every time."

That didn't sound too scandalous to Tally, compared to Gene's criminal troubles in his younger years, but it probably wasn't the best image for a mayor's son.

The customer on the other side of Tally, this one with long, coppery waves, leaned forward to talk to the one telling tales about Gene. "You know, the mayor couldn't have killed him. My husband was with him on the golf course all afternoon. They played eighteen and were behind a slow foursome."

The short-haired original gossip sniffed. "They played in the rain? It rained that afternoon."

"Not too long, I guess. I know it stopped their game early, but they spent the rest of the afternoon in the bar. I know Josef was there with them part of the time."

Short Hair sniffed again, and that conversation was over.

Tally didn't learn much else during her appointment, so she was eager to rush back to Yolanda and find out what her scoop was.

The shop kept both Tally and Andrea busy all morning. It was noon before Tally found time to talk to Yolanda. She texted and Yolanda said she couldn't leave, but Tally should come over. Business at Tally's Olde Tyme Sweets was steady at the moment, but nothing Andrea couldn't handle by herself. Tally thought, not for the first time, how much she missed Mart being there to help out. She also recalled, with appreciation, her steady, thorough working demeanor, her confidence, even if it had bordered on smug arrogance at times. She would have to hire another worker soon.

Tally went out through the front door of her shop and was pleased to see all the foot traffic. Across the street, a young couple strolled into the jewelry shop. A family browsed the window of the art gallery, then went in. People were going in and coming out of the chocolate shop on the corner. That shop was the one that Tally perceived to be her biggest rival, although their wares were quite different. Still, they both sold good things to eat, and she knew she was competition for them—and vice versa.

She crossed her fingers for her own business and walked into Yolanda's shop, fragrant with the smell of lilies at the moment.

"Oh hi, Kevin," she said when she saw the vineyard store manager talking to Yolanda as she worked.

"Just leaving. See you later," Kevin said and left with a wave to both of them.

"What are you working on?" Tally asked.

"Gene's funeral, believe it or not. His mother wants bunches and bunches of lilies for his casket."

"They want a basket for a funeral?"

"No, a spray, but they came to me because they knew I had the flowers. Apparently, Mrs. Faust is on the outs with all the florists in town."

"I imagine she's hard to get along with. I know I don't like her much. Or at all, actually." Tally leaned over to get a full, sweet whiff of the stargazers Yolanda was trimming and inserting into wire mesh and foam for the spray. "Poor Gene." Tally surprised herself when she said it. It came out before she knew it. No one should have the life or the family he'd had. And no one should die like he had. "So they came to you. Do they know you're a suspect in his murder?"

Yolanda shrugged. "Not sure. But according to the women at Fancy's Curls, his mother might have been the one who killed him."

"Do tell."

Yolanda related what they'd said about her coming late and leaving early, changing to a light trim instead of a perm. Then Tally added the information that they had talked about his father possibly killing him too.

"I agree," Tally said. "Poor Gene."

Chapter 14

Soon after Tally walked in the front door of Olde Tyme Sweets after seeing Yolanda, setting off the soft chime she loved to hear, Allen called to invite her out to dinner again. She accepted without stopping to think about whether or not she should. But after the call ended, she wondered if she was getting into something she shouldn't. What did she know about Allen Wendt anyway? But, then again, dinner—what could that hurt?

The place he had mentioned was public, the Rathskeller, in the thick of the touristy part of Fredericksburg and sure to be packed this time of year, even if it was Tuesday night. She had told him she would walk there, since it was so close to her place. She would close up at seven, leave Andrea to do cleanup, again, and concentrate on enjoying herself. She needed a break from worrying about the murders and who could possibly have committed them.

A couple of hours before closing, the shop was full, and Tally seemed busier than she ever had been. Glancing around, she figured out why. Andrea was nowhere to be seen. When the latest wave of customers had passed and there were only a handful of browsers left in the store, Tally pushed through the door to the kitchen and found Andrea on a stool, slumped on the counter of the center island. A faint sobbing sound reached Tally, and she noticed Andrea's heaving shoulders. She must be crying about Gene's death, Tally thought.

When she touched Andrea's shoulder, she flinched and jerked up her head.

"Oh, I'm sorry I scared you," Tally said, backing up a step. "What's wrong? Is there anything I can do?"

"No, there's nothing anyone can do," Andrea wailed. She sniffed and swiped at the tears staining her face.

Tally fetched a tissue from the cupboard. After Andrea wiped her eyes and her nose, she hung her head for a moment, then spoke.

"It's…it's the anniversary of the day my sister died."

So, she was not crying about Gene? Something else? Tally sat on another stool beside her. "I'm so sorry."

Andrea's features hardened. "The tenth anniversary. Of the day she was killed."

"Killed?" Tally's eyes widened, and her mouth dropped open in shock.

"She was killed in a drunk driving accident."

"How awful." Tally hoped she hadn't been driving. "How old was she?"

"She was fourteen."

So, Andrea's sister likely would not have been the driver. Tally didn't know what to say. "Would you like the day off?"

"No. That's okay. I'll get back to work." Andrea hopped off the stool and went to the restroom. She emerged a few minutes later and, true to her word, went back to work.

Tally decided she would be as gentle as she could with the poor girl. She couldn't imagine losing a family member so young, and to violence.

The last hours of the day flew by like a Texas twister, then it was time for her to leave. She grabbed her purse and dashed out to be on time to the Rathskeller.

* * * *

"So, you walked over, right?" Allen said as she approached the entrance. He was lounging against the stone exterior of the place, at the top of the stairs that led down to the German restaurant in the basement of the building that had been there since the 1800s. "My truck is parked out in the alley so I can drive you home if you'd like."

She agreed to that, and they descended into a world filled with the wonderful German aromas of kraut and sausage, and of frying chicken and catfish, too, since it was Texas. They were shown to a table against the rustic stone wall, a waiter dodging them while he balanced a large tray loaded with Jaeger Schnitzel and brats.

Allen didn't seem inclined to discuss the murder of his boss, so Tally figured she would give herself a much-needed break from that topic. They talked about the rain being gone for now, at least they hoped it was. This part of Texas didn't need any more drought, but a lack of rain was preferred when it was tourist season.

Dinner proved to be precisely the relaxing interlude Tally needed. She found herself loosening up and enjoying herself. Allen was intelligent, articulate, and a good dinner companion. She wondered if he would ever be anything more. They seemed to have the same taste in movies, TV shows, and books—unless he was merely agreeing with her to try to get her to like him more.

After they ate, they strolled to Allen's truck, parked behind the restaurant. The sun was setting in a brilliant blaze of colors, reminiscent of one of Yolanda's outfits.

He held the door and assisted her as she climbed up into the seat. However, when he took his own seat and turned the key, the vehicle made a couple of wretched, grinding noises, then fell silent.

Allen swore softly and whipped out his phone. "I know a guy. He can probably be here in a few minutes and give me a jump. It needs a new battery."

True to Allen's prediction, a small pickup with a magnetic sign on the door drove up within about ten minutes. The sign said that the truck belonged to Howie's Garage. A short, compact man jumped out and shook Allen's hand. "Got some trouble?"

Everything around them took on a rosy hue as the sun gave one last burst before fading.

"The battery again, Howie," Allen said in a dejected tone.

"Let's see if she'll jump one more time. But I'm tellin' you, one of these days she won't."

Tally was surprised to learn the battery was female. She was pretty sure her own was male.

Allen said, "It's not that old, Howie."

Howie whipped out some cables and hooked the trucks together. "You know, there was a bad batch of these. This is the same one that's givin' Mrs. Faust fits. Or it was until she got a new one last week. She was throwin' a conniption fit, sayin' she had to get to the divorce lawyer and get her hair done and I don't know what all. But she plain and simple had to have a new battery."

Her hair done? Tally leaned toward Howie. "What day was that? Tuesday?" The day Gene died.

"Yep, it was Tuesday. I know cuz I had bowling that night."

So maybe Mrs. Faust was late to her hair appointment legitimately and not because she was murdering her adopted son. And she was seeing a divorce attorney the same day? Busy woman. Tally figured there would be no reason for her to kill Gene if she was getting a divorce. It sounded like she was planning on leaving both of the men behind. Tally wondered if she would move out of town to make the break complete, although she'd heard the mayor telling her she wouldn't get the house. That made it sound like she wanted to stay.

When Allen started the truck toward Tally's house, he apologized. "I would have a new battery by now if Gene had paid me what he owed me."

Whatever Allen Wendt's virtues, managing his finances didn't seem to be one of them. Missing a paycheck had made him unable to buy a battery for his truck. She wondered if truck batteries cost more than car batteries.

Something on the floorboard rustled when she moved her feet. She peered into the darkness and thought they were lottery tickets.

Her house lights were on when Allen pulled up in front of her home. That meant Cole was there. In fact, as they walked up the sidewalk toward the porch, Cole's voice came from the shadows. The porch light was off. Cole rose from the glider and came down the steps.

"Hey, Sis. Have you eaten?"

She introduced the two men and said she had.

"Did you bring me the leftovers?" he teased.

"Leftovers? No way. I ate everything. Come on inside. I'll fix you something. Do you want to come in, Allen?"

Allen concentrated on the pavement at his feet. "I'd better get going. See you later. Nice meeting you, Cole."

When they got inside and Tally was scrambling eggs with cheese for Cole, she asked him what happened. "Did your Date of the Day stand you up?"

"Aw, Sis, am I that bad?"

"Yeah, you are. You've gone through Mart and Dorella so far. And you've been here all of a week."

"No, I haven't! I'm still seeing Dorella."

"But not tonight?" She set his plate in front of him, then turned to feeding the cat.

"I was…busy tonight." He started shoveling the food into his mouth.

Nigel came running when he heard the kibble clatter into his bowl.

"And she's okay with that?" The small kitchen television was on in the background. An ad touting Faust for mayor came on. The mayor's round, bald head bobbed as he emphasized the words he was speaking. Tally reached for the remote and turned the volume up to hear.

"I'm the man you want to keep our streets clean and crime-free. For many years now I've been an advocate of working with troubled youth to bring about real, lasting reform. If you reelect me as mayor—"

Tally clicked off the set and almost slammed the remote onto the table in her anger at the man.

"Dorella's okay. We're not engaged," Cole said, after he swallowed a big bite. "Oh hell, you'll probably find out. I was being questioned at the police station."

Tally plopped down at the table before she collapsed onto the floor. The *ticktock* of her grandmother's clock from the next room lent insistent punctuation for a few moments. "You? Questioned? They think *you* killed Gene?" She frowned at the thought.

"No, not Gene. They think I might have killed Mart."

Her frown vanished in comprehension. She could see how they might suspect that. The couple had broken up in anger. "You know, until she died, I thought she had probably killed Gene," Tally said.

"She should have. She told him she was pregnant, so he offered to marry her, then backed out. Cold right?."

"But she wasn't pregnant, after all, right?"

"She told me she wasn't, but Detective Rogers told me that the autopsy showed she was."

"Oh no!" Tally clapped her hand to her mouth, horrified. Not only had Mart been murdered, but her baby had lost its life, too. "That makes everything worse. She told you she wasn't, though. I wonder if she knew she was pregnant."

"Whatever, she was through with Gene."

"I can't imagine him marrying anyone."

"From the little I know, they would have made a good pair."

"A good pair? How so?"

"Like Bonnie and Clyde. Two amoral, good-looking people, out to swindle everyone they could."

Tally nodded. He had a point. Nigel jumped into her lap, letting her pet him a few times before trying to make it onto the table and scarf down Cole's eggs and toast. She pulled the big guy off the table and set him on the floor.

"Anyway, do you know a good lawyer?" Cole asked. "Just in case?"

"That's a good idea." Tally promised she would work on that and got up to get some cat treats. She wondered if Yolanda had called a lawyer yet.

Tally pondered the implications of Mart's pregnancy as she tried to fall asleep that night. Did that make it more or less likely for her to have murdered Gene? And had she even known she was truly pregnant? Impossible questions to answer, much as Tally would like to have known the answers to them.

The next morning, Tally remembered that she'd gone to middle school with a woman who was now a secretary for the local celebrity defense lawyer. Not that Fredericksburg had terrific need for a celebrity defense lawyer, but he was the most well-known, having defended a county sheriff against sexual harassment charges—and having gotten him off.

She woke Cole before she left the house to let him know that she would call her friend later, from the shop. He murmured a sleepy thanks, rolled over on the couch, and resumed snoring. Nigel, snuggled in the crook of his legs, gave Tally a sleepy yawn, then resumed his napping also.

Now Tally had to remember what the classmate's name was.

Chapter 15

Yolanda glanced up from the basket she was finishing for a twenty-fifth wedding anniversary celebration. She was proud of the shiny silver bows and the glittery sprayed roses adorning the beautiful basket that was filled with silver-wrapped candies, with an engraved picture frame and a small wall mirror poking up in the back. For this one, she had fastened five silver bells onto pipe-cleaner stalks and had them sticking up in front of the mirror.

Tally walked in the front door. Yolanda greeted her with a smile. "I have a box waiting at the post office, and it might be our plastic candy." She pulled curls onto the ends of the ribbons and considered the basket finished.

"That's gorgeous," Tally said. "You've outdone yourself with it."

"Thanks for coming up with the idea of wrapping your fudge pieces in silver paper. They'll love them. What's up?"

Tally leaned her elbows on Yolanda's counter with a dejected look. "It's Cole. He was questioned yesterday at the police station."

"Questioned? What about?"

"Mart's murder."

Yolanda let her scissors clatter to the countertop. "Oh no. How could that be?"

"It can't. He didn't kill her. But I said I'd try to get him a good lawyer."

"You want Lackey Three, then. Right?" That was what a lot of people called Larimer Lackey III, but never to his face. He was pompous, self-important, and seemed to have a low tolerance for remarks about his name.

"Yes, Lackey. Doesn't a classmate of ours work for him?"

"Oh, yes, his secretary. Nicole."

"All I could think of was Ubermeister."

Yolanda laughed. "Oberlander. That's her last name."

"That's it!" Tally brightened a bit. "Do you have a lawyer, Yo?"

"I haven't gotten one yet. My father wants me to, but I was afraid that would make me look more guilty. Maybe I should."

"I'll call his office and see if I can have lunch or coffee or something with Nicole."

"I'll go with you if you want me to. She goes to our church." She reached to put the scissors on the shelf where the ribbon spools were. "I suppose I should hire him, too."

"Thanks, Yo. I hope she can help my brother. And you."

The three women met at one of the vineyard tasting rooms on Main Street shortly after seven o'clock. Nicole had told Yolanda she was off at five, but could meet them at that later time, after Tally and Yolanda closed up.

Nicole and Tally caught up a bit on mutual high-school classmates, then Yolanda steered the conversation to their purpose.

She picked up her glass of semi-dry red and swirled it, admiring the color and, soon after, the taste. When she set it down, she started. "Tally's brother has a problem I was hoping you could help him with."

"Is he younger than you? I'm pretty sure I remember both of you," Nicole said to Tally.

"We both went through high school here before we moved away."

"I remember he collected strange pets. Bugs and lizards and things." Tally laughed. "He thought he was rescuing them."

"What does he need an attorney for? What's he done?"

"He hasn't done anything. But he went out with Mart Zimmer a few times and—"

"Mart Zimmer! She's the one who was murdered. The second one." Nicole acted horrified. Yolanda thought she would have encountered a murder or two, or more, in her job already and become inured to them.

"Not by him. But he's being questioned about it."

Nicole studied the wall over Tally's shoulder for a moment. Yolanda held her breath.

* * * *

Tally hadn't considered that the lawyer would hesitate to take Cole's case. But here was his legal secretary, going from acting horrified that she was sitting with a killer's sister to looking like she was weighing some unknown factors. Tally buried her nose in her glass, then tossed it back and swigged more of her Pinot Noir. "He didn't kill her, and he needs a defense attorney."

"Yes, he does, if he's being questioned," Nicole said. "Who else are they looking at?" Now she was sounding more reasonable, Tally thought. "For this one? I have no idea. Could you talk to Mr. Lackey and set up a meeting as soon as possible?"

"Sure, I can do that." She set her glass down and fished a notebook out of her purse, then jotted something down. "This whole thing is awfully strange, isn't it?" She waiting for one of them to speak next.

Tally had to agree. "I guess all murders are strange, right? It's not normal."

"But this one involves the mayor. Not Mart's murder, but Gene's, his son's."

"You know that Mart and Gene were seeing each other at one time," Yolanda said.

"So you think the two crimes are related? One of the things I thought bizarre is that there were two murders so close together when we hardly ever get any here."

"They have to be related, don't they?" Tally said. "It would be too strange if they were murdered by separate people for different reasons, and both of them in my shop. Something is going on that no one knows about, that's what I think."

"What's difficult," Yolanda said, "is that there are lots of people to suspect for Gene's killing, but hardly any for Mart."

"Yes," Tally added. "A lot of girlfriends and even his parents."

"You think that his parents might have killed him?" Nicole's eyes grew wide. "That would be something."

"They don't—didn't—seem to like him very much, either one of them," Tally said.

Nicole stared at the table for a moment. "You know, you're right. They didn't. And Josef, the mayor, was supposed to play golf with my boss that day. I remember thinking about that at the time."

"They didn't play golf?" Tally said. She had thought they played a few holes, then went to the clubhouse or bar.

"No, Larry called Josef to cancel because the weatherman said it was going to rain. It did rain a little. I remember him saying later that he wished he hadn't canceled because they probably could have gotten a round in."

Silence descended as Tally thought about this. The husband of the woman at the hairdressers' shop had lied to his wife. Josef was now firmly a suspect again. He couldn't use golf for an alibi.

Nicole set down her half-finished glass and gathered up her purse. "Anyway, I'll talk to Larry about your brother first thing in the morning.

He'll have to find out a few things, then he can call him." She smiled. "That is, I'll be the one calling."

"Wait," Yolanda said. "I might like to hire him, too."

Nicole paused with her hand on her purse. "You're a suspect?"

"Only for Gene's death. So far."

Nicole nodded, as if that made sense. "Sure thing. I'll talk to him about both of you. I don't know if he can take the cases, but I'll catch him first thing in the morning."

Tally gave her Cole's number before she hurried out. She turned to Yolanda. "So, you have to audition for a lawyer? I thought everyone was entitled to representation."

"I'm sure some lawyers pick and choose their clients, and probably turn some down. Why wouldn't they? They have to consider their reputations, and if they take too many losing cases, they'll suffer. And maybe, it would be a conflict of interest to represent both of us?"

Tally asked for another glass of wine.

"You're saying Cole is a losing case? Or you are?"

"No, no." Yolanda held up her palms. "He's not a losing case, and I'm not either, but Lackey doesn't know that."

"Nicole doesn't either, I guess." Tally began on her next glass of wine.

"You can't expect them to. After all, Cole doesn't live here. They don't know him."

"Nicole knows him. She even remembers him from when he was little."

Yolanda twirled her empty glass. "People change."

"Do you think Cole has changed? Do you?" Tally realized she was raising her voice and concentrated on keeping it down. "He's the same loveable person he always was."

"Loveable? He's loveable until he dumps you."

Tally stared at her best friend. What was she saying?

"You have to admit that's true," Yolanda went on, rubbing salt into the wound.

Tally sputtered a bit, but couldn't come up with a good retort. Especially since she knew that Yolanda was right. She had accused her brother of exactly the same thing. "So, you think he killed Mart?"

"No, no, I don't think that! I'm saying they don't know him. That's all I'm saying."

She was saying a lot more than that, but Tally was getting a headache and wanted to go home. "I have to leave," she said, then paid her bill and walked out.

On her way home, she realized she wasn't walking in a straight line. She probably shouldn't have had that third glass of wine. Or was the last one the fourth? Yolanda had stopped way before she had. She had stayed, Tally supposed, to keep her company, but she couldn't get their argument out of her head. Yolanda, it seemed, hadn't been questioned for Mart's murder. Maybe she was off the hook because Cole was on it? Tally wanted everyone to know, by looking at him, that her brother didn't kill anyone. Was that unreasonable?

Her stomach rumbled. What was unreasonable was having that much wine on an empty stomach. She stopped in at a gas station convenience store for a hot dog, needing something to quickly soak up all those fermented grapes roiling inside her.

As she pulled the door open to enter, she collided with Allen Wendt.

"Allen, sorry!" she said with a hiccup.

He dropped what he was holding, and papers scattered on the floor. She knelt to help him pick them up. They were lotto tickets. Lots and lots of lotto tickets.

"You bought all these?" she asked, handing him the ones she had scooped up.

He helped her stand since she was a bit wobbly. "They're not all for me. Are you okay, Tally?" He leaned close, and she suspected he was sniffing her breath.

"I will be. But I need something to eat now."

He nodded. "I'll see you later." He finished going through the door and left her there wondering how serious his gambling problem was. No wonder he was broke. Next time they had dinner together, she would try to question him. Right now, she couldn't think about anything. Her head was too full of something. Something that felt like helium, only lighter.

Chapter 16

Yolanda's father called her late Wednesday night one minute before she was about to climb into her deep claw-footed bathtub.

"*Cara mia*, have you thought more about the lawyer?" His voice was smooth and coaxing, trying to cajole her into agreeing with him. "I can call the one in Dallas. He's the best in the state."

She wasn't sure yet whether she wanted one or not. In any case, she would prefer to hire one she could afford. "I might get one from here, Papa."

"From where? From Fredericksburg? Are you serious?"

"I want to get one I can afford." She shivered in spite of the steam rising from the tub and filling the small bathroom.

"Not that again." He had changed to his harsh tone. The one that said *Do it because I said so.* "We've been over this."

Yes, they had. They'd argued about this issue, and every other one. Whenever Yolanda wanted to make upgrades in her shop, her papa always wanted to pay for it, then complain later that she spent too much money. When would she be able to resist him? To not feel like a little girl, but the grown woman she was.

It was bad enough they paid for this expensive Sunday House and the rent on her store. The Sunday House was her fault, but she loved the place. She just wished she could pay for it. She knew she would accept them paying for the lawyer, too, eventually, and she didn't like that about herself.

She envied Tally her mostly absentee parents, even though Tally complained about them being so far away most of the time. If only they could both have Happy Medium Parents. But they were what they were.

"Papa, my bathwater is getting cold. Can we talk about this later?" She grabbed a thick towel from the rack and wrapped it around herself. She shivered and sneezed. Was she getting a cold?

"We can't wait too long. From what you've told me, it sounds like the police are about to arrest you."

Yolanda clenched her jaw and bit her lower lip. At least he hadn't brought up Violetta. Perfect Violetta. "Oh no, they won't do that. They might have another suspect now. Or two."

"Who? Anyone I know?"

"No, Papa, I don't know who." Okay, that was a blatant lie. She knew who, and there was only one suspect. Cole.

"I'm so glad I at least have one daughter who doesn't put me through things like this."

There. He did it. He compared her to Violetta. "I have to go now."

After she hung up, she let some cool water out so she could warm up her bath again. She added an extra dose of lavender bath salts for comfort.

* * * *

Tally got a call before she left for work on Thursday from Nicole at the lawyer's office saying he would agree to represent her brother, but they needed to meet to finalize his decision. Tally wondered what this would cost. She was relieved when Nicole said he was tied up with other litigation and couldn't get started on Cole's "case" for another week.

She left it that they would meet on the next Thursday.

"Who was that on the phone?" Cole called from the couch.

Tally had taken the call in the kitchen. Should she tell him what she was doing? Maybe not quite yet. Maybe the police, or herself, would find the real killer before another week went by.

"One of my suppliers. They can't make their delivery until next Thursday."

"Oh, okay." He went back to sleep, and she left for work.

* * * *

Right after work that day, Tally made a run to the grocery store for more cat food and litter, plus some restocking of her own home fridge. She paused, reaching for a can of soup, when she heard a familiar voice in the next aisle. It was Andrea's mother. She would never forget those harsh tones. As she was when Tally first heard her, she was again scolding her daughter.

"Why can't you be like your sister was? Why do you have to be like this? What did I tell you to do?"

"Mom." Andrea's voice was soft. Probably trying to calm her mother down. "We all miss Patsy. We all wish she were here."

"Do you? Do you really miss her? Because I can't see that." The woman's voice was getting louder, more irritated.

"You'll never know how much I miss her," Andrea answered.

"Huh. I'm sure I won't. Now, pick those up and let's get out of here."

They had to be talking about the sister who was killed in a car wreck. Andrea *did* miss her, Tally knew. She'd seen how much she was grieving for her. What a shame that the family was dealing with it so badly. It was hurting Andrea and her mother. Probably her father, too, though Tally had never met him. Maybe he wasn't around anymore? Maybe he had left? Who would want to stick with Andrea's mother?

Tally gave them enough time to leave the store before she continued her shopping.

* * * *

That night Tally found herself agreeing to have a dinner date with Allen again.

As she was coming out her front door, Mrs. Gerg was coming up the front sidewalk bearing another yard sale treasure. This one was a large box. It was bright red and might have been lacquer, but might have been plastic. It wasn't going to fit on the cabinet with the rest of them.

"See what I found, dearie." Mrs. Gerg held it up proudly, with a wide grin on her round face.

"It's big, isn't it?" Tally lingered outside her door, leaving it open so she could stash the latest gift inside.

"Yes, and I got it for a song. I knew you'd love it."

Tally took the offering, realizing that it was, indeed, plastic and trying to think where she would put it where no one would see it. Maybe she could rent a storage space if this kept up.

"Did you see all those people at the Zimmer house last night?"

At Mart Zimmer's house? "No, I didn't go past there."

"The mayor and his wife showed up. I knew they would."

"Showed up for what? What was happening?"

"I imagine it was the wake. For their daughter."

Tally knew that neither Gene's nor Mart's body had been released to their families, but maybe the Zimmers had a wake anyway. That was their right.

"The Zimmers and the Fausts have been good friends for years, you know. Those kind of people stick together."

She meant rich people, Tally assumed. "Do you know them?"

Mrs. Gerg waved a chunky hand. "Oh, I know of them. Everyone in town knows who they are. They don't know me, I'm sure."

"But you know a lot about them?"

"A fair amount. The YSU, you know."

"The what?" Tally asked, ducking inside and setting the box on the floor beside the cabinet that was topped with smaller boxes.

"The YSU, the Yard Sale Underground." Mrs. Gerg winked. "Those of us who go around to them collect all kinds of gossip. You learn a lot about people from what they're selling. Plus, you can talk to them when you're there. They always open up to me, since I buy things from them."

That could be useful. "Have you heard anything about the Fausts?"

"I hear things about them all the time. What do you mean?"

"I mean, in relation to their son's death?"

"Oh, do you mean did they do him harm?" Her round eyes grew rounder. "That's something to consider, isn't it? I'll keep my ears peeled."

Tally thought it might be better to keep her eyes peeled, but didn't want to interrupt.

"I'll snoop around and let you know what I find out."

"If you find out anything important, the police should know."

"Of course. But I'll tell you first." Mrs. Gerg left, happy to be on an important errand.

Tally and Allen got tacos from a taco truck and carried them to the park since the evening was lovely, soft and warm, with no rain. The cicadas were full volume, and fireflies winked in the shrubbery nearby. The whole time they were sitting on a bench under a large live oak tree, making small talk and crunching their tacos, Tally was wondering how to bring up the subject of gambling. She couldn't get the sight out of her head of all those lotto tickets fluttering to the floor. If he had a gambling problem, he probably had money problems. His statement that they weren't all for him hadn't rung true. He'd said himself that he didn't know many people here. When he mentioned that, it made her wonder if he would stay or leave.

"Will you stick around here after you finish up your work?" she asked.

"I'm as finished as I'll get. Gene's father said he wouldn't pay me what I'm owed, so I'm not doing any more of Gene's work. That would be stupid."

He paused for a moment, glaring at the grass beneath their feet as if he wanted to burn a hole in it with his eyes. Or did he want to burn a hole in Josef Faust, Gene's father? He looked up at Tally, and his expression softened. "But if you or Yolanda need any adjustments, I can do that. Is your refrigerator working okay?"

"Yes, after it got that new thermostat part, it's been perfect. Where do you think you'll go?"

He smiled and shook his head. "As usual, I have no idea. I'll tumble down the road and see where I end up."

"That's the life my parents lead. They wander the world and never settle down. I decided I can't do that. I need to put down roots somewhere."

"Here?"

"Why not? I like this town. I do actually have roots here, since I lived here once."

"There are plants that take their roots with them. Did you know that?"

Tally thought for a moment, chewing a mouthful of delicious flavored meat, cheese, lettuce, and crunchy taco shell. "What, besides a tumbleweed?"

"A lot of different plants end up as tumbleweeds. All that means is that it's a plant that breaks off and tumbles when it's dry. One kind came from Russia, Russian thistle, and one is called tumbling oracle, and another name I've heard is wind witch. They don't really take their roots with them, but they take seeds that put roots down when they land somewhere. I like to think they take their future roots with them."

"How do you know so much about tumbleweeds?" Maybe there was more to Allen than she had thought.

He shrugged one shoulder. "I've been called one so many times, I've looked them up. After I learned a little about them, I didn't mind being called that."

"Don't you ever want to have a family? Do you have a family you've left behind?"

"I don't ever miss them. They're not worth it. And no, from what I know about families, I'm better off without one."

His last, forlorn statement hovered in the air above them. Tally could almost see it in the darkness. He must have had a bad family. She was sorry for him. And again, she was so thankful for her own, weird and quirky as they were.

"Some families aren't so bad," Tally said softly, feeling the need to defend hers. "Some are warm and loving and supportive. You know, you can make your own family, find people like that and surround yourself with them."

He stood abruptly. "Not likely." He threw his empty taco wrapper into the trash can next to their bench as hard as he could. She saw that his jaw was clenched. In anger? She leaned away an inch or so, frightened by his rage—it seemed to come and go in a flash. As if to confirm what was in her mind, he gave her a warm smile and held out his hand for her wrapper, to throw it away for her.

He walked her home, but she didn't make an effort to converse much and neither did he. They said good-bye on her porch without touching. By the time she was in the house with the front door locked, she was having serious reservations about going out with Allen Wendt again. There was something scary under his good-looking surface. Maybe tumbleweeds should be avoided, because they tumble on out of your life. She was sure, from their conversation, that Allen would eventually move on.

She knew she shouldn't be, but she was bothered that the Zimmers had had a wake for Mart and didn't invite her. Did they think she had killed their daughter? Maybe they hadn't had a wake. Maybe Mrs. Gerg thought that's what it was, but it wasn't. She checked every online site she could think of and searched every string she thought of, but didn't find any mention of it.

She washed up and changed into her PJs. The house was empty except for the cat. Something bothered her about the silence, then she realized she didn't hear her grandmother's clock. She padded into the living room to wind it, then wandered into the kitchen. Cole had left a note on the kitchen counter: *Out with Dorella. Be in early. Love, Cole.*

It was sweet the way he always signed his notes with "love." She always did the same thing with family. They all did. She sat in the dark, dangling a string for Nigel, waiting for her brother to come home. What did she think about him seeing Dorella? Since she didn't know much about her, it was impossible to form an opinion. All she knew was that Dorella had dated Gene and was angry with him the day she came into the shop the day he was...

That was the day he was killed. And she was angry with him. Did she kill him? She could easily have gone around to the alley, entered the kitchen through the unlocked back door, stabbed him, and left without anyone seeing her. So far, no one had come forward as a witness to his killing. No one had even seen anyone going in or out around the time of his death.

Nigel gave her a pointed stare because she had stopped moving the string. Or maybe his look was because no one had fed him. She got up and went to the kitchen to check his bowl. Sure enough: empty. Poor Nigel.

She heard the front door over the clatter of kibble going into Nigel's metal bowl. The cat daintily started extracting bits of his food from the bowl so he could eat them off the floor. He'd done that before. Tally made a mental note to get a mat to put under his bowl.

"Hey, Sis! Did you have a good night?" Cole came in and carefully set a bag on the kitchen counter.

"Not all that good, but I'll tell you about it later. What's in the bag?"

"Wait till you see it. Dorella made you something. She thought you might like it."

"Me? Why is she giving me anything? I don't even know her."

Cole drew a gorgeous iridescent blue vase from the sack. It started out nicely rounded at the bottom and tapered to a graceful narrow opening that was slightly asymmetrical at the top.

"It's beautiful," Tally said. "But why did she send this to me?"

"She says she has lots and she wanted to give this one to you. Maybe"— he got a sly look on his face—"she wanted to get in good with me."

Tally picked it up, being careful not to drop it. "This looks handmade. Expensive. Why would she have a lot of them?"

"Oh, didn't you know? She's a potter. Works at Potter Paradise on Main Street."

"Really? I thought you said she works at Burger Burger."

"She's part-time at each place."

Tally turned the vase around, liking it more and more. "Thank her for me, okay?" She set it in the middle of the kitchen table to admire.

"Sure will. I'm meeting her after work tomorrow." He pulled out a chair at the kitchen table and motioned her into one, too. "But tell me about your night. What's the matter?"

"I'll tell you, but first, can I ask you a question about Dorella?"

"Sure." Cole kicked off his shoes, and Nigel, already done with his food, raced over to sniff them. Then he jumped onto the table and started batting at the vase.

Tally grabbed it and put it on the counter. She would keep an eye on it, though, and later move it to the mantel beside her grandmother's clock. Nigel had never jumped up there.

"How much do you know about her? About her and Gene?"

"I don't want to know much about that. Why would I?"

Nigel pawed the inside of one of Cole's shoes.

"Why was she so angry with him when she came to my shop?"

He bent down to stroke the huge cat. "What are you talking about?"

"The day Gene was killed, not too long before I discovered him on the kitchen floor, Dorella came in looking for him. She was furious with him for some reason, said to tell him she wanted to talk to him. I never delivered the message."

"Look, Sis. All I know is that she was seeing him. But so was every other young woman in this town. I'll bet they were all mad at him at some point."

"Cole, what if you're seeing the person who killed Gene?"

He shook his head. "Okay, how was your day?"

"Mrs. Gerg stopped by."

"With another valuable handmade, authentic carved chest?" Cole had asked about her growing box collection and she'd told him about her generous, but odd, landlady.

"Yes, unfortunately. Very authentic this time. Authentic plastic." She showed him the large, shiny red box. "But she said something that bothered me. Did you ever meet Mart's parents when you were seeing her?"

Cole shook his head. "It felt like they didn't want me in their house."

"Why not?"

"They think they're somebody. Only the upper crust is invited in. That's what I gathered from Mart. She didn't exactly say she was ashamed of me, but she let me know her parents wouldn't want to meet someone like me. She even used that phrase, 'someone like you.' Weird, huh?"

"Maybe that explains it."

"Explains what?"

"Mrs. Gerg thinks they had a wake yesterday, and the mayor and his wife, plus some other people were there, but I wasn't even informed, let alone invited."

"Sounds about right. I wouldn't worry about that. What did you do tonight?"

"I went out with Allen again." She told him about Allen's own frightening flashes of temper and his obvious gambling. "He has no love for any of the Faust family, father or son."

"And...you think *you* might be dating Gene's killer?"

Tally kicked herself mentally. It wasn't possible that she and Cole were *both* dating his killer. Only one person had murdered Gene Faust. She couldn't suspect everyone who had ever known him. "I don't know what to think." Her shoulders slumped in defeat. How was she going to clear Yolanda...and Cole? She was getting nowhere.

"Let's consider that. Who has the worse temper, Dorella or Allen?" he asked.

Tally kicked herself again, harder. Why had she brought all of this up? "I don't know Allen well enough to know how bad his temper can get. But he has one, and he loses control of it in front of people."

"Hmm. That doesn't sound good. He's also strong, works with his hands."

"It doesn't take much strength to stab someone."

"True," Cole said.

They both thought for a moment, with the loud rumbles of Nigel's purring for background music as he kneaded Cole's shoes.

"How bad is Dorella's temper? Worse than Allen's?" Tally asked.

"That's the question, isn't it? Whose temper would flare up high enough to kill someone?"

"Or high enough to kill two people."

Tally closed her eyes. "I'm tired and going to bed. Gotta work tomorrow." She remembered to put the vase on the mantel on her way to bed.

She had decided. She was not going to go out with Allen again. And she couldn't tell her brother how to live his life. Cole would have to decide about Dorella for himself.

Chapter 17

Tally didn't have to act on her decision the next day. She didn't hear from Allen at all. She did hear from another handsome man, first thing in the morning, but not one she wanted to hear from—Detective Jackson Rogers. When her phone trilled, she was in the kitchen of her shop pouring syrup over the sugar into a pot to begin to boil for Clark Bars. It was all Tally could do to keep from throwing her phone into the sink. But she interrupted her candy making to answer when she saw his ID, knowing she had better not ignore him. After all, he was the police.

He wanted her to come to the station *again* to answer questions. If she didn't know better, she'd think she was a suspect. When she got to the station, he started in as soon as she sat on the hard chair beside his desk. At least she wasn't in an interrogation room.

"We need to go over everyone who was in the shop when Gene was murdered," he said, looking terribly serious.

Tally frowned. "I've told you everyone." She racked her brain trying to remember exactly whom she had listed. "Who did I say?"

"Allen Wendt, Andrea Booker, Martha Zimmer, Yolanda Bella, and Dorella Diggs. But Ms. Diggs didn't go into the kitchen."

"That sounds about right." Then she remembered talking to Cole last night and straightened in her chair.

"You thought of someone else?"

The man was way too observant. "I guess I did. Not someone else, but something else. I just learned about this. Dorella wasn't there at exactly that time. She came in earlier, and she was…looking for him." Was Cole going to be upset that she was implicating Dorella?

"Yes, you said that. Do I have to beat the information out of you?" He smiled to soften his words, and she couldn't help but return his smile.

Tally took a deep breath and plunged ahead. "Well, Dorella...at the time, I'd never met her, didn't know her at all. I only knew that she was looking for Gene and he was busy in the kitchen part of my shop. I didn't want her in there since she was a complete stranger at the time."

"Is she no longer a stranger?"

"Not exactly. She's dating my brother. And he's told me she has a terrible temper. And she was angry at Gene that day. She could have gone around to the back door. It wasn't locked."

"I have contact information for your brother. Is he still around? Still in town?"

Oh great, now she was going to get Cole more deeply involved in this mess. What could she do, though? "He's only in town for a few days."

"Where is he staying?"

"He's staying with me." Of course he was. He was her brother.

"I'd better catch him quick, then." His gray eyes twinkled. Was she noticing how good-looking he was because she'd decided not to see Allen anymore? She shook her head slightly. She wasn't the kind of woman who always had to have a man. Was she? She never had been, and didn't want to start being one now.

Tally got up to leave and went two steps before Detective Rogers called her back.

"You know, I'd like to meet you for coffee after this case is over."

She smiled before she could have a second thought about it, then turned and left. That last bit was unexpected.

* * * *

Yolanda was called to the station that morning, too. From her car in the parking lot, she saw Tally leaving and scrunched down slightly in her seat, hoping Tally wouldn't notice her there. When her friend was gone, Yolanda hurried across the lot to the main doors. She didn't want anyone to know she was still being questioned.

In fact, she had dressed all in black for the occasion. For one thing, she wanted to be clear that she took this business seriously. Her usual bright colors might not convey the gravity needed today. For another thing, she didn't feel cheerful about this and couldn't bring herself to dress in anything but black this morning.

Her lawyer's black Mercedes was close to the door. Her father had called him and insisted he be there with her. It was no use to resist him. At least he had agreed to use Larimer Lackey, and not import someone from Dallas. That would have drawn way too much attention to her.

She halted with her hand on the door. If Tally had just been here, did that mean she was a suspect, too? Or was Tally giving them information about her own best friend, Yolanda? She shook her head and yanked the door open.

Larimer Lackey III was in the foyer, wearing his usual three-piece suit, even though it was summer. He was a little taller than Yolanda and had a gray-streaked goatee, maybe to make up for the fact that the top of his head was shiny and devoid of hair.

When an officer had dragged in an extra chair and Yolanda and Lackey were both seated by his desk, Detective Rogers looked at her with cold steel in his blue eyes. They were the color of a shiny gun, she thought. He started right in on her.

"Tell me again what happened that day." He bent over a thick notebook.

She wasn't going to ask what day he meant. She knew that well enough. Her lawyer nodded. "I went out through the kitchen and saw Gene on the floor."

"You saw him. Had anyone else in the shop seen him at that time?" He looked up and raised his eyebrows.

"I don't think so."

He scribbled a note on his notepad with a stubby pencil. "Then what did you do? Did you react?"

She took a deep breath and chewed her lower lip. Then she dabbed her drippy nose with a tissue. It was time to tell them everything so they could find the killer. She didn't glance at Lackey III before she spoke, in case he would try to stop her. "I saw my ribbon scissors sticking out of him, so I knew he'd been killed with them."

She heard Lackey suck in his breath sharply.

"Do you think he was killed in *your* shop?"

She had already told him this. "I had left my scissors in Tally's kitchen. I'd forgotten all about them."

"But you recognized them."

"Of course."

"How?"

"They're mine. I recognized them."

"I'm asking how you could tell they were yours."

"That's the kind I use. They're extra long, twelve inches. I haven't seen another pair like them anywhere. I sort of lost it. I wasn't thinking straight. I didn't want to see them there a second longer, so I pulled them out."

The detective waited for her to continue. She was lost in thought, though, and didn't notice the silence. Eventually, he had to bring her back. "And you hid the weapon in your cooler."

"No! I didn't hide them there. I didn't take them anywhere. I wiped them off—not good enough, I guess, since there was still a smidge of blood on them."

"And?"

Lackey leaned forward, stroking his goatee so she would notice him, but she ignored him and plunged ahead.

"And I stuck them on the shelf in Tally's cupboard. That's the last I saw of them."

"So…they jumped into your cooler themselves?"

"I have no idea how they got there. I'll try to give you the names of everyone I know who's been in my shop since then. If I can remember them all."

"There is one set of fingerprints visible on the weapon. How do you explain that?"

She didn't like to hear her scissors called a weapon, but had to admit that's what they were.

"I can't explain it for sure. But wouldn't the killer have either wiped them off afterward or have worn gloves?"

Detective Rogers shook his head. "It's hard for me to believe that a killer came prepared with gloves, but didn't bring a weapon."

She avoided looking at the lawyer, even though she could see him staring at her, trying to get her attention, in her peripheral vision. She had to say this. "Maybe he did. Maybe he thought he'd use that instead when he saw it lying there. Or maybe he wrapped the handle in something so he wouldn't leave prints." That sounded perfectly reasonable to Yolanda. What didn't sound reasonable was that someone knew where she'd put them and then moved them. And then Allen had found them in her shop. That gave her an idea. "You're sure Allen didn't kill Gene? He's the one who found them. Maybe he knew where they were."

"I'm not sure of anything right now."

Her lawyer stood. "We're done here."

Yolanda agreed.

As soon as she got inside Bella's Baskets, she texted Tally saying she wanted to bring lunch over to her place for both of them. She had to find out what Tally had said to the detective.

* * * *

Tally welcomed the break, clearing off a place on her island counter for the yummy-smelling Reuben sandwiches, oozing with coleslaw and accompanied by fat kosher dill pickles, that Yolanda brought over. Andrea was done with her lunch break and was handling the sales floor.

Tally poured lemonade for both of them and climbed onto the stool next to her friend, noticing her pinched, worried face. She also noticed Yolanda's black leggings and long black top. She could go to a funeral in that outfit.

"Are you doing okay?" Tally asked.

"No. How could I be? That detective thinks I killed Gene Faust because the killer used my scissors."

Tally hesitated one tick too long, because she knew the detective could be right. He wasn't, she scolded herself. But he could be. "The scissors were right there. Anyone could have used them."

Yolanda nodded and took a small bite. She wiped her left eye as a tear spilled out. "There aren't any fingerprints on them but mine."

"So what?"

"So..."

Tally grabbed a tissue for her and hugged her. "Have you been questioned again?"

"Yes, right after you this morning."

"Oh, you saw me there?"

"I saw you leaving. I hate that man."

Tally smoothed Yolanda's dark, springy curls, then twisted one around her finger like Yolanda sometimes did. "The detective?"

Yolanda nodded under Tally's hand.

"He's only doing his job. He has to keep asking everyone questions."

"Until what? Until someone wears down and admits they did it so he'll stop?"

Tally started to laugh, but realized Yolanda was serious, and distraught. "You would never kill anyone. He'll see that eventually."

Yolanda straightened, and Tally's hand dropped from her head. "What did he ask you about?"

"The same things he asked you, I suppose. He asked me to go over everything again. I think they like to see if our stories match when we've told them eleven thousand times."

That brought a slight smile to Yolanda's sad face.

"Your glass is empty," Tally said. "You want more lemonade?"

Yolanda nodded and Tally hopped off the stool, landing with one foot on the backpack Yolanda had brought with her. "Oops! I hope I didn't break anything."

"Nothing in there to break. Just my shoes."

"Shoes? You carry spare shoes?"

Yolanda shrugged. "I always carry an extra pair. Being on my feet most of the day, I need to change them sometimes."

"Makes sense." Tally went to get the lemonade from the refrigerator, suppressing a shudder. The shoes in the bag were soft, like tennis shoes. When she returned, Yolanda had twirled her seat around to face her.

"I have to tell you something. I had to tell the detective. And my lawyer."

Tally poured carefully, cocking her head to listen to what Yolanda was going to tell her, hoping it wasn't something very bad.

"I told them I took the…weapon."

"You did?" Tally splashed some lemonade onto the counter. "You told them that? Did you have to? So what was the detective's reaction? What does he think now?"

"I did. And now he thinks I killed Gene."

"Of course you didn't. But how did the scissors get into your shop? You didn't put them there? Did you come back and get them later?"

"No, I put them in your cupboard. I have no idea how they got moved."

"No one saw you take them, right?"

"I didn't see anyone there. No one else could have been there. But now, with them turning up in my cooler, that makes me look so suspicious. I hid them here, on a cupboard shelf. That's what I did. I didn't kill anyone." Yolanda fished a wadded tissue from her pocket and blew her nose. Hard. Unattractively.

Tally agreed, but thought Yolanda would look suspicious at any rate, even if she hadn't moved the weapon, since it belonged to her. "If only you had left them there. And screamed so we could come running. Or something."

"I know!" Yolanda started wailing, and Tally gathered her in her arms as they both had a good, long cry.

Chapter 18

When Tally got home after work, she was relieved to find that Cole was gone. Not that she didn't love her brother, but she needed some quiet, alone time in the house to process things. She kicked off her shoes and stretched her legs out on her navy-blue couch, propping herself up on the end pillows. Nigel jumped up, his purr engine revved to top speed.

"I hope you're happy to see me and not telling me that you haven't been fed for ages." She scratched his head between his ears, and he seemed satisfied with that. Good, Cole was feeding him. Her brother could be absentminded about chores.

She wiggled her toes against the fluffy pillow, free of her shoes. "You know, Nigel, carrying around an extra pair of shoes isn't a bad idea. I wonder if I should change during the day. It might do my feet good."

Nigel turned his head in her direction and half closed his bright amber eyes.

"So, you agree. I wonder how you know anything about shoes, though, since you never wear them." A chilling thought froze her for an instant. "Nigel! That shoe in the alley! I wonder if it was…no, I won't even go there." She shook her head to get rid of the thought. It didn't work. She was picturing Yolanda's bag with the extra pair of shoes.

"Okay, buddy, let's brainstorm. We'll assume Yolanda didn't kill Gene. Or Mart. So, who did? Here's the list I gave to Detective Rogers. Allen Wendt, Andrea Booker, Martha Zimmer, and Yolanda Bella. And Dorella."

She held up her pointer finger, not with the hand that was petting the cat. "Okay, Allen. He was angry that Gene wasn't paying him. He couldn't have been too far away. He was around the morning that Gene was killed. If he needed money, he might have been helping Mart steal from me. So, why would he kill her? Because she was going to tell people she knew he killed Gene? Tell people he was stealing money?"

She held up another finger. "How about Andrea? She was there, of course. She was mad at Gene for going out with Mart, but that doesn't make her unique. I guess if she was mad enough about that, she could have killed both of them."

She added a third finger. "Mart Zimmer. Well, she didn't kill herself. If she killed Gene, why would someone else kill her? That doesn't make much sense.

"Yolanda? No." She didn't put up a finger. Her clock ticked, remaining calm and steady, helping keep Tally from sheer panic.

"Dorella?" She put up her pinkie. "I hope not! If so, my brother is probably having dinner right now with a killer.

"What are we going to do, Nigel?"

She noticed his purring had subsided to a gentle whirr. It wasn't even purring. It was snoring. He was fast asleep.

"Wait!" Nigel flinched at her yell. "Gene's parents. I forgot. One of them could have done it. They're the people closest to him, right? Aren't they always the most likely to commit murder?"

Nigel blinked.

"Right, I agree. They seem to have lame alibis. Mayor Faust wasn't on the golf course because it rained. Mrs. Faust wasn't at the hairdressers' place very long—came late and left early. But she had car trouble. Let's think about this. She's unlikely, but maybe possible."

Nigel butted his head against Tally's motionless hand, and she resumed petting him.

Before the pair of couch detectives could resume investigations, the front door flew open and Cole and Dorella came in, laughing about something.

"What's so funny?" Tally asked.

"Oh, you're here," Cole said.

"I live here."

"Right, I didn't know you were home. The lights aren't on. No date with Allen?"

"Not tonight. Probably not in the future, either." Nigel swished his tail. Did her decision annoy him?

"Why?" Cole asked, frowning. "What's wrong?" He switched on two of the lamps.

Tally waved her hand. "Never mind. Dorella, thank you for the vase. I love it. You do beautiful work."

Dorella beamed. "Thank you. It's just a hobby."

"Did you two have a good day? What did you do?"

They looked at each other. "Well," Cole began.

"We've been talking a lot. Your brother is worried about you," Dorella said. "He's afraid this business of Gene dying in your shop is getting to you."

"Why wouldn't it?" Tally stared at her. "I would be pretty cold if it didn't. Weren't you close to him? Isn't it bothering you that he was murdered?" Dorella was annoying her.

Dorella plopped down on the chair across from Tally's and Cole perched on the stuffed arm. "Of course it bothers me. But not in the same way, I wouldn't think. I was mad enough at him to kill him, but I don't seem to be a suspect. The police haven't questioned me."

That, Tally thought, *will change soon.* "They still might." *I'm sure they will after they get done with Yolanda and Cole.*

"I wasn't even there, though."

"Where were you? You were there earlier that day. You came into the shop looking for him."

"Like I said, I was mad at him. I was enraged. I'd just found out that he ran up a few thousand dollars on the credit card I loaned him. There'd been other times when I thought he was using me, but he always sweet-talked me into seeing him again. This time, though…there wasn't enough sweet talk in a sweet tea factory to talk me out of this one. When he obviously didn't even want to talk to me, I left and walked. I walked and walked, for hours."

Dorella didn't know that Tally never even delivered her message. She felt a pang of guilt about that. Tally wondered how many hours she walked. Gene was probably killed a few hours after she left.

Cole asked the question. "How long, Dorella?"

"I didn't keep track, but it was dark when I decided to go home. I was so tired I couldn't be angry anymore. I didn't even eat supper. I fell into bed as soon as I got home and slept all night."

Tally had to admit, her story sounded truthful. If she walked until dark, she couldn't have done it. Maybe Dorella hadn't kill him.

Dorella left soon after that. Cole dropped her at home and came right back.

"What do you think?" he asked Tally, who was petting Nigel, still in a quandary about who could have killed Gene, and still avoiding going to the place in her mind that suspected Yolanda might have done it.

"About what?"

"Dorella. Is she telling the truth or not?"

Tally was surprised Cole questioned his new girlfriend's veracity. He'd always defended her before.

"Do you think so?" she asked. "It sounded like she was, to me."

"It did, didn't it? There's one thing about her, though."

When he didn't go on, Tally had to prompt him. "What do you mean? One thing?"

"Well, she did say, a few times, how mad she was at him. Remember, I told you she has a temper. A bad one. Like a pent-up volcano."

"Has she gotten mad at you?"

"No, not at me. But we were at her place earlier today, and she got a phone call from her credit card company. Gene did a number on her credit rating, and she's trying to get it straightened out. The person on the other end of the line wasn't helpful, I gathered. She stayed calm for a long time, arguing with him, then hung up and threw her phone on the counter."

"Did she break it?"

"No, she didn't throw it that hard."

"So...that doesn't sound too bad."

"It was right after that. She kicked a hole in the door to her bathroom."

"What?"

"I know! She drove her foot right through it. It's not a thick door, but still..."

Quick temper, impetuous, violent. "That sounds like the kind of person who killed Gene. Grabbed Yolanda's scissors and drove them into his chest. Are you changing your mind about her?"

"I don't know." Cole went into the kitchen to get a beer from the fridge.

Tally went into her bedroom to sleep.

Once more, it took ages for Tally's mind to quiet, to slow down enough for her to fall into a troubled sleep.

Chapter 19

Saturday nights were usually Yolanda's dinner nights with her parents. She didn't know a single other adult woman who had dinner with her family every week. She fumed as she changed into a "nice" sundress. Her old-fashioned father thought women should wear dresses. So, even though she gritted her teeth while she pulled a pink- and purple-flowered frock over her head and tied the sash, she did it.

A tickle niggled at her throat, and she almost called to beg off. That wouldn't go over well, and would be more trouble than it was worth. She supposed she felt well enough to endure another family meal.

She drove through the falling dusk to their large house a few miles outside town. After turning in through the gates, she wended her way up the driveway to the rustic, but large main house. The pool beside the house glinted in the dying light. When she got out of her car, her father's booming voice came from that direction.

"Yolanda! We're out here. Come have a cocktail before dinner."

Surprise, surprise. They were always having a cocktail at the pool before dinner, unless it was storming or freezing cold.

She went around to the pool and took a seat beneath the sun umbrella spread above them. Her father handed her a chilled margarita, not bothering to ask if she wanted one. She did, of course. It was the only way she got through these dinners. Her younger sister, Violetta, was home from Dallas for a summer vacation with her family for a couple of weeks.

Yolanda couldn't imagine spending a summer break at the old homestead. She and Violetta were, as her parents noted so often, exact opposites. Sometimes Yolanda wondered if that was because they were seven years apart. But no, watching her sister sip her preferred drink,

Coke, she knew they would not have been a bit more alike even if they had been born a year apart. She had to admit, she didn't understand her baby sister, who didn't drink alcohol and didn't seem to date. Even when she was in college, Yolanda was pretty sure that Violetta hadn't done any of those things. She loved her sister, but didn't understand her. Without their father constantly comparing them, she often wondered if she might like her sister better.

Fireflies blinked and hovered over the pure blue pool water. Yolanda breathed in the smell of chlorine. She liked it. It was clean and fresh to her.

Yolanda studied Violetta's profile. She had a smaller nose than her big sister, which made her prettier, Yolanda thought. But she projected a mousiness from being so shy and quiet. She had the same wild, curly dark brown hair that Yolanda did, but she straightened it. Even her bathing suit was the most modest one on the market, the kind with a skirt. Their mother dressed more daringly than Violetta.

Taking another glance at Violetta, Yolanda changed her mind. Vi usually was so dull and plain she was almost invisible, but there was a spark to her tonight. Her eyes seemed brighter than usual, and she had a pleasant softness on her face. Had she found someone? They had never talked about guys, and Yolanda wouldn't have known how to open that subject with her.

Tonight, her father didn't start in on Yolanda until after the salad, inside at the long table in the vast dining hall.

"Yolanda, are you doing okay for cash?"

"The shop is going great, Papa. I don't need a thing." She coughed. Her throat felt worse. She needed to quit talking and rest. Fat chance right now.

"How about rent? Did you make enough last month to pay the current rent?" He concentrated on the roll he was buttering instead of looking at her as he spoke.

Yolanda pursed her lips and bit her upper teeth into her lower lip before answering. "No, Papa. Not quite." Her bottom lip hurt. She'd been biting it too much lately and both her lips were sore and badly chapped.

"I'll write you a check after dinner. Remind me." He still didn't look at her. And he wouldn't forget to give her the check. To shame her and make sure the point was driven home. She was merely a woman, a "girl" to him, and couldn't earn herself a living.

Yolanda had, when she first started the shop, appealed to her mother to try to get him to lay off and let her ask when she needed money.

"But Yolie, dear, you would probably never ask. You might lose your shop and that would upset you, wouldn't it?"

Her mother didn't have any higher opinion of her ability to be an adult than her father did. She so often envied Tally with her absent parents. Tally thought they sometimes forgot she existed. If only Yolanda's parents would do that!

* * * *

There was an odd tapping at Tally's door. Not really knocking, but a couple of uneven taps followed by two rapid ones. Was a woodpecker rapping on her door? She listened and the pattern was repeated.

When she opened the door, Mrs. Gerg was there, empty-handed for once. The woman stuck a stubby forefinger to her lips and glanced around. "Let me in," she whispered.

Why was she acting so oddly? Tally wondered. She held the door open wide for Mrs. Gerg to get her considerable girth inside.

"What's going on? Why did you knock like that?"

"Shh! Close the door," Mrs. Gerg said, still whispering and winking repeatedly, screwing up her face.

After Tally did that, Mrs. Gerg reverted to her normal voice. "I knocked in code. It's Morse code."

Comprehension started dawning. "Was that Morse code for YSU, the Yard Sale Underground?" Maybe the woman had some information for her.

"No, not that. It's Morse for CI."

"CI?"

"I'm your Confidential Informant."

"Ah, my CI."

"Don't you watch the police shows on TV?"

"Not that much," Tally said, although she had heard the term CI. Had she created a monster, asking Mrs. Gerg to spy for her?

"I have some intel," she said. "I heard there's going to be a big yard sale, a huge one. And guess where?"

"I can't."

"The mayor's house. Mrs. Faust has kicked him out, and she's telling people she's going to sell all his belongings."

That sounded vindictive. How would that affect his re-election campaign? "Do you know that for sure?"

"It's a rumor, but it's a good one. Mind you, that woman doesn't always do what she says she'll do. She's kicked him out before and taken him back in. So..." Mrs. Gerg shrugged. "She might not go through with it. But if she does, it'll be a great yard sale."

Tally was sure it would be. She decided to reserve judgment on Mrs. Gerg's discovery and believe it when and if it happened.

"Thanks for telling me," she said, ushering Mrs. Gerg out the door.

"No problem. I'll report in when I have more intel."

Yes, Tally had created a monster.

* * * *

Yolanda felt awful by the time she got home from the dinner at her parents' house. Her throat was so scratchy it hurt to swallow. She made some tea and poured a generous amount of honey into it, then added some wine for fortification.

Her phone buzzed as she began to sip. It was her sister's number.

"Violetta? Are you okay?" Her sister never called her.

"Yo, I need to talk to someone."

"Tonight? I'm getting a sore throat. I can barely croak right now."

"That's okay. I'll talk and you listen."

This didn't sound like her sister at all. She wasn't the talker, Yolanda was. But she agreed. "Is something the matter?" She had thought her sister acted happier than usual at the Saturday dinner. Had she been wrong?

"Not yet, but it might be." There was a moment of silence. Yolanda perched on the edge of her living room couch and pictured her sister gathering her courage to speak out. Was she going to tell her that she *had* found a guy? "I've been seeing someone." Bingo.

"Vi, that's wonderful. I'm so happy for you." In spite of her sore throat, she had to congratulate her little sister on this.

"I'm very happy. I've never felt like this before. The whole world seems like a different place. A wonderful place."

"When do we get to meet him?"

"Not a him, Yo. Her name is Eden. Eden Casey. Isn't that a beautiful name?"

Not a him. Yolanda was taken aback. She hadn't expected this. "If you're happy, I'm happy for you, Vi." And she was. There had been such life in Violetta's eyes. Yolanda had known it was from love, from finding a soul mate. "Where does she live?"

"In Dallas."

Of course. That's where Violetta lived. "When do we get to..." Oh. That was the problem. Yolanda pictured Violetta introducing a girlfriend to their parents.

"Yes, oh. Eden wants to meet my family. I've met hers, and they're wonderful people. But what would Papa say? And Mother?"

"I don't know for sure, but it might not be a good idea. Can we somehow introduce this gradually?" Yolanda was still feeling shocked at the sudden knowledge. She could only imagine how their parents would overreact. Because they were good at that, experts. Especially their papa.

"I'm so glad I told you, Yo. I had to tell someone in the family."

"I'm glad you told me, too. We'll figure this out. Let me think about it."

Yolanda sipped her tea after they hung up and after she added a bit more wine to it. There were going to be a lot of consequences to this, but she couldn't help but feel good for her sister. She had always loved her, but she felt that she liked her a lot more tonight. After all, Vi had trusted her with her heart.

Chapter 20

Mid-morning on Sunday, Tally felt her phone going off in her apron pocket right after she had finished a transaction and sent a happy customer away with a box of her own version of Clark Bars. She didn't recognize the number, but answered it anyway.

"Ms. Holt, could you meet me for coffee some time this afternoon? Someplace close to where you work?"

It was the detective. He must be calling on his cell phone, she thought. What did he want now? At least he didn't want her to come to the station. Was he being considerate? If so, why? "I'm sure I could arrange that. What time?"

"I'm off today. What's good for you?"

That seemed strange. "Maybe after I close up, around seven fifteen or so?"

"Sounds good. How about the coffee shop a couple of blocks from you?"

So, yet another time, she left Andrea in charge of closing the store while she trudged through the early evening heat to a meeting with the detective, although this time it was at the Java Joe Corral, the place she had met Allen a while ago. She didn't know how many more times she could stand being questioned.

Kevin ran out as she passed Bear Mountain Vineyards. "Is Yolanda okay? She didn't open up today."

"I have to go meet with the police right now. I'll get hold of her later."

"Let me know if there's anything I can do." He seemed to be genuinely worried about Yolanda.

But then, Tally was worried, too. She couldn't call her now. She was too distracted. She would call her right after she got done seeing the detective.

Her heart pounded as she pulled the door of Java Joe Corral open and was met with a burst of dark, coffee aroma.

His gray eyes twinkled when he saw her enter. A little of her fear lifted. He was in the back of the shop, gesturing to the table next to him.

"Good to see you outside the police station," he said after she wended her way there through the passage of tables and chairs. His smile came off as a bit tentative. "Here, do you want to sit here?" He sounded nervous.

"Maybe over there? I like sitting by the window." She led the way to an empty table at the front of the store. He followed behind, more slowly.

"Is this okay?" she asked.

"Sure," he said. He held her chair, then sat in his, moving it a few inches so that he wasn't completely framed by the window. Did he not want people to see him here?

Then it dawned on Tally. Bingo! This wasn't an interrogation. This was a date.

"I thought of asking you to bring me some of your candy, but I didn't know exactly what I wanted. Maybe we can stop there after coffee and I'll pick up some things."

Tally's smile was automatic. A date *and* a sale. This day was looking up.

After Detective Rogers ("please call me Jackson") brought lattes to their table, they chatted a bit about Fredericksburg.

"What are those old, tiny houses?" he asked. "They're odd. There are quite a few of them, and I've never seen any others like that."

Tally thought for a moment. "Oh, you mean the Sunday Houses? Are you not from here?"

"I grew up in Dallas. My grandparents on my dad's side came from this town, and I visited a few times as a small child before they passed away. But my grandparents weren't much for touring their own town. I guess I never noticed them as a child. It's been years since I've been here."

"How long have you been in Fredericksburg? Did you just move here?"

"A few months ago. This is only my second felony case in this town."

Tally wondered what the first one had been.

"So, tell me about these Sunday Houses," he said.

"I don't know if they exist anywhere else, but here in Fredericksburg, they were built by the local farmers in the 1800s so they would have a place to stay in town for the weekend when they came in to go to church. There weren't any churches out in the country. They're all in town. So the farmers had to come to town for Sunday. Some of them had to drive far and stayed the whole weekend. That's why they're small, they're second houses."

"They seem like they're in good shape."

"Yes, they're well preserved. A lot of them are rented out to tourists now."

"I'd love to see inside one," he said.

She felt a text ping her phone and slipped it out of her jeans pocket to sneak a peek. It was from Yolanda.

"Do you have to take that?" he asked.

She hadn't been as surreptitious as she thought she'd been. "Do you mind? It's from Yolanda." Tally clamped her lips together, too late. Maybe she shouldn't mention the main suspect right here and right now. But something was wrong if Yolanda hadn't worked today.

Yolanda had texted that she was home with a sore throat and asked if Tally could please bring her some cough syrup from the drugstore, and maybe some lip balm, too. Tally told her she could, in about an hour. Yolanda was agreeable. Being sick was better than being in jail, she texted.

Tally had an idea. "Say," she said, sticking the phone into her pocket, "I need to bring some medicine to Yolanda. She's home sick. And…she lives in a Sunday House. Would you like to stop by to see the inside?" Maybe if Jackson visited Yo at her home, it would humanize her to him and he could think of her as something other than a murderer.

"Sure. That would be interesting."

Or, he might catch something from Yolanda. Which would serve him right for suspecting her and Cole. Tally wouldn't mention how expensive the Sunday House was to rent, or how wealthy Yo's family was. He probably already knew.

After a stop to grab a bottle of cough medicine and a tube of lip balm, Jackson drove to the Sunday House.

Jackson looked the place over as they came up the sidewalk to the porch of the tiny place. The yellow-painted wood siding glowed in the streetlamp. A staircase ran up the wall at their right to a door that led to the second half-story.

"Why does she want to live in such a small space?" he asked.

"It's got an addition on the rear that you can't see. And it's plenty of room for one person." Although Tally's house, which was not large, was much larger than this one. "It's got a living area, kitchen, bedroom, and bath."

"What's on the second floor?"

"That used to be where the wives and children slept, while the men slept downstairs. But it's an extra room for Yolanda. She uses it for storage."

Yolanda met them at the door wrapped in a fluffy white robe, her nose red and her eyes runny. "Do you want to come in?" she croaked.

"You look terrible," Tally said. "Are you sure you want us to come in?"

"Us?" Yolanda looked startled, and Tally realized she hadn't seen the detective. "Um, no, you'd better not." Yolanda coughed hoarsely and took the drugstore bag from her. She motioned Tally to come closer, though.

Tally didn't want to be too near Yolanda's germs, but she leaned her head toward Yo's puffy, red face. Jackson stepped away to give them privacy. She thought that was considerate of him.

"What is wrong with you?" she whispered. Tally inched a bit closer to hear her. "Why are you going around with the policeman? Why did you bring him here? To search my place?"

"Don't be silly," she said, also whispering. "We were having some coffee and he said he'd like to see a Sunday House."

"So you wanted to show him *mine*? I'm about to give up on your whole family. You, your rotten brother, your crazy parents."

Tally straightened up and talked aloud. "What about my brother? And my parents? Okay, my parents are odd, but what do you have against my brother?"

"You don't even know, do you? You've never known. I should date him and drop him cold so he can find out how it feels. I really should."

Yolanda slammed the door in Tally's gaping face.

Detective Rogers, who had been standing a few feet away for their private conversation, stepped up to Tally and touched her back. "What was that all about?"

"Well…" Tally shook her head. "She's right about one thing. I have no idea what it was about. Maybe feeling sick is making her extra cranky. Maybe you can see her place another time."

"That would be best. Neither one of us wants to catch whatever it is she has. It's looks like nasty stuff."

"Poor Yolanda." Poor Tally. What on earth was wrong with her friend? This was no way to make a good impression on Jackson Rogers.

The ride home was uneventful. He thanked her for the glimpse he'd gotten of Yolanda's Sunday House. He stopped his car in front of her home, and she let herself out. She spotted Andrea, out jogging in the dark, turning the corner at the far end of the block.

Cole wasn't there, but had left the living room television on, playing softly to an audience of one. Nigel. Another campaign ad for Mayor Josef Faust's reelection was running. She was getting tired of them, of the thoughts that they unleashed in her. What if he had murdered his son for sympathy, to win the election? Or what if he had murdered him so Gene wouldn't continue embarrassing him and ruining his chances at winning? She snatched up the remote and switched off the set. The house settled into the relative silence of the soft *ticktock* from the clock on the mantel.

Nigel, who was perched on the table in front of the television, flicked his ears and swished his tail, annoyed that the interesting lights and movements had been switched off, she thought.

She pondered Yolanda's odd behavior for a long time as she slowly ate a light supper. Somehow she would have to find out exactly what had gone on between her brother and her friend. Yolanda had been her best friend in the time before Tally moved away, but she'd been gone for a few years. People changed. Maybe she didn't know who Yolanda was now.

A clap of thunder announced a brief, heavy downpour. It was unusual to get this much rain in July in Texas. At least they weren't in drought right now. That was devastating on the wine crop, and everything else. The deluge was short-lived. That part was usual.

As the rain let up and retreated to dripping from the eaves, Tally shrugged off her questions about Yolanda's behavior and changed the direction of her thoughts. Curious about Detective Rogers's other big case, she picked up her tablet from the end table and searched for it. A list of local crimes came up, but none of them murders. Had he said it was a murder case? She thought back. No, he said this was his second "felony" case. So maybe this was his first murder here? She wondered if it was the first murder case in his career. She hoped not. That might mean he didn't know how to solve one.

Chapter 21

Tally woke up partway when she heard Cole come in. He'd probably been out with Dorella, she thought. A glance at her bedside clock told her it was two a.m. The lateness of the hour wasn't a problem for Cole, but she wondered if Dorella had to work in the morning. Tally had to, for sure. She lay awake for at least an hour listening to a light rain dripping through the rainspout outside her window.

The alarm clock roused her early, after a too short night. She had a thought of waking Cole up, since he was part of the reason she'd missed her sleep. But, she had to admit to herself, only part of the reason. Truly, her mind had been whirring and her stomach churning at all the uncertainty and accusations. She wasn't used to Yolanda being angry with her. She was suspicious of Allen after beginning to form an attachment to him. She wasn't even sure she could trust Andrea, or Dorella. Maybe she should keep good relations with Cole before she alienated everyone she knew.

Nigel, whose warm body had been curled up behind her knees, yawned and stretched, curling his pink tongue and squinting his eyes. When he began working his claws into her bedspread, she shooed him to the floor and got up to stagger through a shower and breakfast.

The cat raised his voice as she started to leave.

"Oh, I forgot your breakfast. Sorry." She filled his water bowl and poured out some food. The glare Nigel gave her made her pause. She had poured the food into the water. After everything was cleaned up and the water and kibble were in the proper places, she gave him a couple of strokes and dashed out the door.

She arrived at work a few minutes after her normal time, but she was usually quite early, so she wasn't actually late. When Andrea showed up well past the hour, Tally pounced on her.

"You're late," she stated, unnecessarily, her voice sounding harsh to her. "Is everything all right?"

Andrea took a breath, and her face pinched in on itself. "Oh dear. I'm sorry. It won't happen again." She stuffed her bag under the shelf, then changed her mind and pulled it out again. "I need to use the restroom. I'll be right back." She seemed distraught.

Tally was in a bad mood. She didn't have to inflict it on her employee. She softened. "I know you won't be late again. It's okay. We've only had a couple of customers. Don't worry about it."

Where was the gentle, friendly young woman that Andrea had been before Gene wooed and dumped her? She'd been so weepy and even volatile ever since his death. Then Tally remembered that the tenth anniversary of her sister's death had also hit her hard. Maybe she needed more time to regain her equilibrium after all of that.

At about two in the afternoon, Tally was surprised to see Detective Jackson Rogers come through the front door. She was alone on the sales floor while Andrea took a break in the kitchen. She broke into a grin that disappeared as soon as she saw the severe set of his jaw. And the other policeman tramping in behind him.

"Can...can I help you?" She tried to smile again, but only achieved a forced grin.

The detective ducked his head before talking to her. Was he being shy? No, that couldn't be. Embarrassed?

"Tally, Ms. Holt..."

Ms. Holt? What was going on? Why was he calling her that?

"...I have a confession to make. I've talked to my commander, and he's...surprised we only searched the kitchen, the shop, and—for Mart—the restroom."

"And the alley," she said. "You searched the alley. You found the shoe there."

He nodded slowly. "Yes, we did. But I've been told to look around again, with your permission, and include the whole premises."

"What else is there? Just my office."

He nodded again. "Would it be all right if we did that?"

He turned his smoky gray eyes on her, full force. Poor guy. He got in trouble for not looking for clues where there wouldn't be clues anyway.

"Sure." She lifted her right shoulder. "I don't see why not."

His smile seemed as forced as hers. "You're saving my day, Tally. I'd have to get a search warrant if you'd said no."

She returned his smile, trying to cheer him up. "No problem. Maybe you can balance my books while you're in the office."

"Officer Edwards, you stay here." He abruptly strode past her into the kitchen, leaving Tally with the uniformed man—a large, imposing, beefy man—with a scowl on his pockmarked face. She thought he looked unhappy and wondered if he had ever shot anyone. Now, why had that thought popped into her head? She wiped her hands on her smock, realizing that they were sweaty.

Andrea strolled through the kitchen door. "What's going on? There's a policeman in your office."

"I know. He's… He's here on police business." She put her hand up and scratched behind her ear. She felt nervous, for some reason.

"What kind of police business?"

"I don't know exactly. They're dotting Is and crossing Ts. That's all."

Andrea frowned. "Are you sure?"

She was rescued from her puzzling conversation by a family of four coming in for Whoopie Pies. She motioned Andrea forward to wait on them, since her hands were a bit shaky.

What was going on? Did he come here just to search the office? Why? She decided to brave Officer Edwards.

"Do you know why he's looking in there?" she asked him.

"Got a confidential tip today."

"From who?"

"Can't talk to you about that." A man of few words, obviously.

"Oh. Okay." What an exasperating man. A tip? Someone called the police and told them to search here? That didn't make sense.

Rogers emerged through the kitchen door into the shop holding a bulging paper evidence bag. He gave a dark scowl to his partner, who unclipped a set of handcuffs from his belt and told Tally to turn around.

"What? What are you doing? Are you arresting me?" She was too stunned to move. Edwards grabbed her arm and spun her around so he could click the hard, cold metal onto her wrists.

"Andrea, call my brother." She breathlessly gave Andrea the number. Andrea, thank goodness, grabbed an order pad and wrote it down.

"Should I close the shop?" Andrea asked as they were marching Tally out the front door.

"I don't know. No. Maybe. Ask Cole." She shouted frantically over her shoulder as she went through the door, her heart hammering like a frantic woodpecker. "Call Cole! And Yolanda!"

Chapter 22

Yolanda glanced up from tucking a silver jingle bell into the basket she was finishing for a fortieth birthday present. The theme was the cruise the husband was going to surprise his wife with, and the basket contained palm fronds, a jar of beach sand, some flip-flops, and the tickets.

She had had a nice, long phone conversation with her sister. That didn't happen very often. Had it, she wondered, ever happened before? The difference in their ages made sure they didn't have a lot to talk about. What they did have in common was the family, their mother and father.

From what Violetta said, it seemed their father was finally expanding his chronic disapproval to his younger daughter.

"It was a big mistake letting him get a peek at my credit card bill," Violetta had said.

"I agree with that. Have you racked up a big balance?"

"It's not all that big, but I can't pay it off in a month."

"Two months?"

"Well, maybe six or seven. I needed some furniture. According to Papa, I should have kept sitting on the floor until I saved up for a couch and chairs."

"I know," Yolanda said, sympathizing with her sister. "Haven't you heard him hitting the ceiling about my credit card bills?"

"Bills?"

"Well…yes. I have more than one. If you do, don't *ever* let him learn about that."

"Yolie." Her voice grew somber. "I'm worried about you. What's happening with that murder thing?"

That was sweet, Yolanda had to admit. "They have another suspect."

"I thought they had several more."

"That's what I let Dad believe. But I honestly don't think the person they're hammering at now did it."

"So who did?"

"I have no idea, but I hope they find out soon."

"If you didn't do it, they can't arrest you, can they?"

Of course they could. But she didn't want to worry Violetta. "No, Vi, they won't arrest me. Don't worry about me. And keep your bills away from Papa or I'll start to worry about you."

As Yolanda straightened the bow a final time, she relished the warm feeling she had from her talk with her sister. Maybe families weren't so bad. She gazed out the window at the hot pavement. You could see heat rising from it in distorted waves.

Yolanda felt so much better after swigging the cough syrup Tally had brought her. And her lips felt smooth and silky from the lip balm. She would try not to chew on them so much, but she needed less stress for that to happen.

She gazed out the front window, then did a double take. Tally was being led to the back seat of a police car by that detective. And she had handcuffs on!

Yolanda stood frozen, wanting to dash out and see what was going on, but not wanting to draw attention to herself any more than had already happened.

After the uniformed cop had pushed Tally's head down and closed the back door, Yolanda moved closer to her front window and looked out, feeling helpless and confused. The car drove away toward the police station. She stood still for a few moments, then ran next door to see if Andrea knew anything.

Her tug on the door was met with resistance, so she pulled harder. It was locked. Was Andrea inside? She must have locked the door immediately behind Tally's exit. Yolanda pounded on the door, but no one responded.

The words she had flung at her best friend last night haunted her. Sure, Cole had treated her bad in school, years ago, but he treated all the girls bad in those days. And probably now, too. That was no excuse to go off on Tally. She had brought her the medicine, and it had worked a miracle. Once her cough was tamed, she'd started to feel better. This morning she slept late, but felt good enough by mid-morning to come in to work. She wasn't even sniffling anymore. She'd kept telling herself she needed to call Tally and apologize. Maybe take her out to lunch, but lunchtime came and went.

Now what should she do? She had to help Tally. Without giving herself a chance to chicken out, she called her father.

"Papa, it looks like Tally's been arrested."

"Arrested? For the murders?"

"I don't know. I saw her leave with two police officers and she had handcuffs on."

"That's not good. Should I call Lackey?"

Yolanda twisted a strand of hair with the hand that didn't hold the phone. "What do you think? Would that make her look more guilty?" That had been, after all, her own objection to her father getting the lawyer for herself.

"Something must be making her look guilty if she's handcuffed," he said. "They took her away in handcuffs. Doesn't that sound bad?"

"I...guess."

"*Cara mia*, do you think she did this?"

"No!"

"Not so loud. Are you certain?"

"You know what? Let's hold off. I need to find out what's going on."

She cut the connection before he could say anything else. A car pulled up, and Andrea ran out of Olde Tyme Sweets and climbed in. An older woman was driving, the same one who often dropped her off in the mornings. She was probably Andrea's mother, the one Tally had talked about being so ugly to her daughter.

Every family had its own dynamic, and some were difficult to understand from the outside. Andrea seemed as much a mama's girl as Yolanda was a daddy's girl, but the vibes were very different in their cases.

Taking a deep breath, trying to swallow her pride with a big gulp, Yolanda raised her phone to call Cole, then realized she didn't have his number. She flipped the *Closed* sign on her door and drove to Tally's house to try to find him.

She had a long wait. Cole wasn't there, so she waited in her car for him to arrive from wherever he was. Surely he'd be there eventually.

Yolanda waited two hours, trying to decide every five minutes whether to leave or not. Her phone startled her, and she realized she had dozed off. The number was unfamiliar.

"Yes?" Her greeting was tentative, as it always was with an unknown caller.

"Yo! Can you come get me?"

It was Tally. "Where are you?"

"I'm at the police station. I don't have my car here and I can't reach Cole."

Yolanda said she would be right there and started her engine as she was disconnecting the call.

Tally was standing outside the station when she pulled up to the entrance. Tally ran to the car and climbed in, starting to sob before she finished fastening her seat belt. Yolanda reached over to hug her friend and felt

Tally's body quaking in her arms. They clutched for no more than a few seconds when Yolanda was startled by a horn honking behind her. "I guess I'm blocking the way." Yolanda patted Tally on the shoulder, shifted into gear, and drove out of the parking lot. "Where to, Tally? Your house? Andrea closed up your shop and left."

"That's okay." Tally's voice was thin through her tight throat and her tears. "Yes, my house, I guess."

"What happened? Can you talk about it?" Yolanda threw frequent glances her way as she drove toward Tally's place.

"Detective Rogers found a tennis shoe in my office. A tennis shoe. It must be the mate to the one they found outside the back door when Gene was killed."

"Why were they in your office? Were they looking for it?"

"They must have been. Officer Edwards said they got an anonymous tip."

"Someone told them to look there? I've wondered where the mate was. Wait, it was in your office? The whole time?"

"I have no idea. I never saw it."

"So they just showed up, walked in, and found it?"

"They had a tip and they can't tell me who gave it to them."

"How could anyone else know what's in your office? That's weird."

"Maybe it was hidden somewhere. I kept asking them where it was, but they never told me. They wanted *me* to tell *them*. But I can't. I don't know!"

"They? How many people questioned you?"

"Detective Rogers and the other cop. Edwards, his name is."

"Two against one."

"It was awful." Tally started sobbing again, more loudly than before.

Yolanda felt completely helpless. She knew Tally hadn't killed anyone. And she herself hadn't either. What was happening?

Chapter 23

Tally sat on the couch in the dark, her legs tucked up under her. Her awful heaving sobs had stopped, but tears still ran down her face. A box of tissues sat on the end table, but she had quit dabbing her face fifteen minutes ago, leaving a pile of tissues on the cushion beside her.

She figured she was lucky she hadn't been arrested and thrown into a cell. If not for killing Gene—and maybe Mart, too—then for concealing evidence, which was how it appeared. The shoes weren't her size. Maybe that was why she'd been released.

Nigel crouched in her lap, watching her. He stretched up and licked a tear as it reached her jawline.

She smiled. "You silly boy. You're making me laugh. I love you."

She vaguely wondered where Cole was, but didn't try calling him again. A pain gnawed at her stomach. Was it from tension or hunger? She didn't feel like eating, even though it had been many hours since her breakfast.

The sun had set long ago but she hadn't turned on any lights. The shadows suited her mood better.

Nigel made her smile again when he turned his attention to the pile of tissues on the couch and batted them, one by one, to the floor.

Eventually, though, he jumped down with a thud and headed toward the kitchen, starting to meow. His meows were as loud as his purring. He was acting like he did when he was hungry, even if she wasn't.

She put her feet on the floor and pushed herself up to go the kitchen to scoop food into his big bowl and refill his water. From there, she heard the front door unlock and open.

"Cole?" she called.

"Why are the lights out? Did we lose power?" He came into the kitchen, flipped the overhead light switch on, and plopped into a chair. "What's going on, Sis?"

She turned and he saw her tearstained face.

"Whoa. Now what's happened? Someone else die? Get killed?"

"No. It's just… I was taken in and questioned again."

"Okay. And?"

"They took me in wearing handcuffs. They found the mate to the tennis shoe in my office."

"In *your* office?"

She nodded. "In my office. At the shop."

"Where in your office?"

"I don't know. I didn't see them find it. They wouldn't let me back there. I had to stay in the front while the detective searched."

Cole jumped up and hugged Tally. "Hey, they found the shoe. All right. That doesn't mean anything. They have to find out how it got there. And who it belongs to."

She chuckled, half crying again. "I wish they would. They think I put it there."

"That's stupid. If you killed Gene, why would you keep incriminating evidence in your own office?"

"Because I didn't think they'd ever look there?"

Cole pushed her an arm's length away. "Wait. What are you saying?"

"No, I'm not saying I put it there. But if I did, that would be why. But I didn't."

"That detective likes you, I can tell. He's not going to come down hard on you."

"Guess again." Tally pulled a spoon from the flatware drawer and a container of chocolate-chunk ice cream from the freezer and started eating it from the carton. She had thought he had some feelings for her, too. But if he had, they were over now. Those smoky, warm gray eyes were nothing but hard metal during that interrogation.

She sat across from her brother at the kitchen table. "I assume they didn't arrest me only because the shoe is a tad bit too long. What am I going to do, Cole?"

The doorbell rang. "I'll get it," Cole said.

She heard two men's voices at the front door, Cole and someone else. Her curiosity got the better of her. She stuck the ice cream back into the freezer and went to see who was there. The sight of Allen Wendt in her doorway made her pause. What was he doing here?

Cole had switched on a lamp, and Allen caught sight of her.

"Are you okay? What happened?"

"What do you mean?" she asked.

"I was on a job on that side of town, at an apartment building that had a plumbing problem. I saw that cop take you into the station and you were cuffed. I thought I'd drop by and see if you were home. And how you're doing."

"She's pretty upset," Cole said. "You want me to tell him, Sis?"

She nodded and curled up in the corner of the couch while Cole related everything to Allen about the shoe and her questioning.

Allen looked at her when he was finished. "Do they really think you would have killed Gene?"

"And Mart," she said. "It seemed like that when they were drilling me over and over."

Allen looked down and shook his head. "What's going on anyway? That's stupid. You didn't kill anyone."

"Well, who did?" Tally cried. "Someone did. And everyone is under suspicion until someone finds out who."

The clock ticked on the mantel in the silence following her outburst. The three sat and racked their brains while the ticking urged them on, reminding them that each second wasted could never be retrieved.

Cole broke the silence. "Should we make a list?"

Tally and Allen both looked at him. "What kind of list?" she asked.

"A list of suspects."

"Oh," she said. "And put down why they could have done it and why they couldn't? For Gene or for Mart?"

"Let's start with Gene. Let's also try to figure out what the police know."

Allen tapped his foot. "So we can figure out what the cops will do next."

"Exactly," Cole said.

Tally thought that would be a waste of time. She'd done the same thing in her mind so many times, she couldn't count them. And it hadn't gotten her anywhere. Aloud, though, she agreed. What else could they do? She crawled out of the corner of the couch to retrieve a pad of paper and a pen from the kitchen.

"Who's the secretary?" She raised her eyebrows at Cole, expecting him to volunteer.

"I'll do it," Allen said.

She hadn't expected that, but handed the paper and pen to him and perched on the edge of the couch cushion. It didn't seem right that he was participating in this, since, in her mind, he was as good a suspect as anyone.

What if he was the one who had killed both of them? On the other hand, what if Allen thought she was the killer? She seemed to be the best suspect right now, for the police. At least no one suspected Cole. He hadn't been in town yet when Gene died. And he wouldn't have killed Mart. No, he wouldn't have. She knew he wouldn't have. What she hated was suspecting everyone.

"So," Cole began. "We're starting with Gene. Who do we list?"

"I'll give you the names I gave the police," Tally said. She remembered Gene and Allen arguing before the murder, but she hadn't mentioned that to the detective and didn't mention it now either. "I told them Allen was there, of course, and Dorella."

"Dorella was in your kitchen?" Cole said. "When was that?"

"No, not in the kitchen. She was only in the front. But she was mad at Gene."

"So you don't need to write her down," Cole said.

"Yes, you do," Tally insisted. "The back door was unlocked and she could have gone around to the alley."

Cole stood up and threw his hands in the air. "If you put it that way, anyone in Fredericksburg could have gone in and killed him."

Chapter 24

Allen broke the tie. "We need to include everyone who is likely to be suspected by the police. I'll add Dorella's name. So, for Gene's murder, we have her and me."

Nigel sauntered into the room and rubbed against Allen's leg. Allen reached down absentmindedly and gently pushed him away, but Nigel was persistent.

Tally saw Allen write his own name under Dorella's. "I also told the police that Yolanda, Andrea, and Mart were around near the time he died."

Allen dutifully added their names, then looked up at her. "And?"

"I give. And?"

"You were there."

Tally let out a breath and collapsed slightly. "Yes, I was, and I seem to be a suspect now, too." She considered her brother. "You're the only one of us who isn't."

Allen squinted and tilted his head at Cole. Was he considering that he could be a suspect, as well?

"Don't look at me." Cole held his hands up to block Allen's eyes. "I wasn't in town yet."

Nigel gave up on Allen, who kept nudging him away, and the cat jumped onto the couch next to Cole.

"When did you get here?" Allen asked Cole.

"That night."

Tally spoke up for him. "He got to my house two or three hours after I found the body. And Gene was murdered some time before I found him."

Allen shrugged. "Okay, I'll leave you off, Cole. Now what? We have a list of names."

"Now," Cole said, "we go through each one and see what motive and opportunity they have. Right, Sis?"

Nigel crept into Cole's lap, where he was rewarded with a head rub.

"Not quite," Tally said. "I mean, we're not quite done with our list. There are two more suspects, Gene's adopted mother and father."

"What motive did his parents have to kill their son?" Cole asked, incredulity in his horrified eyes.

Everyone in the room grew quiet at the thought. Then Nigel's roaring purr broke the silence.

"He's not their biological son," Tally said. "He was adopted as a teenager, and it doesn't look like either of them ever bonded with him. Yolanda and I have been trying to see if they could have done it, and their alibis are thin."

"Wow. It's a wonder he lived as long as he did, with that many enemies," Cole said. "I almost feel sorry for the guy."

"I know. Me too," Tally agreed.

"What do I put down?" Allen asked.

Cole told him to make columns for motive and opportunity. "Do you have a better motive than not bonding, Sis?"

"There's the mayor's upcoming election, and Gene has been embarrassing him, being seen with lots of different women in, I imagine, his convertible, if not other places. I also know that he took money from them. I don't know if that's common knowledge, but I know that he has. Mayor Faust wanted to be rid of him and had even petitioned to have the adoption annulled."

"Can you do that?" Cole asked.

"I have no idea. His mother didn't like Gene at all, from what I can tell. She's been trying to divorce her husband and wants the house. I heard her say she was afraid they would both lose everything because of Gene."

"Why would that be?" Allen said, raising his head from his note taking.

"I don't know that, either," Tally said. Maybe they knew he was stealing money and had never reformed, when reform was the purpose in adopting him—to show what a loving family could accomplish, presumably. But when she had stated their so-called motives out loud, they didn't seem too solid. "Maybe both of them would have simply rather ignored him than have killed him."

"Let's talk about Dorella," Cole said.

She seemed a better suspect than his parents. "She was spitting mad at him right before he was killed. And you've said she has quite a temper, right?"

Cole had to admit that. "Yeah, she kicked a hole in a door."

"You saw her do that?" Allen asked.

"No, but I saw the hole and she told me she did it."

"She's got the temperament then, doesn't she?" Allen looked to Tally, and she agreed.

"What was she mad about?" Allen asked. "When she was at your shop, not when she kicked in her door."

"Charges he'd racked up on her credit card bill," Cole said. "Not a motive for murder, I don't think. When she kicked in the door, she was mad at the credit card company for not handling her complaint the way she wanted them to."

She knew he was reluctant to ascribe a solid motive to Dorella, and she was glad he didn't feel he could. They seemed pretty serious together, as serious as Cole ever got about anyone, so it was a good thing she couldn't be considered a good candidate.

"I wrote Mart's name down, but I don't think I should have," Allen said.

"I'm not sure," Tally said. "Could she have killed Gene, and then someone else have killed her?"

"Anything's possible," Cole said. "But do you really think that happened?"

"I don't know."

"There's a lot you don't know."

"Yes, there is!" Tally was exasperated with her brother. "You're not helping. We're trying to consider *all* the possibilities, aren't we?" Cole didn't answer. "Well, aren't we? Mart actually had a pretty good motive if she thought she was pregnant with Gene's baby. And if she was stealing money from me for an abortion."

"Let's talk about the money," Cole said. "That's a good motive for murder."

Tally got a sudden stomachache, remembering the argument her brother had had with Mart about the money he lent her for that abortion. "I'm certain that both Mart and Gene were stealing from me, but I can't prove it."

"Then you have good motives for getting rid of both of them, don't you?" Allen was scribbling on the list.

"There's one more," Cole said. "Andrea."

"Jealousy for her, plain and simple," Tally said. "She thought Gene had a thing for her, but then she found out he had things for every female who looked at him."

"This isn't getting us anywhere." Cole stood, depositing Nigel on the floor.

Nigel laid his ears flat onto his furry head and strutted over to rub Tally's leg, his tail held high. She reached down and petted the big cat. She'd known this process wouldn't get them anywhere. She'd tried it over and over with this exact same result.

Chapter 25

After Allen left, leaving the list of suspects lying prominently on the coffee table, Cole announced to Tally that he was going to get something to eat somewhere else. Did he want to avoid being with his sister because he thought she was a murderer? Murderess? Whatever? When he was gone, she switched off the lamp and went into the kitchen.

She scrambled an egg and toasted a piece of bread, rounding off her meal with a banana that was on its last good day. She wasn't even hungry for that small meal, but Nigel's appetite was fine. He complained until she filled his bowl.

"Glad someone's appetite is unaffected by all these tragedies," she said to him. He had a cute habit of waiting politely until after his bowl was filled before digging in. Maybe he was afraid she would stop serving him if he started in too early.

After she and Nigel were both finished, she wandered into the living room to switch on the television. She hadn't turned on the lamp again, and heading toward the couch, she tripped and nearly fell headlong, catching herself on the arm of the couch.

When she turned the lamp on, she saw that she had tripped over her own shoes. When she had curled up on the couch, she had kicked them off. Picking up the offending footwear, it occurred to her that it was mostly due to footwear that she was a suspect, specifically that tennis shoe mate that someone had hidden in her office.

That was it!

If she could solve that mystery—figure out whose shoe it was and who had put it in her office—she should be able to point the police to the real killer.

Closing her eyes, she pictured the shoe. It had been a bit larger than the ones she wore. For a fleeting moment, she realized that didn't mean she wasn't still a suspect. You could wear shoes that were too big for you. She pushed that thought firmly down.

It couldn't have been Mart's. She'd been tall and willowy, with long, narrow feet. The shoe was at least a medium width. For those who were in the shop a lot, who worked there, that left...Andrea. Andrea was taller than Tally, and she...yes! She carried a shoe bag and sometimes changed shoes.

Now she had to really think back. Tally squeezed her eyes shut and drummed her fingers full speed on the arm of the couch, trying to recall every detail of the day of Gene's death. Had Andrea been wearing tennies when she came in? Tally thought she had. Had she worn them when she left?

The clock ticked. Nigel's tongue made slight moist sounds as he licked the pads of his feet.

A faint squeaking sound. She recalled a faint squeaking sound. The sound of Andrea's rubber soles as she left through the kitchen. She *had* been wearing tennies. Were they Chuck Taylors? Maybe. Tally returned to her recollection. Something was missing. When Andrea left through the back door, it should have squeaked loudly. It badly needed oiling. Tally had heard Andrea's shoes, but she hadn't heard the door squeak. Andrea hadn't left right away. If she'd left later, Tally hadn't heard. She hadn't been listening after that—she had gotten busy with customers.

The door had also screeched as Allen left, shortly before Andrea. But it was silent as Andrea walked through the kitchen, and didn't make any noise when she should have been going out the door.

Did she even go out the door right then?

Could Andrea have stayed in the kitchen and killed Gene? Why? Because he was seeing other women? That couldn't be it. She was missing something important.

* * * *

At six thirty, about half an hour before closing on Tuesday afternoon, Cole texted Tally and offered to bring her something to eat at her store. She was glad to hear from him, since she wasn't sure they were on good terms after last night. He was apparently at Burger Burger, no doubt to see Dorella. She texted back that she was starving because she hadn't had time to eat lunch. She'd also overslept and hadn't had much breakfast. She requested a cheeseburger and onion rings, and he arrived promptly with her meal.

As he came in the front door, she motioned him into the kitchen to eat. Making sure Andrea was occupied in the salesroom, she followed Cole to the office and closed the door for maximum privacy. She sat at her desk and Cole took the only other chair. Between bites, she told Cole her theory about the shoes and Andrea, as quietly as she could.

He rested his elbows on his knees to attack his own burger. "But why would she kill him? What's going on in her life? What's she like? I don't know her at all."

"I don't know a whole lot about her. I know she lives at home and doesn't have a good relationship with her mother."

"That's got nothing to do with Gene's murder."

"True. She's been upset lately because it was the anniversary of her sister's death."

"Her sister died? How?"

"In a car wreck. The girl was only fourteen. She died way too young, and Andrea had a right to mourn her on the anniversary."

Cole set his burger on the edge of her desk and pulled out his phone. "Let's see if we can find out what happened to her sister."

Tally got up and moved to stand over his shoulder to see what his search brought up.

"Do you know what her name was?" he asked.

"I'm not sure, but the last name is Booker."

"How long ago did she die?"

Tally was getting tired of not knowing anything. "Wait, Yolanda told me. She said it was the tenth anniversary of her death. Yolanda noted that it was a big milestone for Andrea's family. Maybe that's why she and her mother have been tangling so often, from grief over losing her too young."

Cole thumbed his phone for a few seconds. "Got it. Patsy Booker, age fourteen. Killed in a car wreck."

"Oh dear, that's terrible."

"The driver was a teenage boy. Patsy left behind her mother and an eight-year-old sister, Andrea. Her father was not alive."

"I've wondered about her father. Yes, that's definitely her. Does it say what happened? Was the driver drunk?"

"This article doesn't even identify the driver. Let me look some more."

Tally sat in her chair and picked at the breading on one of her onion rings while Cole continued to search.

"Oh my God." Cole stared at Tally, his eyes wide. "The driver's name was Gene. Gene Schwartz."

"That was his name before he was adopted! Gene killed Andrea's sister?"

"One reporter was scandalized because the driver was let go with a light punishment."

"Why?"

"Because Josef Faust decided to adopt him and take responsibility. The reporter says he probably paid the Booker family a bunch of money."

"You know, Dorella called him Gene Schwartz when she came in looking for him. I remember thinking she must have known him for a long time, back when that was his name."

"Was Andrea there when she said that?"

"Yes, she was working with me in the front. And—I just remembered this—she said she felt sick and left soon after that. In the middle of her shift."

Cole puffed out a big breath. "This all fits. We may have found our killer."

The back door squeaked loudly. Tally realized they hadn't been keeping their voices down. She jumped up and peeked into the kitchen. No one was there. She pushed the door open to the salesroom. The only ones there were a young couple who came in regularly for Moon Pies.

"I'll be with you in a minute," she called to them.

"No rush," the young man answered.

Andrea was gone.

Tally waited on the couple, then flipped the sign to close the shop. It was after seven o'clock anyway.

She stumbled into the kitchen, to the corner, and sank into her cozy reading chair, letting her head fall onto the cushion behind her. She felt sick to her stomach.

Chapter 26

Tally and Cole left together out the back door, and she locked her shop up tight. Tally peered up and down the alley to see if Andrea was lurking anywhere. After all, if she'd already killed two people, what would stop her from killing one or two more? It was still light enough to tell that no one was there.

"Where are you headed?" she asked Cole, hoping he'd go to her house.

"I need to give Dorella a ride home from work in about twenty minutes. I'll see you at home in...maybe an hour? Is that good?"

"Sure." It would have to be, but she didn't like it.

Cole walked down the alley and around the corner to retrieve his car from where he'd parked at the curb in front. She got into her little Chevy and locked the doors before starting the engine.

She was afraid.

More than anything, she wanted to go straight home. But no one was there. Maybe that wasn't a good idea. She'd gotten a phone call in the morning that there was an order at the grocer waiting for her to pick up. She had planned to do that this afternoon while Andrea minded the store, as it was needed for tomorrow. If she opened for business tomorrow. They'd been too busy for her to leave. So it was still waiting at the store, and the store was open late.

She drove out of the alley, turned, and headed toward the grocery store. It wasn't far. She would pick up her order, then she would go home and take the supplies in to the shop later.

However, leaving the grocery store with her arms full of bags, she spotted a familiar car at the other side of the parking lot. It was Andrea's mother's car, the one that often dropped her off and picked her up. She shoved the supplies into her trunk and drove out to the street.

The car followed her.

She tried to see who was driving. Andrea and her mother were about the same height and build. But Andrea's hair was long and straight, and her mother's was cut short. The window was down in the car behind her and she could see Andrea's long hair blowing about in the wind. Tally turned down a side street to drive to her house. Andrea followed her.

She didn't dare go home. Where could she go?

* * * *

Yolanda had seen Cole go into Tally's Olde Tyme Sweets out the front window of Bella's Baskets. She still felt bad about blowing up at Tally over something that happened so long ago. What was wrong with her? Sure, she was feeling awfully sick that night, but still. Was that an excuse? She should have gotten over a high school crush and a petty slight by now. She wanted to wait until she saw Cole leave, then go over and talk to Tally. To patch things up a bit more. Maybe they could talk about Cole dumping her, and maybe Yolanda could be rational about it this time. She certainly owed Tally an apology. They'd been best friends for so many years.

She had another good excuse for talking to Tally. She had finally gone to the post office and picked up the samples of the fake food, the fudge and Clark Bars. She would like Tally to come over to see them. She thought they looked pretty good, but maybe they could be better. If she could find another company that made something similar, she should dig into that.

Her cold was still hanging on, but she felt much better. She'd thoroughly disinfected the three baskets she created today before the customers picked them up.

She hung around, tidying up, waiting to see Cole leave out the front door. Instead, she eventually saw Andrea come around from the alley and get into her mother's car, which was parked at the curb. Andrea must have driven it today. She didn't drive off, though. She kept sitting in her car. While Yolanda pondered what Andrea was waiting for, Cole came around from the alley too. He got into his car and drove away before she could consider whether or not she wanted to go out and talk to him. No, she wanted to see Tally first. Then, maybe, Cole.

Soon, Andrea pulled away from the curb and drove slowly down the street.

Now she could go over and talk to Tally. But the shop was dark, and no one answered her knock. Tally must have left. Before or after Andrea? What on earth was going on? She would put it off for a while and call Tally later. She decided she couldn't do anything more then. She wanted to go home.

Chapter 27

Tally barreled along through the town, going up and down side streets, taking corners too fast, trying to get away. But she couldn't manage to leave Andrea behind. She was breathing heavily, in short pants, her heart thumping in her chest. The sun was getting low. The rays slanted through Tally's windshield when she headed west, so that she had a hard time seeing the traffic lights. When they both stopped for a light, a glance in the rearview mirror showed Andrea's face, caught in clear relief as the fading sun hit it. Nothing about that reassured Tally. Andrea's mouth was set in a grim line, and her eyes had the glint of a crazed person. Another red light was ahead. Tally stopped, ready to bolt as soon as it turned. This time Andrea rolled forward and bumped Tally's car. As soon as the light turned green, Tally shot away and made a hard right turn. Andrea followed.

She realized she was headed out of town. She couldn't go home to her empty house with an angry Andrea right behind her. Tally grew more and more certain the young woman had killed Gene and Mart both.

Her radio played music faintly. She was going so fast she could barely hear it. Hoping it would calm her somewhat, she dialed up the volume. The news came on when it turned nine o'clock.

She listened to the announcer's grave voice. "Local authorities, responding to a call from a neighbor, found a body in a Fredericksburg residence late this afternoon."

Another dead person?

"The neighbor hadn't seen the victim all day and they usually have coffee mid-morning, the neighbor said. The woman, Mrs. Ellen Booker, wasn't responding to phone calls or texts."

Booker! Ellen Booker!

"Police broke into the house after seeing Mrs. Booker's body through a front window. It is thought that she died recently, sometime today. Foul play is expected. Police are looking for her daughter, Andrea Booker, to get some more information. If anyone—"

Tally hit the button to turn off the car radio and stepped on the gas. She needed to turn around and drive straight to the police station.

The traffic was steady coming toward her. She looked in vain for a side street to use for turning around, but was now out of town where side streets were scarce. She was also going too fast to make a turn. Andrea was directly on her tail, occasionally nudging her rear bumper. How could she turn around? What was she going to do? She had to get rid of Andrea and get to the police.

She fumbled her phone out of her purse on the seat beside her and held it up to dial 911. She got the 9 and the 1 pushed, but then a jolt from behind knocked the phone from her hands. Her cell flew to the floor and landed next to the passenger door. There was no way she could reach it.

Tears of frustration blurred her vision. She jerked the wheel to make a U-turn at a break in the oncoming traffic. Andrea swerved to the left to block her. Tally would be T-boned if she continued. Might even roll. She straightened out and sped ahead, driving north. Going faster and faster.

* * * *

Yolanda's mother called her to tell her that a woman named Booker had been found dead. "Doesn't someone with that name work for Tally? Andrea?" she said. "Is that the same Andrea Booker?"

Yolanda felt the hair on her nape stand up. "Andrea," she whispered. "It's Andrea."

"Yes, that's what I said. Andrea Booker. Well, do you know if it's the same person?" Her mother was getting impatient with her. But that was nothing new. She couldn't talk to her mother right now.

"Mother, I have to call someone. Thanks for telling me."

Yolanda dialed Tally. No answer. She texted their emergency code, *ASAP*. Nothing. Where was Tally? Where was Andrea? What should she do?

* * * *

The sun had set. The sky was getting darker. Tally sped through the tiny ghost town of Crabapple. "I'm halfway to Enchanted Rock," she mumbled to herself. "I wonder if..."

Could she? Could she get far enough away from Andrea to hide at Enchanted Rock? She stepped on the gas, called for every last ounce of power from her little Sonic. It responded and shot ahead. There were finally no cars in front of them as she completely floored it. A glance at the dashboard told her that at least she had a full tank of gas.

She dared a glance in the rearview mirror. Andrea was falling behind. Tally was getting away from her! Her grip tightened even more desperately on the steering wheel. Her arms shook. She kept driving down Highway 965, heading for the state park that she knew so well. She hoped Andrea didn't know it.

She slowed enough to turn into the entrance to Enchanted Rock State Natural Area, as it was called, then careened around the curves to the parking lot at the foot of Summit Trail. She encountered less than a half dozen cars. The park would close soon and, since it was mostly dark now, all but a few stragglers were gone. Her car screeched to a halt. She grabbed her phone from the floorboard and bolted out the door, running for the trail. Andrea wasn't in sight. She would call 911 as soon as she had enough distance between her and her relentless pursuer.

The trails at the park were marked as well as they could be, but since some of them ran over bare rock, they were hard to follow, even in full daylight. Tally counted on Andrea not being able to make out the trails in the gray dusk.

As quietly as she could, Tally jogged up the trail. It soon became steep. Summit Trail, the most difficult one in the park, led to the top of Enchanted Rock. Soon she was breathing loudly. She had climbed this trail many times, but had never run up it at full speed. Her pants and puffs and gasps were so loud she wondered if she would hear the fabled wailing if it happened that night.

The Plains Indians had been coming to this place for ten thousand years, and legends had built up around the huge granite outcropping. It had become endowed with magical and spiritual powers. One legend was that, if a person spent the night on the rock, he or she would become invisible. Tally wished she could become invisible at that moment, but just for the night, not forever.

Another superstition was that if a person climbed the rock with bad intentions, bad luck would befall them. Surely running away from a murderer didn't imply bad intent. Being a murderer should count for bad intentions, though.

The one Tally hoped wouldn't come into play right now was the fable about the wailing woman, a white woman who had been kidnapped by Native Americans and who screamed at night. Skeptics, or maybe scientifically minded people, insisted that the rocks were cooling off at night, or maybe shifting, to produce the eerie noises. Other tales involved human sacrifices. Tally wouldn't think about any of that right now.

As she ascended, the top of the dome of pink granite caught the last dying rays of sunlight. Tally stopped for a few seconds to listen, letting her breathing regulate, trying to tell if she could hear Andrea behind her. She still gripped her phone in her right fist. She raised it and punched 911. Nothing happened. She squinted at the face of her phone. There was no reception.

A shriek came from below her. Was it Andrea? Or was it the ghost of the kidnapped woman? Or one of the sacrificial victims?

Tally took a huge gulp of cool air. It tasted like the night and like dirt and like dry desert plants. She renewed her efforts and ran on, slipping slightly on the smooth rock every few steps as the darkness made it harder and harder to see her footing. It would make it hard for Andrea, too.

Chapter 28

Yolanda couldn't sit still. She had to do something. She drove to Tally's house. The lights were off. It was completely dark. Though she heard the cat meowing inside, no one came to the door. She went past the shop, but it was dark, too.

What to do? Where to go?

She drove to the police station. It was late, and only a few cars were in the lot. When she ran in and asked for Detective Rogers, she was told he had gone home.

"I need to talk to someone," she said, a sob catching in her throat.

The severe, bespectacled woman behind the glass asked what she wanted to talk about, in a bored tone.

"It's about the murders."

"Murders?" She looked mildly interested.

"Yes. Gene Faust and Mart Zimmer. My friend Tally Holt may be in trouble."

"Trouble? Why do you think that? What sort of trouble?" The woman looked even more interested now.

"I think Andrea Booker may be after Tally."

"Andrea Booker?" The woman was a regular echo chamber.

"She might be... I think she's following Tally. I saw her drive away, and I can't find Tally anywhere."

The woman had picked up her internal phone. "Where did you see them?"

Yolanda told the woman when and where she had seen Andrea, but that had been at least an hour ago. Where would they be now? She had no idea.

"I'll call Detective Rogers and you can talk to him."

Yolanda sat on a hard plastic chair, chewing on her bottom lip until it was about to bleed. She cringed at the thought of bleeding lips. Blood—that horrid, vivid red ooze that frightened her so. With a shudder, she forced herself to clamp her lips together and keep her teeth off them.

* * * *

The summit was in sight. Tally slowed slightly, out of breath now. It had been years since she had climbed this steep trail.

That's when she heard light footfalls coming up the path behind her. That's also when she remembered that Andrea was a jogger. This hike had probably given her no trouble, and she had likely been able to follow the sound of Tally's huffing and puffing.

Tally's mind raced. She didn't want to go to the top, where her body would be silhouetted against the sky. Her breath now mostly under control, she stole quietly downward, at an oblique angle to her former path. At this point, there was nothing but bare rock face. No place to hide. If she could get lower, she would encounter some scrub and some scree that might conceal her.

Somehow, after only a few minutes, she managed to reach a jumble of rocks without encountering Andrea. She hunkered down and listened. Did she hear faint footsteps proceeding upward? Maybe. A huge owl swooped out of the sky toward her and she stifled a cry. When she heard the scrambling of a small rodent near her feet, she realized what the owl had been after.

Shielding the screen with her hand, she checked for cell reception on her phone. She had a tiny bit.

She dialed 911. When the operator answered, she whispered her name and said that she was being chased by a killer at Enchanted Rock. She wasn't sure the woman heard or understood her, but she broke the connection quickly, afraid Andrea would hear her.

Now what?

* * * *

"Ms. Bella, how can I help you?"

Yolanda knew the detective had been called away from something better than this, probably dinner or watching TV. But he was being kind and considerate by coming to the station to talk to her.

"I'm afraid Tally is in danger." Her breathless words tumbled out. "I can't reach her. I saw Andrea drive out from the shop, and Tally was already gone. What if she's following her? Anyone who heard the news about Andrea killing her mother knows by now that she probably killed the others, too."

"Whoa. Slow down. We don't know that Andrea is responsible for her mother's death."

"Seriously?" Yolanda jumped up and stuck her face in his. "You don't know that? I do."

He raised one hand, palm out. "Hold on. Here, come into my office where we can talk."

She followed him, took a seat, then started to hyperventilate. "I know she's in danger, Detective. I can feel it."

"Do you know where she is?"

Yolanda shook her head, and tears sprang from her eyes. "What can we do?"

* * * *

Footsteps. Tally caught her breath. Not too loudly, she hoped. Andrea was heading her way. She had to move.

Tally got up and scrambled, crouching, down the hill, off trail completely, trying to avoid prickly pear cacti and the small depressions in the rocks that caught water. She crept downward as fast as she could, but kept hearing the footfalls behind her.

It was too dark to see the ground now. She was going too fast. She was going to fall or—*splash*. She stepped in a vernal pool. Andrea had to have heard that.

Tally changed direction and ran across the hill, parallel to the ground. Maybe she could confuse Andrea.

"I heard that!" Andrea shouted. "I know where you are." Her voice was closer than Tally had thought. "I have a gun. You won't get away."

She had a gun! The one she'd used to kill her mother that morning?

Adrenaline surged. Tally moved with lightning speed, zigging up and zagging down. She had no idea where she was now, but she was nowhere near a trail.

* * * *

"Detective Rogers?" The woman from reception was at his door, frowning down at a piece of paper in her hand. "A nine-one-one call came in that you should know about. The caller said she was Tally Holt."

The policeman jumped up and snatched the piece of paper from the woman's hand. "Where is she? Did you pinpoint her location?"

"Very strange. It seems to be coming from north of here, maybe around Enchanted Rock. The connection was bad, but it seems she's in the vicinity of Enchanted Rock."

"Tally loves that place. She knows all the trails there," Yolanda said.

Rogers headed for his door.

"I'm coming with you," Yolanda said, trying to follow him out the door.

"No, you're not!" Rogers barked. "You stay right here."

In less than a minute, his car was out of sight, leaving the sound of his siren and the aftermath of his strobing lights in its wake.

Yolanda tried the reception desk woman one more time. "What else did she say on the phone?"

"I can't give you that information."

The woman was maddening. Yolanda wasn't going to sit here staring at her. "Call me if you decide you can tell me anything about my best friend, who is in a lot of trouble right now. Here's my number." She scribbled her number on the sign-in sheet, threw the pen down with more force than necessary, and left.

Chapter 29

A bullet whined off a rock above Tally. She shuddered, then stumbled on, running on adrenaline and fear. Another shot rang out, also uphill from her. Andrea didn't know exactly where Tally was. That was good. She wanted it to stay that way.

Could she head downhill? Straight downhill? If Andrea thought she was still going across the rock, could she get away? Could she get to her car?

She stopped for a moment to collect her thoughts. She mustn't give in to panic. She had to keep her wits about her. Andrea was running toward her, but slightly uphill from Tally's position. Tally squatted next to a boulder that had fallen there long, long ago. Grasses had grown up around it. She worked her way into the tall, dry grass. It rustled, but faintly.

Andrea passed by, still pursuing the same route. She shot two more times, once hitting another rock.

Tally waited for a count of twenty, then stole out of her hiding place and hurried downhill as carefully as she could. A faint, high, thin sound came through the night. Tally stopped to listen for more sounds of a possible ghost. This sound grew louder and more distinct. It was a police siren!

She wanted to run pell-mell downhill as fast as she could, but Andrea might shoot her before she made it to the bottom if she gave away her position. She continued with caution.

Her shin ran into a prickly pear, and she yelped. Tally froze, her blood running cold, every sense on alert.

Andrea's maddeningly calm voice came through the dark. She was very close.

"There you are. Now I have you."

Andrea's shape was above her, about fifteen feet away. Tally could make out the glint of a pistol in the starlight. Andrea held it steady, not trembling, pointing it directly at Tally.

"Ah, revenge is so sweet. Just like they say it is. I'm getting back at everyone. Everyone. Getting my revenge for everything. I took care of the others. And now I have you."

Tally faced Andrea and slowly took few steps backward, still moving down the hill, putting the prickly pear between them. "Yes, you have me. I'm not armed, Andrea. You can't shoot me when I'm not armed."

Andrea's laugh sounded crazy. "But that's the best way to shoot someone. When they're not armed. Was Gene Schwartz armed? No. Or Mart? No again. Do you think my sister was armed when Gene killed her?"

"Gene killed your sister?" Tally knew she was talking about the car wreck years ago, but had to keep Andrea talking. The siren was closer. Andrea didn't seem to hear it.

"Didn't you know that? Maybe you weren't living here then. He was drunk. He crashed his car. She died. He didn't. He went on to live a full life. She was dead. He killed her, and he didn't even pay for it. There wasn't even a trial. The mayor rescued him. Poor little juvenile delinquent."

"That wasn't right. Gene should have gone to jail."

"He should have died, too! And he did. I took care of that. I got revenge for Patsy. But…but he killed me, too. He killed our whole family. My mom turned into a different person. A horrible one. We'd always gotten along so well before that. Since the wreck, she's been mad that I lived and Patsy didn't. She would never get off my case. I couldn't take it anymore. I finally had to take care of her." Andrea was silent for a moment as they slowly continued downhill, Tally still walking backward. "Now you know everything. You're a loose end."

"Andrea, other people know. They know you killed your mom."

"No, they don't. They can't prove it. When you're gone, I'll be free."

Tally hadn't heard the siren for a few minutes. Was the police car not coming here? She hadn't heard it go past. Maybe it was Detective Rogers and he had turned off the siren and was on his way to rescue her right now. And maybe he wasn't.

Tally kept moving. Not too quickly, since she couldn't see where she was going. Andrea came after her slowly, still pointing the gun at her.

Andrea started talking again, still sounding dangerously demented. "I'll be totally free. All of this will be over. It will be behind me. I can go on with my life. No more problems. No more—"

Andrea yelped as she finally stepped into the patch of prickly pear.

In a fraction of a second, Tally was on her, grabbing the gun away and shoving her deeper into the cruel thorns.

A warm hand clasped her shoulder.

"Good work. I'll take it now." Detective Rogers was behind her.

Tally collapsed onto the ground, grateful that there were no prickly pears where she landed.

Chapter 30

Nigel jumped into Tally's lap, purring at the top of his…purring apparatus. She wondered if that sound came from his throat or his lungs. She leaned her head on the back of her worn navy-blue couch and closed her eyes.

"Are you all right?" Yolanda sat next to her, balancing a plate of fruit, crackers, and cheese.

Tally smiled and nodded without opening her eyes. "I'm still bone-tired today, but I'll be okay. I'm alive and whole."

The night before, Andrea had been arrested and shoved into the back seat of the police car by Detective Rogers. Other officers and technicians set up lights and swarmed across the rock surface collecting evidence. Tally had ridden into town in the front seat of his car, and they had both listened to Andrea screaming at them during the whole ride. She insisted she hadn't meant to harm Tally, that she hadn't shot her mother, that Rogers was making a big mistake.

Yolanda, who had followed the detective to Enchanted Rock, and then followed them down the highway to the station, had taken Tally home and made her a cup of cocoa. It was crowned with half a package of marshmallows, it seemed to Tally. Yolanda knew how much Tally loved marshmallows. Tally had eaten them off the top, sipped half of the lovely chocolatey liquid, stumbled to her bed, fallen on it fully clothed, and slept until morning.

When she woke up, Cole was in the kitchen feeding Nigel.

"Want breakfast, Sis? I can do up an omelet. I bought croissants and bacon to celebrate."

"What are we celebrating?" Tally asked, rubbing the sleep from her eyes and smoothing her rumpled clothing, the same outfit she'd worn yesterday and slept in all night.

"You, silly. You're alive and you caught the killer."

"That's not exactly what happened, but, okay. We'll say that." She didn't consider that she had "caught the killer." She had gotten lucky and hadn't gotten killed herself.

"Yes, you did. No one else did."

"Andrea kept talking about getting her revenge. 'Revenge is sweet,' she said."

"Not as sweet as locking up a killer."

"No, I guess not." She gobbled down Cole's culinary masterpiece, then changed into her pajamas and went back to bed. A momentary thought flitted through her mind. *What about my shop?* Then she pushed it aside and fell fast asleep.

When she woke up again, Cole was waiting for her. "Need to tell you this," he said.

He grew serious, and Tally wondered what had gone wrong. "Why? What happened?"

"It hasn't happened yet."

"It's bad, though, right?" She was almost dressed, but sat on her bed to put on sandals.

Then he smiled, putting his dimples into action. "No, not exactly bad. But I don't know how this is going to work out. I need to leave to get started on my next job."

"Now?" She stood up and started brushing her hair.

Nigel wandered into her bedroom and jumped onto the bed for a bath.

"I was planning on leaving tomorrow or the next day. But now..."

"Now what? You're driving me crazy. Tell me."

"It's Mom and Dad."

Tally plopped onto her bed. Nigel stopped for a moment, moved a few inches away from Tally, and resumed his ablutions. "They heard, right?"

"I don't know how. But they left a message that they're on their way here. I mean, it's not bad news. It'll be good to see them. But I do need to leave for my job. It's in Albuquerque. It takes a while to get there."

"It doesn't take that long."

"I guess. Anyway, Dad says they'll get here tomorrow."

"Can't you see them for a day, then leave? That should be okay."

Cole walked to the kitchen, and Tally finished getting ready for the gathering that Yolanda had warned her was coming.

"The cat, Cole," she called. "Are you taking Nigel with you?"

He didn't answer.

In the late afternoon, Yolanda showed up, accompanied by her sister, Violetta.

"It's good to see you, Vi," Tally said, surprised they were hanging out together.

The two sisters both started setting things out on the dining table. Paper plates, hors d'oeuvres, wine bottles, and plastic cups.

"Everyone's coming," Yolanda said to Tally. "We all want to congratulate you."

"We're still celebrating?"

"We haven't started yet." Yolanda had outdone herself, dressed in a gauzy chiffon creation of all the colors a sunrise could be. Tally had never seen it before.

Yolanda pulled Tally into the kitchen for a private chat. "I need to tell you something," she said in a mysterious tone.

Tally asked if something was the matter.

"Yes and no. We'll need reinforcements. Vi has a special friend who is going to visit here next weekend."

"Vi? A boyfriend?" Tally was delighted for Violetta.

"Not exactly. She's dating another woman."

"Oh! That's a surprise." Tally thought for a moment. "Good for her then, for finding out that's what she wants."

"I know, but my parents!"

"Oh yeah, your parents."

"So, I'm going to either invite you or ask you to drop over while they're there, okay?"

"Sure. Tell Vi she can count on me. I know what parents are like."

Dorella was the next to arrive, and she helped set out the food. Her neighbors and several of the shopkeepers from near Olde Tyme Sweets came. Yolanda's mother and father soon arrived. Allen Wendt showed up, even Detective Rogers.

Tally asked him if he thought Andrea had done all the killings—Gene, Mart, and her mother.

"Come over here." He led Tally off into the corner. "I can't reveal any details, but you can rest easy. Within a few days the chief will announce that we are confident we have the person responsible in custody. We're still piecing together movements and phone calls, and we have to determine exactly when she planted the shoes and the murder weapon, but she's not denying anything."

"Does she have a lawyer?"

"A public defender. If she admits to everything, then it's all but over. But I can't tell you anything more. I shouldn't have told you this much, but I don't want you to worry that someone else will be killed in your place of business. This is over."

"Two questions."

He nodded.

"Did Andrea phone in the anonymous tip about the shoe in my office?"

The detective gave a slight grin. "That's a good guess."

He probably couldn't tell her outright. "Then I suppose she put it there, too?"

The grin stayed, but he didn't give an answer.

"And I suppose she came across the scissors on the shelf where Yolanda stuck them and moved them to her shop. Come to think of it, she ran over there when she knew Yo was out doing a delivery. Am I right?"

He gave her another enigmatic smile and a squeeze on her shoulder.

At his smile and his touch, a weight of at least a half ton floated off Tally's shoulders, went right through the ceiling, and disappeared into space. Well, she felt fifteen pounds lighter at least.

Mrs. Gerg put in a short appearance, arriving with her hands full, as usual. "Tally, I got this for you. I knew you'd like it. I can't stay. There's a huge sale three blocks away, and they're closing up pretty soon."

"Thank you for coming," Tally said. "What's this?" It was wrapped in newspaper and wasn't the right shape for another box.

"Open it and see." Mrs. Gerg handed the package to Tally with a proud smile pushing up her round cheeks.

Tally tore off the newspaper, which was taped together. It wasn't the shape of a box, but it was a box. A long, thin one.

"You could keep nice long candles in that one," she suggested.

"Yes...I guess I could."

"It was the least I could do after you captured that awful killer," she said with an exaggerated wink.

"Thanks so much, Mrs. Gerg." Tally managed to squeeze the new arrival onto the edge of the cabinet without knocking any other boxes off.

"I'll be going now. Wish me luck!" She trudged out the front door, down the two steps, and off to the next yard sale.

Tally crossed her fingers that there wouldn't be any boxes for sale at this one.

"Is Yolanda here?" Tally turned to see that Kevin Miller had come in, bearing a box of wine bottles from his shop.

Tally didn't see her. "She's in the kitchen, I guess. Do you want to take those in there?"

"Sure." He gave a big smile and made his way through the crowd to Tally's kitchen.

She realized that he always asked about Yolanda when she saw him. What was that all about? She'd have to give that some thought. He was very nice, seemed successful, and was pretty good-looking. Yolanda could do a lot worse. They would have to talk.

"Oh my God." Yolanda poked Tally when a middle-aged woman with thick spectacles, wearing a mid-calf skirt, came in the door a little later.

"Who is she?" Tally whispered.

"She's the woman from the police station. I thought she hated me."

"Maybe she likes *me*."

Tally went forward to greet her. "Hi, I'm Tally Holt. Welcome to my home."

"I know who you are. I'm very glad to see you well." The woman shook Tally's hand without cracking a smile, not telling her what her name was.

Tally met Yolanda at the punch bowl a minute later. "She's odd, isn't she?"

"I'll say."

They watched her meet the other people in the room. Tally and Yolanda were astounded and amused when she broke into a huge smile upon meeting Cole.

As soon as the nameless Police Station Woman left, the mayor and his wife walked in.

"Did you invite everyone in town?" Tally asked Yolanda. She didn't know how she felt about having those two here.

"I guess word got out," Yolanda said, scooping a generous dollop of crab dip onto a sturdy cracker.

Nigel hovered near the table, catching the occasional spill. He looked smug and satisfied, cleaning his whiskers in between forays.

Mayor Faust glanced around the room, then headed straight for Tally. "Here's the little lady who caught my son's killer," he boomed, orating to the whole room. He stuck his hand out to shake.

Tally cringed at being called a "little lady." She reluctantly, but politely, shook his hand, wearing a strained smile. He didn't seem to notice. His own toothy grin never wavered.

Mrs. Faust simpered behind him. "Yes, we're so grateful that justice was done for our poor son."

The poor son you wish you'd never taken in. Tally couldn't help the thought, but shook her hand, too. "Help yourself to whatever you want."

She gestured toward the spread on her dining room table that had reached impressive proportions.

Mrs. Faust turned toward the table and picked up a paper plate.

"I'm afraid we have to run," the mayor said. "I wanted to stop in and officially congratulate you. I'll see if the city can give you a commendation."

"Oh, please, no," Tally said quickly. "I'd rather not. That's not necessary."

Detective Rogers stepped close to the mayor and spoke quietly. "Let's not do anything to jeopardize the trial of Andrea Booker. Publicity needs to be kept to a minimum right now."

The mayor nodded, putting on a sage expression, and the Fausts swept out.

The air loosened up after they left, and the party began in earnest.

Sneak Peek

Don't miss the next Vintage Sweets Mystery
DEADLY SWEET TOOTH
by
Kaye George,
coming your way in
September 2020!

Twinkies Recipe

Make the cake portion first.

4 eggs
1/2 cup butter

1 cup water
1 box of instant vanilla pudding mix
1 boxed yellow cake mix

Beat the eggs, add butter and mix well.
Add next three ingredients and stir well.
Batter will be thick.

Bake the cake portion.
Preheat oven to 350 degrees.
Grease and flour two 10x15 jelly roll pans.
Pour half the batter into each prepared pan and spread.
Bake 15–20 minutes or until toothpick comes out clean.
Cool on wire rack.

Next make the filling.

1/2 cup butter, room temperature
1 (8 ounce) package cream cheese, room temperature
5 cups confectioners' sugar

1 (8 ounce) container frozen whipped topping, thawed
1 teaspoon vanilla extract

Mix butter and cream cheese. Sift the confectioners' sugar and add. Beat well.

Add whipped topping and vanilla and stir.

Combine.

After the cakes are cooled, spread the filling on one layer. Place the second layer on top.

Cut into bars.

If you don't eat these right away, you can wrap them in plastic and store them in the freezer. They're good cold!

Adapted from Allrecipes.com by Tyler

If you enjoyed REVENGE IS SWEET, you won't want to miss
the second book in the
VINTAGE SWEETS MYSTERIES
by Kaye George—
DEADLY SWEET TOOTH,
coming to you in
June 2020.

Turn the page for a quick peek at this wonderful new mystery!

Chapter 1

Tally Holt had been hoping he wouldn't show up today.

While Tally was talking, pacing the floor as she heard the news she didn't want to hear, Yolanda burst into Tally's office from the kitchen of Tally's shop.

"Who was that on the phone?" asked Yolanda Bella, Tally's best friend.

Tally's friend owned Bella's Baskets, the gift basket business that was located next door to Tally's vintage sweet shop on Main Street in Fredericksburg, Texas.

Yolanda flounced into the office guest chair, her bright orange and yellow skirt billowing as she sat. *Flamboyant* was the only word for the way Yolanda dressed, in bright colors that always seemed to swish around her when she moved. They looked good with her dark coloring—wild dark brown curls and flashing eyes that were so dark, they were almost black. Tally was quite a contrast with her usual jeans and T-shirt, but, as they say, opposites attract. The two, now in their mid-thirties, had been best friends going back to their public school days.

"It was my brother, Cole," Tally said, stuffing her phone into her pocket.

Yolanda frowned. There was no love lost between those two. "Is he coming early?"

Tally nodded, slumping into her desk chair. "I'm afraid so. I guess it's good he wants to help, but we don't need him. He was supposed to come late Friday, and now he thinks he'll get here earlier." She took a deep breath, inhaling the delicious scents of her shop, chocolate and caramel dominating today. The lingering warm fragrance had a calming effect, and her shoulders lost some of their tension.

"I thought he was tied up until Friday night. Isn't he doing a big installation in Albuquerque?"

"He was. He finished early." Tally neatened the thick stack of job applications that included those she had been dealing with for the last three hours. "I think what he really wants to do is see Dorella."

"That's good. That'll keep him out of our hair."

"You mean, keep him out of *your* hair, don't you?" Yolanda, Tally knew, would prefer for Cole to stay in Albuquerque forever. They didn't have a good history. Tally loved her brother, she just wasn't ready for him to come quite yet. There was so much to deal with.

"Hey," Yolanda said, "was the woman I saw leaving just now applying to help cater? Have y'all had a good turnout?"

That was a problem. "Yes and no. I mean, I've had lots of people apply for the job, but there aren't very many I'd consider hiring to help with the reception."

Tally shuffled the job applications, pulling out the ones she'd flagged with sticky notes. They were for promising interviewees, the ones who hadn't interrupted the session for a cell phone call, hadn't texted the whole time, hadn't worn rumpled (or, in one case, dirty) clothing. The chosen few had sat up straight and paid attention to her and thoughtfully answered her questions. The number of those applicants was discouragingly small.

The reception was coming up soon, in three days. Tally wanted it to be perfect since it was such a special occasion. Hiring people was not her favorite part of being a small business owner. But it was a necessary part. The job she was interviewing people for today was a bit different. She had decided that the two or three she picked to do the reception would be considered later for a position at Tally's Olde Tyme Sweets, her vintage candy shop. Depending on how they worked out at the reception.

"How many did you talk to today?" Yolanda asked.

"Six. That's all I had time for."

"The one I saw didn't look half bad."

"I'll admit she was one of the better ones. I wish I had time to interview a whole lot more, but I have a shop to run."

"It'll be much better when you get some help in here. You're doing everything yourself."

Yolanda had an assistant, a young man named Raul, but Tally was running her place all by herself lately, having had a run of bad luck with assistants. It was mid-August, and the high tourist season was in full swing. Tally needed more help to order supplies, make her candies and sweets, sell them, and do all the cleaning and straightening that needed to be constantly attended to.

"I have to get out of my office," Tally said. "I've been cooped up here for three hours." She had closed an hour early, at six, to do the interviews.

"Are you hungry? Let's go out and get a late supper." Yolanda jumped up. "How about that new place? Do you remember the name?"

"You mean Burger Kitchen?"

"Yes, that's it. Raul has eaten there, and I think Kevin has, too."

"Perfect. Let's do it." Tally took one more look at the applications, stuck three of them into her purse, and followed Yolanda. After she locked the back door from the inside, they went out through the shop at the front, Tally pausing a moment to enjoy looking over the salesroom she had worked so hard on, had poured her heart and her money into.

Muted pinks and lilacs swirled across the walls, accented with chocolate brown shelving, and lit with cute lights whose shades looked like Mason jars. The glass display cases gleamed. They'd better, Tally thought, since she had polished them after closing, as she did every night. She and Yolanda walked across the rustic wide-plank flooring to the front door and left, accompanied by the soft chimes activated by opening the door.

"Oh gosh, Nigel! I forgot about him," Tally said when they were on the sidewalk outside. "He'll be rummaging through the cupboards and opening cereal boxes if I don't get home and feed him. I'll meet you there."

"Do you mind if Kevin joins us?" Yolanda asked.

Tally smiled. She didn't mind at all. "Of course not."

In fact, she was delighted that a relationship was developing between Yolanda and Kevin Miller. He was the proprietor of Bear Mountain Vineyards, the wine shop on the other side of Bella's Baskets. Yolanda was in business for herself, too, marketing special occasion baskets. The two women were able to collaborate sometimes, using Tally's treats to help fill the baskets. It was only a week or so ago that Tally realized something was happening between the two of them. Kevin was older than Yolanda, maybe by ten years or so, but they hit it off well.

It was a quarter past nine, well after sunset. Even though the sun had set, the hot air rippled with excited shoppers and locals on their way to get something to eat or drink, or to see some of the entertainment offerings in the quaint Texas tourist town. The area around Fredericksburg was studded with many wineries, and the German town boasted quite a few tasting rooms.

"See you in about twenty minutes." Tally turned to go the other direction to her rental house, which was only four blocks away.

"We'll save you a seat."

When Tally opened the front door to her small, neat ranch house, she wasn't met with the noisy greeting that had become usual over the last few weeks that Nigel had lived with her.

He's mad, she thought. *That won't be good.* She threw her purse onto the couch, peering around the living room for him.

"Here, Nigel," she crooned. "Come get your dinner." It wasn't until she poured the kibble into his bowl that he appeared, drawn by the clatter. The huge, black-and-white Maine coon cat gave a disgusted glance in her direction, then went straight to his task, extracting morsels and setting them gently on the mat so he could eat them. Tally had finally gotten a couple of mats for his dining pleasure so she could toss them into the washing machine when they got full of kibble crumbs. Before the mats, she had to scrub the floor around his food and water bowls every other day.

He was not about to do anything so common as to eat from his own food bowl.

She smiled at the haughty cat. Her life had been simpler, but, she had to admit, duller, before Nigel came to live with her. She enjoyed talking to him, telling him her problems and her joys. He seemed to listen intently when she talked to him, giving her wise looks, always agreeing with her own viewpoints. He was a satisfying companion.

Tally waited for Nigel to get halfway through his dinner, then told him she'd be back soon. He gave her a skeptical look.

"No, really, I will." At least she hoped she would.

He turned his tail end to her and left the room. She knew he'd come finish his meal after she left. Nigel wasn't one to leave kibble uneaten in his bowl.

Tomorrow was another big day, and after her late meal with Yolanda and Kevin, she needed to get home to ponder the job applications and, maybe, get a good night's sleep before another busy day at Tally's Olde Tyme Sweets.

Tally walked quickly to Burger Kitchen through the soft night air, the warmth caressing her tired body and feeling so much better than the hot daytime air of August in this part of Texas.

Yolanda and Kevin were seated near the back and waved her over. Kevin gave her a smile through his *au courant* dark scruffy beard. He was of medium height, unimposing, and, as far as Tally could tell, a genuinely nice guy. He was, as usual, dressed all in black—black jeans and a black button-up shirt with the sleeves rolled up a few inches.

"I got you an iced tea," Yolanda said, taking a sip of her own.

Tally was thirsty from her two short walks and gulped half the glass down. It tasted wonderful. The restaurant served their special blend, slightly sweet with a hint of peach flavoring.

"Now, what do you have?" Yolanda asked when Tally set her sweating glass on the paper coaster. "I saw you stick some papers in your purse. Any good prospects?"

"A few," Tally said. She fished them out of her purse and handed them to Yolanda. "Look them over and see what you think."

"Have you heard from your parents today?" Kevin asked.

The waiter brought them a basket of steaming bread, and Kevin helped himself to a crusty roll.

Tally's roving musician/actor/dancer parents, Nancy and Bob Holt, were on their way home after many months on the road. They were coming in from Marrakesh in Morocco, where they had performed for a few days after their shows on the beach in Bali ended. The reception Tally was planning, with the help of Yolanda and Kevin, would be to celebrate their rare homecoming. She wanted it to be a special occasion for them. They had been gone for months, had never seen her shop, and she hoped they would be impressed. She had sold a successful bakery in Austin to buy her place here, and she knew they didn't think it had been a good idea, even though this was their hometown and Tally had spent a good part of her childhood in this Texas Hill Country town.

"They're on a flight today, then stopping for a day in Spain and coming here from there," Tally said.

Kevin shook his head. "They sure gallivant around, don't they?"

"That's all they do. They never stay anywhere very long." Tally took a piece of steaming corn bread, her favorite, and started to butter it, letting it melt in before she took the first luscious bite.

"Y'all should put Cole to work since he's coming early," Yolanda said.

"He says he'll help me. We'll see if that happens."

"They're his parents, too. You can't blame him for wanting to help out."

"Wasn't this reception his idea?" Kevin asked, taking another warm roll.

"I guess it was," Tally said. "But I agreed to set it up. I thought he wouldn't be able to do much while he was building a sculpture in Albuquerque."

"I'm glad he'll be here," Kevin said. "We need all the hands we can get."

Tally drummed her fingers on the table, hoping that Kevin might be able to get more labor out of Tally's little brother than she would be likely to. Even though she was his big sister, she hadn't been able to boss him around for quite a few years now. Every single person in her family was the independent type.

She was half dreading the reception. Her parents would fly in, get a few hours' sleep, and go straight to the party the next day—their choice. Tally knew they would be jet-lagged and the affair might be a dull flop. Then again, maybe she was wrong. They were so used to traveling, maybe they had conquered jet lag and would be ready to party. It was now Wednesday night, Cole would be here early Thursday, and her parents would arrive on Friday. She had left the hiring of the help until almost too late, she knew. Actually, she hadn't even considered they would need help until Yolanda mentioned it. Yolanda was a great detail person, luckily.

"This has me rattled," Tally said. "I think I've let it get a lot bigger than I should have."

"You don't look a bit rattled," Kevin said with a smile. "You never do."

Tally knew she often looked cool, calm, and collected when she was a jangle of nerves inside. Maybe that came from being onstage at such a young age. She was glad to be out of that life, but she had to admit the days when her parents used to give her and Cole parts in their acts had resulted in some useful takeaways. Cole and Yolanda were the two people on the planet who could always tell when she was upset, and she was thankful for that. She would make the best of Cole being underfoot—no, not underfoot—being here and helping. Yes, that was it. Helping.

Her other worry was what this would do to her business. Missing a day of sales, and on a Saturday, would leave a big hole in her income. And she needed all of her income while her shop was still gathering steam and becoming known in the town.

"Let's talk about the reception," Yolanda said. "What are y'all going to serve?"

"My own products, of course," Tally answered. "I'll do some Mary Janes and Whoopie Pies. What else?"

Kevin said, "I think you should have your Clark Bars. I like that fudge with Baileys in it, too. I have a Petit Syrah that would be good with the fudge. If you do Twinkies, I'll bring some Riesling."

They discussed sweet treats and wine for a few more minutes until Tally changed the subject.

"Okay," she said, pointing to the three sheets of paper spread on the table. "What do you think of the applicants?"

Yolanda looked them over and held one up. "This one."

"Let me see." Kevin wiped his fingers so the butter from his roll wouldn't get on it. "Greer Tomson," he read. "She didn't graduate from high school. Is that a problem?"

"I'm not sure," Tally said. "The other two I liked are a bit younger. One is eighteen and the other one twenty. Greer has lots of work experience, so that might be good."

"Maybe too much," Yolanda said, frowning at the paper in her hand. "She seems to change jobs a lot."

"You're right," Kevin agreed, reaching for the paperwork from the other two and looking it over. "But she's the only one with retail experience."

"The good thing is," Tally said, "that I can try her out at the reception and then decide if I want to hire her to work in the store."

The server came and took their orders—hamburger, cheeseburger, and veggie burger.

"Back to the hired help," Kevin said, staying on point. "Are you just using one person at the reception?"

Tally gave it some thought. "What do both of you think? Do we need more?"

"What can you afford?" Yolanda asked. She was much better at managing money than Tally was. In fact, she helped Tally with the books in her shop whenever she couldn't make things balance.

"You probably know that better than I do." Tally laughed, and Kevin chuckled.

"I think you're doing pretty darn well lately. You could hire all three, just for that day, then decide which two you want to keep."

Tally liked that idea. Like buying three pair of shoes, then returning the one or two pair that hurt her feet after an hour on the carpet at home. She decided to call all three and offer them jobs for Saturday. She would do it first thing in the morning.

As the three friends were winding up their dinner and waiting for the bill, a couple they all knew came through the door and were seated at a table near them. The pair looked like Jack Sprat and his wife, reversed. The woman was thin, with what looked like a perpetual frown on her creased face, which was topped by short gray curls that always made Tally think of a mop. The man, in contrast, was bald, potbellied, and wore a jovial expression on his round face. Friendly eyes twinkled under his bushy eyebrows. The woman sat facing them, glanced in their direction, gathered her frown lines to new depths, loudly cleared her throat, then concentrated on her menu.

Kevin saw Tally's own frown and gave her a questioning look.

"Later," she said.

"Yes, later," Yolanda added.

Yolanda was surprised, but glad, when Kevin took her elbow and guided her out of the restaurant, just like they were an old married couple. She was beginning to look at him with a different perspective. He was older than she was, but seemed interested. She could do a lot worse, and she liked Kevin a lot.

When they were outside the restaurant, Kevin asked again. "Do you not like the Abrahams?"

Yolanda started to answer, but Tally beat her to it. "Lennie is okay," she said, "but I can't stand his wife, Frances. She's had it in for my mother since I can remember."

"Tally's right," Yolanda said. "She finds something mean to say about Tally's mom every time they're in town."

"What's her problem?" Kevin asked. "I've heard only good things about your mom from several of my customers. They're excited she's going to be in town. I thought everyone liked her. Both of your parents, really."

They were walking toward Tally's house first, since she lived the closest. Yolanda wondered if Kevin was going to come to her place and stay for a while. Or overnight. The tree frogs were in full voice, their songs ringing above them through the night from the live oaks and crape myrtles that lined the streets. The air was deliciously cooler than the mid-nineties high of the day. The thermometer was heading down to the upper sixties, and Yolanda wished she had a sweater on.

"That's one of the problems," Yolanda said. "Everyone likes Nancy, but hardly anyone likes Fran. Nancy is an old girlfriend of Fran's husband. Lennie still acts very friendly when he sees Nancy, which doesn't help anything."

Kevin pulled his head back and frowned. "Nancy is Mrs. Holt's first name? And she was a girlfriend of Mr. Abraham's?"

Yolanda and Tally both nodded.

Kevin continued, "That must have been a long time ago. You're, what, in your thirties? So it had to be more than thirty years ago."

"Yes," Tally said. "Fran has been a thorn in my mom's side for their whole lives."

"One problem Fran has is competition," Yolanda said. "They're both performers, after all."

Yolanda had known Frances Abraham her whole life. Mrs. Abraham presently directed the local theater group and ruled it with an iron fist. To anyone she considered competition, she was extra nasty. She had sent more than one aspiring starlet home in tears, wanting all the starring roles for herself. That became more and more problematic as she aged and her face became more and more set into permanent harsh lines that you could now see even beyond the stage. She had verbally attacked Yolanda's own sister, Violetta, so harshly and so often that Vi had dropped out of the one production she had tried out for. She'd been slated to have a starring role, too, but she couldn't work under Fran. Yolanda remembered her little sister coming home in tears after every rehearsal until she quit.

"I've wondered, before, why Lennie puts up with her," Kevin said. "They come into Bear Mountain sometimes and whatever wine he picks out, she nixes. She's the boss."

"From working with them, I can tell you this," Yolanda answered. "He mostly ignores her. Just hammers the sets together and paints them and doesn't pay attention to what goes on in front of his scenery."

"I'd forgotten," Tally said to Yolanda. "You were in some of her plays, weren't you?"

"A few years ago, when I was much younger. I didn't like working with her, but I stuck it out for a short time. Three productions one summer. I think most people who are in her productions put up with her because they love the stage."

"No one forgets the past in a small town like this," Kevin said.

"And she's not a bad director, just a limelight hog," Yolanda said.

"Too skinny for a hog," Kevin answered, and they all laughed.

They rounded the corner to Tally's block of East Shubert and she stopped. "It's a day early! He's here already!" Her brother's Volvo sat in her driveway.

Meet the Author

Photo Credit: Megan Russow

One of Kaye George's quirky claims to fame is having lived in nine states, many of which begin with the letter "M."

A native Californian, Kaye moved to Moline, Illinois, at the tender age of three months. After college at Northwestern University in Evanston, Illinois, and marriage to Cliff during finals week their senior year, she and Cliff touched down in Sumter, SC; Lompoc, CA (very briefly); and Great Falls, Montana, during his Air Force career.

Kaye is also a violinist, an online mystery reviewer, an award winning short story writer, and the author of four different mystery series with three different publishers and one self-published. She has accrued three Agatha Award nominations and one finalist position for the Silver Falchion, as well as national bestseller status with her Fat Cat series written as Janet Cantrell.

Visit her at https://kayegeorge.wixsite.com/kaye-george.

CPSIA information can be obtained
at www.ICGtesting.com
Printed in the USA
LVHW042104310720
662090LV00003B/339